Royal Secrets

Royal Secrets

a novel

TRACI HUNTER ABRAMSON

Covenant Communications, Inc.

For
Mac & Rebecca
and
Scott & Sheila

Two fairytale romances
that ended much too soon

Acknowledgments

First, I want to thank all the readers who insisted the story from *Royal Target* needed to continue. You were absolutely right.

Thank you to my family for your constant support, especially Luke, Hunter, Parker, and Gabriel for teaching me all about little boys and their hopes and dreams. Thanks to Ed and Janice Parker for the inspiration behind the You Are Here maps needed in some houses and for always providing me a home away from home. Also, thank you to Tiffany Hunter and Rebecca Cummings for sharing your trials of single parenthood.

Thanks to Julie Robb for suggesting I use the name Alora, and thanks to everyone on Facebook who gave me suggestions when I needed to name a horse. Jeff Schrade won that impromptu contest, so thanks, Jeff.

As always, thank you to the wonderful people at Covenant for giving me the opportunity to do what I love.

Finally, my continued appreciation goes to Samantha Van Walraven and Rebecca Cummings for your constant willingness to help me turn an idea into a story. I don't know what I would do without you.

Prologue

"THAT'S THE ONE." THE VOICE was all business with a harsh edge of irritation.

"Are you sure?" The younger man hesitated as he looked at the fenced yard, at the tricycle parked on the sidewalk leading to the Tudor-style house. A single candle flickered in each window, and a decorative wreath hung on the door. "It looks like kids live here."

His jaw clenched, and heat flashed in his eyes. "Sometimes children have to pay for the crimes of their parents."

"But . . ."

"Don't let yourself be fooled." He looked past the tricycle to the sparkling white lights that adorned the outside of the house. "This is a house of spies and infidels. There are no innocents."

* * *

Alora DeSanto shifted her baby, Dante, on her hip and kept a firm grip on two-year-old Giancarlo's hand as she waited in line to pick up Dante's prescription. Strep throat on Christmas Eve. She could only shake her head and hope the antibiotics the doctor had just prescribed would work miracles overnight so Dante wouldn't be miserable for his first Christmas.

"I want to go home," Giancarlo whined, his little lip poking out in a pout.

She looked down at him sympathetically. Both sets of his grandparents were home right now with her husband, Carlo, and her brother who had just arrived from Italy. Giancarlo had wanted so badly to stay home with everyone, but she had worried that he too was running a fever.

"Just be patient for a few more minutes, okay?" Alora gave his hand a little squeeze. "Then we'll go home, and you can have that hot chocolate Papa promised you."

Her cell phone vibrated in her pocket, and she debated briefly whether it was worth it to let go of Giancarlo's hand to try to answer it. With a sigh, she looked down at Giancarlo and said, "Stay right here with me." Then she released his hand and pulled her phone free, her eyes remaining on her older son. "Hello?"

Carlo's voice came over the line. "Hi, honey. Where are you?"

"In line at the pharmacy. Dante has strep."

"Poor little guy." Sympathy hung in his voice. "I hate to ask, but is there any way you can pick up a gallon of milk on your way home? There's no way we have enough to make it through tomorrow."

"I'll try, but no guarantees."

"If you can't, I can always—" Carlo's voice cut off.

"Carlo?" Alora waited a second. When there was no response, she held her phone out to see that the call had ended.

The pharmacist motioned to her that it was her turn, and she went to the counter to pay and collect the medicine. She was halfway to the door of the pharmacy when her phone rang again. She dug it out of her pocket once more, this time surprised to see that it was her neighbor's phone number illuminating her screen rather than her husband's. "Hi, Marie."

"Alora!" Marie's voice came out in a rush. "Thank goodness you're okay! Are the children with you? And Carlo?"

"The kids are with me, but Carlo is at home," Alora said, her focus still more on her children than on the phone call.

"Alora, it's your house." Marie's voice broke on a sob. "Oh, I'm sorry. I'm so sorry."

"Marie, what are you talking about? What about my house?" Alora hesitated, her mind replaying Marie's earlier comment. "Why wouldn't I be okay? What's wrong?" Alora's pace quickened. "Marie. Tell me what's wrong."

"There was an explosion." Marie's voice broke again. "Alora, it's gone. Your house is gone."

Alora's face paled. Her phone dropped unnoticed to the floor, and she scooped Giancarlo up with her free hand. With a child in each arm, she rushed to her car and somehow managed to buckle her children into their car seats despite the terror clawing through her. Prayers raced through her mind as she somehow navigated the streets of Paris toward her home.

Ten minutes later her car screeched to a halt three houses away from her own. Fire trucks were parked haphazardly in the street, obstructing the view of her house. Two police cars blocked the road, their lights flashing. Dozens of people had gathered outside, and several policemen were stringing out yellow caution tape, apparently to keep everyone back.

"Mama! Look! Firemen!" Giancarlo unbuckled himself and scrambled out of the car as Alora quickly grabbed the baby from his car seat and managed to grab Giancarlo's hand before he could race past her.

She could hear the crackling of the fire, could feel the heat emanating from beyond the barricade. Smoke lingered in the air, not the pleasant campfire scent but the acrid smell of firecrackers and burning gasoline.

Alora's eyes frantically searched the crowd as she pushed her way forward, her muscles trembling. Panic and raging fear dominated, even as she fought to keep a glimmer of hope alive. She ignored the sympathetic looks her neighbors offered, her heart sinking with each step. When she reached the front of the crowd, all she could do was stare.

Tears streaked down her face unnoticed, her grip instinctively tightening on her children.

Ash and soot filled the air where her house once stood, blackened bricks and debris littering the yard and street. Flames licked at what was once the northwest corner of the house, and a mangled tricycle wheel was imbedded in the fence.

A neighbor talking to a policeman pointed at her, but she barely noticed. Once again, her eyes frantically searched the crowd.

Clutching her children close to her, she watched a policeman approach, his face grave.

Silent prayers rambled through her brain, but deep in her heart, she already knew what the policeman was going to tell her. There were no survivors.

Chapter 1

ALORA GLANCED AROUND THE PARK, looking for anything out of place. For more than three years, she and her children had remained safe, living in a small apartment on the outskirts of Zena, Italy, only a few miles from where she had grown up. Every day she awoke wondering if she would ever find a way to feel safe again, a way to feel alive again. And even after all this time, she still didn't know who was responsible for tearing her world apart.

For months after the bombing, she had searched for information. The CIA had shared their suspicions that Carlo's cover had been blown due to an inadvertent disclosure by his brother and sister-in-law. Beyond those basic facts, she didn't know if the Agency truly hadn't uncovered any more leads or if they were simply unwilling to share the information they did have.

Alora remembered how her brother-in-law had been mad that they wouldn't come to the United States for Christmas that year, especially when their parents had chosen to spend the holidays in Paris with them. Carlo had finally broken down and admitted that he was CIA and tried to explain that his work made it impossible for him to travel right then. Alora knew that conversation had cost Carlo his life.

She reached the playground and leaned down to tie her four-year-old son's shoelace. The moment she finished, Dante dashed toward the swings where his older brother was already playing. When she straightened, her dark hair caught in the breeze. Standing beside her, Janessa Rogers adjusted the baseball cap on her head.

"I feel ridiculous," Janessa said in Italian as she pushed her dark sunglasses higher on her nose.

A smile tugged at Alora's lips. "At least you've been trained to blend in. That must help when trying to get around the paparazzi."

"I don't think the Agency expected me to use my training for this," Janessa said with humor in her voice.

Alora nodded in agreement. The CIA had trained them both well in a variety of skills, but typically, their expertise focused on survival tactics. Today Janessa was simply hoping for privacy. Her recent engagement to Prince Garrett Fortier of Meridia had put Janessa firmly in the spotlight, a place she had previously been trained to avoid.

Although both women had worked undercover for the CIA, their career paths had been markedly different. Janessa worked as an operative and a linguist, while Alora had primarily worked in finance. Janessa was American by birth. Alora was American by marriage.

After losing Carlo, the CIA had offered to transfer her back to the United States, but instead, she had opted to leave the Agency and return to her native Italy, to the city where she had been raised. Of all her friends from the CIA, only Janessa had made the effort to keep in touch after the tragedy.

Although Janessa normally visited several times a year, Alora had been surprised when Janessa had written to tell her she was coming. Not only was Janessa recently engaged, but Alora suspected she was also involved in saving Queen Marta of Meridia from a recent kidnapping attempt.

Alora didn't typically keep up with the headlines, but she hadn't missed the news last month when Queen Marta had nearly died at the hands of her captors.

"Are you going to tell me what really happened between you and Prince Garrett?"

Sarcasm coated Janessa's voice. "You mean you don't believe everything you read in the tabloids?"

"You know I never read those things." Alora's eyebrows lifted inquisitively, only a trace of sadness visible in her eyes. "But I'm not buying the story I read in the newspaper about you knowing him for two years. My guess is some kind of undercover op."

Janessa shook her head. "You know I can neither confirm nor deny such an assumption."

"Of course not," Alora said cryptically. "Then tell me how things are now."

"Great! I love him. He loves me. We're planning our happily ever after."

"Can you really be sure there will be a happily ever after?" Alora asked gently. "I thought you of all people would never settle for less than a temple marriage."

Something flashed in Janessa's eyes but was quickly gone. She drew a deep breath and said simply, "I can only tell you that when I prayed about marrying Garrett, the only answer I received was yes."

Alora studied her, knowing that Janessa was holding something back. When she didn't offer any more details, Alora gave her a tentative smile. "Then I will wish you every happiness. Still, I wish I were showing up at the temple instead of a cathedral to see you marry."

"I know." Janessa nodded in understanding and promptly changed the subject. "Tell me, how are you holding up?"

Alora looked down at the ground. "Okay."

Janessa didn't say anything. She simply stared until Alora looked up and their eyes met.

Alora let out a sigh. "Okay, so things are difficult."

"Talk to me."

She shrugged her narrow shoulders and then gestured with her left hand where a ring still occupied her finger. "Giancarlo still has nightmares about fires. Dante doesn't even remember Carlo, and I don't know how to begin to make up for the fact that they have to grow up without a father." A sigh escaped her. "I go to church on Sundays, and they can hardly sit through sacrament meeting. Sometimes I wonder why I even bother."

"You've always said how important it is to you for your kids to learn to love the gospel. I know it may not always feel like it, but you're giving them that." Janessa reached out and put her hand on Alora's arm. "You really are doing a wonderful job with both of your boys."

Alora shook her head, tears forming in her eyes. She hated that even after all of this time, her emotions were always so close to the surface.

"You are," Janessa repeated. "But maybe it's time for a change of scenery."

"What do you mean?"

"I have an idea I wanted to run past you, one I hope will help both of us."

Alora looked at her, her interest piqued. "I'm listening."

* * *

Prince Stefano Fortier of Meridia emerged from the back of the limousine, followed by his younger brother, Prince Garrett. Cameras began flashing immediately, but neither man noticed. They had never known a time when the paparazzi hadn't been part of their lives. Both men assumed the press followed them because of their titles. Neither understood that they were the type of men that fairytales were built on: tall and dark, with chiseled features that often graced the covers of magazines.

Stefano took a step forward and waited as Garrett turned to offer a hand to his fiancée, Janessa Rogers. He could feel the media's attention shift to the young couple. Garrett and Janessa were a modern-day fairytale, one on which the media often speculated. The public would never know, of course, that the engagement had started out as a publicity stunt. Nor would the information ever be revealed that Janessa was a CIA operative who had come to Meridia to help protect the royal family.

Secrets of the past would be kept, only adding to the intrigue of the romance between his brother and the vibrant, red-haired beauty who had captured his heart. Witnessing them together was like seeing magic, something intangible that was almost too good to be real.

Garrett and Janessa's wedding wouldn't take place until next year, but today his country was celebrating another royal marriage, that of his cousin Philippe and his longtime girlfriend, Elaina.

Stefano turned as their limousine pulled away and another arrived carrying his parents. Additional security personnel scurried into position before King Eduard and Queen Marta joined their family on the sidewalk outside of Meridia's National Cathedral.

Cameras continued to flash as the family began their procession toward the massive church built of native stone and impressive stained glass. The heavy wooden doors were already open, the church's air conditioning competing against the humid July weather. The royal family followed an usher to a pew at the front of the church, the heavy doors closed, and within seconds, the wedding march began.

Stefano stood with the rest of the congregation and watched as Elaina's father escorted her down the aisle. Her dress was modern, the edge of her veil skimming her bare shoulders, her nose slightly upturned as though she too had already adopted Philippe's superiority complex. How different the two families were, Stefano thought. His father had taught him and Garrett to serve. His Uncle Elam's family expected to be served.

Stefano had no doubt that his brother's wedding would look and feel completely different from this stiffly formal affair they were currently attending. Janessa's dress would certainly be more conservative than Elaina's, since Garrett and Janessa would be privately married first in the Mormon temple. Then, following the laws of their land, they would have a second ceremony in this very church.

Stefano didn't understand Garrett and Janessa's insistence on a temple wedding, but apparently, it was important to Mormons, or Latter-day Saints as they liked to be called. Then again, he couldn't claim to comprehend much about his brother's new religion. Garrett had definitely changed a lot over the past few months, and Stefano could admit that he had never seen his brother happier. Janessa seemed to bring out the best in him, and Stefano was willing to entertain the idea that Garrett's newfound faith played a part in his contentment.

Although Garrett and Janessa would have both been happy to bypass the large public wedding, personally, Stefano was glad they weren't limiting themselves to the temple ceremony. If he had his way, the public would remain unaware that his brother had joined the LDS Church until long after he and Janessa married.

Chapter 2

Two men stood in the shadows of the church as the bride and groom pulled away in the limousine that would transport them to their reception. The taller of the two lowered his voice and kept his eyes on the people mulling near the church entrance. "Ambrose has arrived."

Warily, the older man watched King Eduard and Queen Marta make their way out to their waiting limo. Guards flanked the royal couple, and from the right angle, at least one sniper could be seen on the roof across the street to protect against any unforeseen threat. He spoke in hushed tones when he asked, "Are you sure this is going to work? Bringing in someone who dines with terrorists on a regular basis seems risky to me."

"He's the best at what he does, and we need him. Neither of us knows how to make a precision bomb that can go undetected by security sweeps."

"I still don't know about this."

"It's very simple. If we let things go as they are, the Americans will be running this country and the monarchy will be little more than puppets on a string." His voice was dark and passionate. "This is the only way. This monarchy is dying, and it's up to us to make sure we're in control when the last drop of blood is shed."

* * *

Stefano moved through the crowd at the reception, greeting guests smoothly and listening to snippets of the conversations around him. As expected at such an event, the women seemed content to discuss fashion and the men seemed unable to digress from politics.

The latest political topics appeared to center on his father's recent decision to refuse to allow a local company to harvest the oil discovered in their territorial waters. As the president of Meridia's environmental agency,

Stefano agreed with his father's decision completely. In fact, he had encouraged it.

Offshore drilling was risky, especially in the area where the oil deposits had been discovered. A single spill could instantly ruin Meridia's tourism industry, and the payoff simply wasn't worth the risk. Besides, the royal family solely owned and operated the oil industry in the northern region of the country. The company interested in drilling offshore was run by a group of local businessmen in partnership with Caspian Oil, a Libyan-based company.

A study of Caspian Oil's past ventures had raised concerns that the company would put profits before the safety and welfare of the environment and Meridia's citizens. Those concerns had ultimately resulted in the denial of their drilling plans. Shortly after the denial was issued, Meridia's ruling council had enacted laws to prohibit such ventures in the future.

"Prince Stefano, it's been a long time." Jacques Neuville reached out and shook Stefano's hand.

"Yes, it has. How have you been?" Stefano kept his voice polite and managed to gloss over his dislike for his former college classmate. They had both pursued their undergraduate degrees in petroleum engineering, but their views always seemed to be polar opposites, especially regarding the ever difficult topic of balancing economic progress with environmental protection. Not surprisingly, Jacques had aligned himself with Caspian Oil in their pursuit of offshore drilling.

"I am doing well. My wife and I just had our second child a few months ago, and business is booming."

"Are you still working with oil pipelines?"

He nodded. "My company mainly works with the pipelines in France and Italy. Of course, we had hoped to expand into Meridia if the offshore drilling had been approved." He shrugged casually. "But since that didn't happen, I'm making do with other options."

"It's always good to have multiple options," Stefano said mildly. "Give my best to your family."

"I will."

Stefano started through the crowd once more, this time only making it a few feet before the reigning archbishop greeted him. The archbishop was still dressed in his traditional black robes, a heavy gold cross hanging around his neck and coming to rest on his protruding stomach. Round-rimmed glasses perched on his nose, the dark eyes behind those glasses always serious.

"Prince Stefano. It is such an honor to be here with all your family for such a joyous occasion."

Stefano nodded. "Thank you for performing the ceremony today, Archbishop Leone. It was lovely."

"It is always a privilege." He motioned to Garrett across the room. "Has your brother set a wedding date yet?"

"They mentioned next summer," Stefano said vaguely. "I'm sure you'll be among the first to know when they're ready to finalize their plans."

"I'll look forward to assisting them," Archbishop Leone said graciously. "I hope you enjoy the rest of your evening."

"You too." Stefano shifted away from the crowd until he managed to find a quiet corner. He wasn't there thirty seconds before his brother stepped beside him, his company smile pasted on his face. Garrett lowered his voice and asked, "Is it time to leave yet? I don't think I can handle getting cornered by our new cousin-in-law again."

"Was she fishing for invitations?"

"You could say that." Garrett gave a slight nod. "She doesn't seem to understand that even though Philippe wears the title of prince, he has never assumed any family responsibility to warrant his inclusion in state affairs. He never even served in the military."

"I don't think she cares about his responsibilities. She just wants the perks."

"Including frequent invitations to the palace and unlimited access to the chateau in Bellamo," Garrett said with a hint of frustration.

"In other words, she wants to use our homes as her vacation spots."

"I think if we gave her the chance, she'd move in permanently," Garrett muttered.

Stefano nodded in agreement. "Unfortunately, Philippe hasn't always been much better." Then his attention shifted across the room, and his eyes lit with humor. "Face it, Garrett. Not everyone can be as fortunate as you."

Garrett turned, and his smile was instant and genuine when he saw Janessa moving through the crowd toward him. Her hair flowed loosely over her shoulders, and her blue gown shimmered as she moved.

She returned his smile, and humor laced her voice as she addressed both men in Italian. "What are the two most handsome men doing standing in the corner of the room?"

"We were just waiting for you." Garrett leaned down and kissed her cheek.

"Of course you were." Janessa looked from Garrett to Stefano. "So what were you two so deep in conversation about?"

"Our new cousin-in-law wants to move in with us."

"What?"

"She mentioned that it might be prudent for her and Philippe to come live at the chateau until after we get married. After all, we don't want to give the public the wrong impression."

"She wants to be your chaperone?" Stefano asked before Janessa could respond. "You two aren't even living in the same wing of the chateau. You're in the family quarters, and Janessa stays in the guest quarters. Besides, I'm there as often as not."

"I know, but I think she sees this as an opportunity to gain a foothold there."

"Actually," Janessa began tentatively. "It wouldn't be a bad idea to have someone staying with us for now, especially if I had someone who would be willing to help with the wedding plans."

Garrett looked at her, horrified. He lowered his voice and spoke in hushed tones. "Janessa, you can't expect me to have my cousin and his new wife come live with us. Philippe has never been anything but a spoiled brat."

"I don't know Philippe well enough to have an opinion about him, but I wasn't thinking about Philippe and Elaina."

"Then who?"

"Alora DeSanto."

"Your friend from Italy?"

Janessa nodded. "She's incredibly organized, and I think the change would do her a lot of good. Besides, she's an accountant by profession, so she wouldn't have any trouble taking care of the business side of things."

"Have I told you lately how much I love you?" Garrett asked with a grin. "You may have just saved my sanity."

"Oh really?"

"You could invite a toad to move in with us, and I would be thrilled, as long as it keeps Philippe out of our house. Besides, you don't have to ask my permission to have a friend stay at the chateau. It's your home too. She's welcome to come and stay as long as you like," Garrett told her. "We both know you need an assistant. You only have to tell Martino that she's your choice to have her put on the payroll."

"And we all know she'll be worth every penny if she helps keep Philippe and Elaina from trying to move in," Stefano added.

Garrett nodded. "Exactly."

"Looks like they're headed this way." Stefano gave a subtle nod toward the bride and groom.

"Janessa, I've been hoping to talk to you." Elaina leaned forward and kissed the air beside her cheek.

"You look lovely." Janessa motioned to Elaina's gown.

"I'm sure you will make an adequate bride when your time comes," Philippe said as though he had rehearsed the words, his voice carrying a combination of arrogance and disdain.

Janessa gave Garrett's hand a squeeze. "I was just talking to Garrett about plans for our wedding."

"Really?" Elaina's eyebrows lifted slightly. "Have you set a date?"

"Not yet, but I just returned from Italy yesterday. The friend I was visiting has agreed to act as my personal assistant. She will be moving into the chateau until after Garrett and I are married."

"Oh." Elaina's Cupid's bow mouth formed a perfect *O*. "Garrett and I were actually discussing the possibility of Philippe and me moving into the chateau."

"Elaina, that is so kind of you to offer to sacrifice like that for us, but I couldn't possibly let you do that," Janessa said smoothly. "After all, you and Philippe have a life to start together, and you certainly don't want to do that in someone else's home."

Before Elaina could respond, Garrett spoke. "Janessa, we really need to get going. Both of us have to be up early tomorrow."

"You're right." Janessa nodded and then looked over at Elaina and Philippe. "Congratulations again on your marriage. I wish you both every happiness."

"*Grazie*," Philippe said stiffly.

Stefano banked down on his instant irritation with his cousin and wondered again how he and Philippe could be from the same family. With considerable effort, Stefano managed to smile at Philippe and Elaina as he exchanged his good-byes. Then he motioned to one of his guards and let himself be escorted to the door.

Chapter 3

STEFANO URGED HIS HORSE UP the path, the sound of crashing waves growing stronger, the scent of the sea carrying on the wind. The palace was behind him now, barely visible through the thick foliage that covered the steep hills leading up to his home.

"Steady, Midnight," he murmured to the black stallion beneath him as they slowed to a walk. They moved out into the grassy field near the ruins of the castle that had once housed Stefano's ancestors. He didn't know why he always felt drawn to this place: it could be that the last man to rule from the ancient castle was also named Stefano or that the ruins served as a reminder of his duty as the future king to protect the citizens of Meridia.

Only one wall of the castle was still intact, a remnant of an earlier time, a time when warring religions had nearly torn his country apart. He thought of his own brother's fight for religious freedom, Garrett's conversion to the LDS Church still weighing heavily on his mind. His family hadn't attended church regularly in years, but he had never considered the possibility of any of them turning their backs on the religion that had been a constant in his family for centuries.

In medieval times, his family had appointed the archbishop, and the monarchy had been actively involved in nearly every aspect of the church. Those close ties had loosened through the generations, the most recent adjustments coming several years before his father took the throne.

Although the changes only occurred twenty years ago, the reasons behind them had already been reduced to a combination of facts and legend. According to the family stories, a falling out had occurred between Stefano's grandfather, King Alejandro, and the presiding archbishop at the time. Frustrated that several clergy members in the Meridian Church were trying to influence state policy, King Alejandro had insisted that all state and church operations be separated. In an effort to make the transition run smoothly, he also created a liaison position between the royal family and the church.

Since Stefano's father, Eduard, was already actively involved in the politics of Meridia, King Alejandro had appointed his youngest son, Elam, to serve as the liaison. Stefano couldn't be sure if Elam had ever been anything more than a figurehead, but regardless, the public perception was that the Meridian Church was still very much integrated in state affairs.

Stefano turned his horse toward the cliffs on the west side of the ruins, dismounting when he reached the spot where the grass gave way to rock. The salt-scented wind whipped through his dark hair as the waves of the Mediterranean crashed beneath him. Stefano looked out over the water, his eyes lingering on the dark rain clouds in the distance. A storm was coming, but it wasn't the rain he feared. Rather, he worried about the political tempest most surely brewing on the horizon.

The ruling council could be fickle at times, and the presence of U.S. naval vessels in Meridian waters had already caused some ripples of dissent among them. Didn't they see that his father was taking this country into a new era while still preserving centuries of tradition? The exploration of oil in the mountains had given Meridia's citizens a new industry without impeding the stunning coastlines that had made the country a popular tourist spot for Europeans for decades.

His parents had used much of their increased wealth from their oil profits to invest in both the country's infrastructure and local businesses and the arts, yet the villages that dotted the countryside continued to maintain their culture and charm. Traditions ran deep in Meridia, and change was rarely easy.

Glancing back at the ruins behind him, Stefano couldn't help but worry about what would happen when his brother's baptism into the LDS Church came to light. Only a handful of people knew of his brother's conversion, all of them Mormons except for his immediate family. He was amazed that these relative strangers were protecting his brother's privacy so fiercely. Stefano wished he trusted his extended family as much as he had come to trust Garrett's newfound Mormon friends. Unfortunately, he knew his Uncle Elam and Aunt Victoria to be narrow-minded in most things. Their only child, Philippe, was simply self-absorbed.

Stefano imagined that, given the opportunity, his cousin and his new bride would be more than happy to see Garrett banished from the royal family so they could step in and take his place. It wouldn't happen, of course, but Stefano's distrust of his extended family was cause for concern. The news was bound to become public eventually, and the family needed to be unified to keep Garrett's religion from becoming a spark for political unrest.

Midnight shied back from the edge, and Stefano patted his neck, murmuring soft reassurances. He swung himself back into the saddle and wondered what the future would hold for this little piece of earth his family had ruled for centuries.

* * *

King Eduard settled back on the couch beside his wife as their sons and Janessa walked into their sitting room. He motioned for them to sit and then addressed his future daughter-in-law in his native Italian. "I know you prefer not to work on Sundays, but I felt it prudent for all of us to meet before you and Garrett return to the chateau tomorrow."

Janessa's eyes lit with humor as she sat on the loveseat across from him. "Believe me, I am not a stranger to having family meetings on Sundays."

"Is everything okay?" Garrett asked.

"I'm not sure." Eduard lifted a file from the table beside him. "I was looking over our monthly financial reports earlier this week, and I'm concerned that there may be some unexplained irregularities."

"What kind of irregularities?" Stefano asked.

"The first thing that caught my attention was the expense report for the gala." Eduard passed copies of the report to everyone. "Look at the amount listed under security for the event."

Garrett's eyebrows lifted. "Two hundred thousand euros?"

"That can't be right." Stefano shook his head. "The basic security staff is funded through the regular household budget at the chateau, and most of the other security personnel were on loan from the U.S. government. Any reimbursement we sent would have posted as a foreign funds transfer."

"Exactly." Eduard nodded. "So where did this charge come from? I estimate our share of traditional costs would have been less than twenty thousand."

"Could it be a posting error?" Janessa asked. "One extra zero and you would go from twenty thousand to two hundred thousand."

"That's what I first thought had happened, but then I started looking at some of our other accounts. A similar problem occurred for the Christmas party at the winter villa last year."

"How much was it over?"

"I would estimate about forty thousand, although some of the other expenses looked high as well," Eduard told them. "My concern isn't only about the possibility that someone is skimming funds from our accounts but also that our quarterly audits have not revealed any problems."

"Is it possible that the auditors are involved?"

"I don't know. We've been using the same company for more than a decade. Either they're involved or someone has faked the documentation adequately enough that the auditors missed the discrepancies," Eduard explained. "Had I not personally approved the budget for security for both of these events, I never would have noticed the irregularities."

"It sounds like we may need to bring in another auditing firm," Stefano said.

Eduard shook his head. "If we bring in new auditors now, we may never find out who's behind this. If it's someone within the family, I want proof before I make any accusations."

Garrett's eyes widened. "You think it might be Uncle Elam or Aunt Victoria?"

"Or Philippe." Eduard nodded, his expression solemn. "I hope that isn't the case, but the fact remains that all of them at one time or another have had access to family funds. They have also been living beyond their means for some time. I was asked several times to help with the cost of Philippe's wedding. While we did make a modest contribution, I don't see how they were able to afford it without some help."

"Did the audit reports for the Meridian Church show any problems?" Stefano asked now. "If Uncle Elam is the one skimming funds from the various accounts, it's possible he's been dipping into church funds as well."

"I was wondering the same thing," Eduard said. "The new reports are due next week. Stefano, you've always had a good eye for finances. I hoped you might look them over and let me know if you see anything unusual."

"Of course, Father."

"Is there anything I can do to help?" Janessa asked.

"I would like to keep this matter private, but if there is any way you can access your agency's reports on my family, I would appreciate it."

"You want me to see if the CIA has been spying on your family?"

"Janessa, I am perfectly aware that all intelligence agencies keep dossiers on the ruling classes of various countries," Eduard stated in a matter-of-fact tone. "What I want to know is if the CIA has uncovered anything that might explain these anomalies."

"I will certainly see what I can do." Janessa started to lean back in her seat, but then awareness lit her eyes. "There is one more thing I might be able to offer."

"What's that?"

"My friend Alora has agreed to move to Bellamo. I asked her to assist me in my wedding plans and serve as my assistant."

"Yes, you mentioned that last night," Stefano commented.

"I think I also mentioned that she worked in accounting before her husband died," Janessa reminded him. "She might be a valuable resource if you decide you want someone to look into the financial reports without conducting a formal audit."

Eduard considered this newest information and gave a noncommittal nod. "We'll certainly keep that in mind."

Beside him, Marta laid a hand on his arm. "Now, if we have this business taken care of, can I interest all of you in some lunch? After spending last night socializing, I would love nothing better than to enjoy some time alone with my family."

Eduard took his wife's hand in his and brought it to his lips. "I think that is one request we are all happy to grant."

Chapter 4

JANESSA ENTERED THE KITCHEN IN the chateau, her stomach grumbling as she breathed in the aroma of fresh bread. Her mood instantly brightened when she saw Patrice pulling a batch of fresh croissants out of the oven. Janessa spoke in French, Patrice's native language, and smiled at the older woman. "*Bonjour.*"

"Giannessa." Patrice's smile was instant. "I didn't know you were back from Italy."

"Garrett and I came home late last night."

Patrice's eyebrows lifted. "Did you go to Philippe's wedding on Saturday?"

"I did." The corners of Janessa's lips lifted slightly. "In fact, Elaina approached Garrett at the reception about moving in here until after our wedding."

"What?" Patrice's face showed alarm. "You aren't going to let those people live here, are you?"

Janessa laughed and shook her head. "No. Garrett wasn't any more excited about the idea than you are."

"Thank goodness." Patrice let out a sigh of relief as she transferred the fresh croissants into a basket. "I don't think I could keep up with them, especially while Enrico is still recovering."

"How is your husband doing?" Janessa asked. Enrico typically served as the driver for the chateau, but a serious injury had kept him from his duties the past several weeks.

"Better, but the doctor said it will be a few more weeks before he can return to work."

"We'll be happy to see him up and around again, but you make sure he doesn't try to do too much too fast." Janessa reached for one of the croissants, tossing it from one hand to the other to keep from burning her fingers.

Patrice rolled her eyes and opened a cabinet to retrieve a plate for Janessa. She handed it to her along with some fresh butter. "What do you have planned for today?"

"I need to head over to the naval base in a few minutes, but I wanted to talk to you about something first." Janessa broke open her croissant, steam rising from the center. She spread some butter on one half before turning her attention back to Patrice. "I spoke to Garrett last night about having a friend of mine move in here, but I want to make sure it's okay with you."

"You don't need my permission." Patrice looked at her, clearly surprised to have the soon-to-be princess asking the hired help for approval.

"But I do need your opinion," Janessa insisted. "Alora wouldn't be coming alone. Her two sons would come with her."

Patrice shifted away from the stove to face Janessa. "And her husband?"

"He died more than three years ago. House fire," Janessa told her. "The boys are really sweet, but they are also young. Giancarlo is six, and Dante is only four. I was hoping Alora could move in, help with the wedding plans, and try to keep me organized. Unfortunately, that also means you would have little ones underfoot. And I don't know a lot about the schools here. Giancarlo is ready to start first grade, and I thought it would be good for Dante to attend some kind of preschool."

"The Renaissance Academy is only a ten minute drive from here. They don't start classes until late September, and they do have a preschool." She gave a definitive nod. "And it's about time we have children running around here again."

"I'm glad you think so." Janessa grinned at her and then motioned to the clock hanging on the wall. "I'd better get going, or I'll be late. Garrett said to tell you he should be home by lunchtime, and Stefano should arrive sometime this afternoon."

Patrice nodded. "When will your friend arrive?"

"Hopefully next week."

"I'll speak with housekeeping about preparing quarters for them," Patrice told her.

"You're a gem." Janessa leaned forward and kissed her cheek. Then she grabbed a napkin and scooped up the rest of her croissant to take with her. "I'll see you tonight."

* * *

Garrett studied the remains of the marble-sized transmitting device in his hand. Yesterday his father had raised concerns that something wasn't right with their finances, and now Garrett was faced with the likely possibility that someone had been spying on his family in their own home. He looked up at Martino, the man who managed the chateau's day-to-day operations as well as its security. "Where was this found?"

"This one was located within the framework of a curtain rod in the dining hall. Levi found seven others at various locations around the chateau," Martino said, referring to the CIA operative who had worked with Janessa to enhance the chateau's security over the past few months.

Garrett glanced around his office and lowered his voice. "Do you think it's safe to talk here now?"

Martino nodded. "We checked out all the offices actively being used, and they were clean."

"Do we have an assessment yet of how much sensitive information could have been compromised?" Garrett asked.

"We believe it to be minimal. All of the listening devices were found in common areas." His tone turned apologetic. "I'm sorry, Your Highness. Levi suggested we do a full security sweep when he arrived in May, but we didn't feel it was as important as enhancing our other safety measures."

"It's not your fault, Martino," Garrett assured him. "The last few months have been stressful for all of us, and we've all been doing the best we can." He considered for a moment. "Is there any way to know where these were made or how long they've been here?"

"Levi believes the technology to be somewhat outdated, but because these bugs are difficult to detect, they are still popular. He said the battery power in them indicates they would have been placed about two years ago," Martino told him. "We had some remodeling done around that time, along with some painting and a deep cleaning. Maybe one of those contractors planted the listening devices."

"I want you and Levi to start looking through those contracts and run the names of all the people who worked here during that period," Garrett told him. "Did Levi say anything else about who might have made them?"

"No. They're common enough that they're hard to track, but Levi did say this type of listening device needs a transmitter nearby to operate properly. We might have more luck identifying the origin of that."

"Has a transmitter been found?"

"Not yet, but we'll keep looking."

"Let me know if you find anything." Garrett closed his hand around the metal fragments in his palm and prayed that this was simply a souvenir from the people who had orchestrated a recent kidnapping, people who were no longer in a position to threaten his family.

* * *

Stefano leaned back against the soft leather seat in the back of the limousine that would take him from the palace overlooking the capital city of Calene to his family's summer home in Bellamo. The two-hour drive had become a frequent one over the past few weeks since his father and the United States secretary of the navy had signed the final agreement for the new U.S. naval base.

Negotiations had been ongoing for several years before Janessa Rogers had arrived and facilitated the current agreement. Her purpose for coming to Meridia had been to enhance security for his family, but she had exercised her initiative and proposed an option for the U.S. naval base that her government had not previously considered: retrofitting a portion of Meridia's current naval base in Bellamo for their use rather than building a new facility.

Since that time, Stefano had been actively engaged in working with the environmental agencies in Meridia to ensure that their shoreline would be protected while Garrett and Janessa worked tirelessly to ensure the base's security. While Stefano could see significant benefits from the United States developing a presence in Bellamo, he also knew the Americans were popular terrorist targets. No one in Meridia wanted their country to be known as the location of a successful terrorist attack.

Stefano indulged himself and looked out the window as his driver began the descent from the cliffs, where the palace was located, down into the village below. Adobe-style homes topped with red tiled roofs were scattered along the hillside, overlooking the brilliant blue of the Mediterranean. Boats were scarce on the water today, presumably because of the dark clouds threatening overhead.

They made it only a few miles past the village before fat raindrops splattered against the windshield and the driver flipped on the wipers. Stefano supposed his brother and future sister-in-law had been wise after all to make the trip late last night instead of waiting to travel with him this morning. They had been anxious to get home, as that's how they both thought of the chateau now.

Over the past few months, Garrett had transitioned to living there full time even though the chateau had once been used only as the royal family's summer home. Garrett would always have a place in the palace in Calene, but for Janessa, their ancestral home would never be more than a place to visit.

Stefano settled back in his seat, opened his briefcase, and pulled out the latest proposal for environmental testing off the coast of Bellamo. He barely noticed the flash of a dark car passing them on the narrow road, but when his driver slammed on the brakes, Stefano looked up suddenly. His heart jumped into his throat when he felt the car swerve and spin, sliding at full speed toward a cluster of palm trees.

The driver fought for control but to no avail. In an instant, the sleek limousine careened off the road, followed by the crunch of metal.

* * *

King Eduard stood in the private waiting room of the hospital in Calene, feeling an uncomfortable sense of déjà vu. He had walked into the hospital a king, but now he was simply a worried father, one who was desperate for news. Only weeks ago, his wife had been in a hospital bed fighting for her life, and Eduard remembered all too well those long minutes while they had waited for news.

Queen Marta gripped his hand now, and Eduard could feel the tension vibrating through her. That tension heightened when the doctor entered moments later.

"Your Majesties." Dr. Casale bowed slightly.

"How is Stefano?" Marta asked before the doctor could continue.

"He's going to be fine," the doctor assured her. "Thankfully he was wearing his seat belt, and the worst of the impact was on the other side of the car. He has a broken clavicle and some bruised ribs, but other than being uncomfortable for a while, he's doing remarkably well considering the severity of the accident."

Relief swept through Eduard. "What about the driver?"

"I'm afraid he is in serious condition," Dr. Casale said gravely. "He's being prepped for surgery right now."

"How did this happen?"

"The emergency personnel said it appears that the driver lost control on the wet road. We did get our toxicology report back, and there isn't any evidence that the driver had any drugs or alcohol in his system," he told them. "I imagine the police who responded will be able to give you more details."

"*Grazie, dottore*," Marta said. "Can we see Stefano now?"

"The nurse is doing some blood work, but as soon as she is finished, someone will come get you. We should be able to release him within an hour or two."

"Why is the nurse doing blood work for a broken collar bone and some bruised ribs?"

"It's standard procedure," Dr. Casale assured him. "The nurse will be out to show you to your son's room shortly."

"*Grazie*," King Eduard said, effectively dismissing the doctor. Then he led his wife to a sofa on the side of the room.

They had barely sat down when the police chief entered the room and approached them.

"*Mi scusi*, Your Majesties." He bowed then held out a single sheet of paper. "I wanted to bring you our preliminary accident report."

"What did you find out?" King Eduard asked, glancing down at the typewritten page.

"Our findings are inconclusive at this point. I'm afraid no one witnessed the accident, and the only skid marks we found belonged to the limousine. Until we can question the driver, we can't be sure what caused him to brake so suddenly."

"Was there any evidence of another vehicle involved?"

"No, sir." The police chief shook his head. "The limousine wasn't struck by another vehicle."

"So you think the driver simply lost control."

"It looks that way," he said tentatively.

"You don't think so though, do you?"

The chief hesitated briefly. Then he chose his words carefully. "I find it unsettling that an experienced driver, especially one who has been working for the royal family for so long, would lose control on a familiar road."

King Eduard's jaw clenched briefly. "You think this could be an attempt on my son's life."

"Sir, it would be premature to make such an assumption."

"But the possibility exists."

He shrugged slightly. "The accident happened a short distance from Viale Settimo. We did find some muddy tracks near that intersection, but we have no way of knowing if the vehicle that made them was involved."

"Perhaps it would be prudent for the royal family to go into seclusion for a few days to give you time to explore the possibilities," Eduard considered. "I think Prince Stefano would do well to spend a few weeks recovering at the chateau with his brother."

"Sir, I think that is an excellent idea."

Chapter 5

ALORA STARED AT THE MEAGER furnishings of her one-bedroom apartment and considered what else she wanted to pack. For the first time in three years, she actually felt like she was looking forward instead of dwelling on her past. Her clothing was already neatly packed into suitcases, and the majority of the kids' toys were boxed up.

Right after finalizing the details of her new job with Janessa, Alora had visited her landlord and told him she was moving. She hadn't worked since losing Carlo, and what was left from the life insurance money was dwindling fast. Still, over the past few years, it had been enough to pay rent and put food on the table. The boys' clothes might always be secondhand, but at least they had a parent at home who loved them.

"Mama! Mama!" Giancarlo rushed into the room, a toy in each hand. "Are we really going to live in a castle?"

"Well, it's not a castle, but a prince lives there." She leaned down so she could look into the dark eyes that reminded her so much of his father's. With a sigh, she reached for him and pulled him close for a hug.

He snuggled into her for a second and then squirmed free. "Can we go see it now?"

A smile tugged at her lips. "We have to pack first."

"Tomorrow, then?"

"I thought we would wait until next week."

"Pleeeease?" He asked, dragging out the word as he looked up at her hopefully.

Alora wanted to hold firm to her original plan, but as she looked around at the shabby furniture, she realized she was as anxious as her son to take a step forward into their new life. "Tell you what. If you'll keep an eye on your brother while I get organized, maybe we can leave a few days early."

"Tomorrow?"

"Maybe tomorrow, but I'm going to need you to be a good helper."

"I can help you, Mama."

"I know you can." She gave in to the urge to smile. "You go play with your brother now, and I'll come help you pack your things in a couple minutes."

"Okay!"

Alora watched him race back into the bedroom and considered for a moment. Janessa had said to come as soon as she could manage it. As she looked around the room once more, she decided that perhaps Giancarlo had the right idea. Maybe tomorrow should be the start of their new life.

* * *

The walls were closing in. Stefano recognized the frustrating sensation of feeling trapped. He had felt it often throughout his life, especially since reaching adulthood. Now, with the prospect of staying within the walls of the chateau for the next few days, he struggled against those familiar bonds. The file in his lap was little more than a blur as he tried to ignore the pain from his shoulder and ribs. He shifted to try to get more comfortable, only to have another sharp pain shoot through him.

Gritting his teeth, he focused on the French doors that were open wide to let in the scent of the sea and the gardens below. On the balcony, exotic flowers with vibrant colors spilled out of a huge pottery urn. Beyond the stone balcony, the magnificent blue of the Mediterranean contrasted against pristine white sand.

He wanted to be out on the water right now, working the sails of his boat, a glass of wine in his hand. Of course, sailing would be out of the question for the next several weeks, and he wouldn't be able to drink as long as he was dependant on the pain medicine the doctor had prescribed. Not that he drank often, but he certainly preferred to make his own decisions when it came to his social life rather than have his doctor dictate them for him.

His attention shifted when a knock sounded at the door. Before he had a chance to respond, Garrett pushed it open and walked into the sitting room. "How are you feeling?"

Stefano looked up at him and winced again as he closed the file in his lap and set it on the end table beside him. "Sore."

"That isn't surprising." Garrett dropped into the seat across from his brother. "Patrice said to tell you she was making you some chicken cordon bleu for dinner."

"Chicken cordon bleu is your favorite dinner, not mine."

"Yeah, I know." Garrett grinned. "What can I say? I can't help it if Patrice loves me best."

Stefano narrowed his eyes. "I'd tell you that you're a selfish brat, but you'd probably take it as a compliment."

"Probably," Garrett agreed with a chuckle. "Would it make you feel any better if I told you Janessa convinced Patrice to make that raspberry cheesecake you like so much?"

"Maybe," Stefano said, slightly mollified. He tapped a finger impatiently on the file in his lap. "I don't know how Mother and Father can expect me to just sit around for the next few days."

"From what I heard, it's going to be more like a few weeks," Garrett said with a touch of sympathy. "Apparently the police chief wants some more time to look into your accident, especially since you thought you saw another car right before it happened."

Stefano's heart sank. "As I told Father, I'm not sure I really saw another car. I was working in the backseat when my driver slammed on the brakes."

"But the fact remains that something caused him to hit the brakes," Garrett reminded him, his tone now serious. "Besides, it will be easier for you to work on the environmental studies if you don't have to keep commuting back and forth between here and the palace."

"I suppose," Stefano conceded, "but I don't know how I can look into those financial matters Father's worried about."

"I know you won't have access to the church's books or the ones at the winter palace, but the records for the gala would be here. I'm sure Martino can help you track them down." Garrett shrugged. "A little work will help you keep your mind off the pain."

"Easy for you to say." Stefano grimaced as he shifted in his seat. "Any news about my driver?"

Garrett shook his head sympathetically. "Last I heard, he had come out of surgery okay, but he still hasn't regained consciousness. I'll ask Martino to keep you up to date. I'm heading out of town today."

"Where are you going?"

"I'm taking Janessa on a little trip." Garrett's lips curved up. "It's a surprise."

Stefano considered his future sister-in-law's profession and looked at his brother skeptically. "Do you really think you can surprise her?"

"I'm sure going to try."

* * *

"Archbishop Leone." Janessa extended her hand to the older man and wondered if he ever went anywhere without wearing his religious robes and heavy metal crucifix. "Please come in and sit down." She motioned to the parlor and added, "Thank you so much for coming here to Bellamo. I appreciate you going out of your way like this."

"It is my pleasure." His normally serious expression warmed when he smiled. He waited for her to sit down before choosing the chair beside her. "How is Prince Stefano? I heard of his accident."

"He's recovering," Janessa stated simply. Her training kept her from elaborating even though she knew the royal family trusted this man, that he had been in their confidence for more than twenty years.

"I know everyone hopes to see him up and around again soon," he said, apparently content with her answer. "Now, I understand you and Prince Garrett are ready to set a date for your wedding."

Janessa nodded. She couldn't tell him, of course, that the driving factor was the estimated completion date of the new LDS temple in Meridia. Garrett's conversion to The Church of Jesus Christ of Latter-day Saints was still being treated like top secret material, and the royal family didn't seem to think that would change anytime soon.

The information would get out eventually, but this man across from her wasn't likely to welcome the news no matter how mild-mannered he might seem. "We were thinking about the second Friday in June."

"A summer wedding." The archbishop smiled his approval. "I'm sure it will be absolutely perfect."

Janessa thought of the new temple that would overlook the Mediterranean. She granted the older man a smile. "I'm sure it will."

* * *

Dr. Casale stared down at the single sheet of paper he held, rereading the lab results for the third time. The numbers couldn't be right. They just couldn't. If they were, life in his country would be forever altered.

He looked up at the lab technician who had run the test and saw by her pale face that she believed the report to be accurate.

"I want you to redo the test. Let's make sure this is right."

Belinda Parnelli spoke slowly, cautiously. "I already ran them three times. I even used the backup blood sample to make sure. I'm sorry, sir, but the results are accurate."

"Who else knows about this?"

"No one," she said, anxiety humming through her voice.

"Let's make sure it stays that way."

"What are you going to tell the prince?"

"The truth."

She shook her head sympathetically. "This is going to be a nightmare for him when the public finds out."

Dr. Casale looked up at her once more, and his voice was stern. "The public isn't going to find out about this. Ever. Do I make myself clear?"

Belinda took an automatic step back and swallowed hard. "Yes, sir."

"Good." He waved toward the hallway. "Now, I want you to go back to the lab and destroy all of the files on this and dispose of the blood samples. I don't want any records that can link these results back to the royal family."

She stared at him for a moment and then reluctantly nodded. "I'll take care of it."

* * *

Janessa opened the door to the chateau's security office with a sense of anticipation. Her talk with Patrice that morning had helped ease some of her logistical concerns about bringing Alora to Bellamo. Now she hoped to dispense with some concerns of a more emotional nature.

As she expected, fellow CIA agent Levi Marin was sitting at his desk in the corner of the room while two guards watched the various television monitors on the wall. Levi glanced up, his dark eyes curious. He looked completely professional and almost aloof, wearing an expression she had seen him adopt frequently over the past few years as they had worked various undercover operations together.

"Levi, could I see you for a minute?" Janessa asked from just inside the threshold.

"Of course." Levi pushed back from his desk and turned to the two security guards across the room. "I'll be right back."

Levi stepped out into the hall with her and closed the door behind him. Automatically, he lowered his voice. "Is everything okay?"

"I just wanted you to know I've asked Alora DeSanto to move in here and be my assistant."

"DeSanto?" Levi's eyes widened. Even though he had never met the woman, he was well aware of the tragedy that had resulted several years earlier when her husband's cover had been leaked. "Are you sure that's a good idea?"

"Yes, I am." Janessa nodded. "The queen insists that I need an assistant to help me manage my schedule and the wedding plans, but with my work at the base, I need someone who has both a security clearance and the right language skills."

"She hasn't worked for us since the bombing," Levi pointed out. "Her clearances won't be valid anymore."

"I know, but it will be easier to get them reinstated than to start from scratch with someone else." Janessa's eyes met Levi's. "Besides that, she's a friend."

Levi nodded in understanding. "Is that the only reason you wanted to talk to me, or is there something else?"

"Actually, yes." Janessa nodded. "I know you were planning to transfer out of here in a few weeks, but I was wondering if you would be willing to stay on awhile longer if Director Palmer will approve it."

The corners of his lips lifted. "You must have read my mind. I spoke with personnel this morning and asked if my position here could be extended."

"What did they say?"

Levi glanced down the hall to make sure they were still really alone. "The Agency is still concerned about possible security issues at the base, so I've been approved for at least a six-month extension."

"That's great. I don't think I'm quite ready to be without backup," Janessa told him with a wry smile. "Are you going to keep working from here, or will you transfer over to the base offices?"

"As long as the royal family will allow it, I'll work from here. My cover working in security is already intact, and there's no reason I need to be onsite, especially since the base is only a five-minute drive from here," Levi told her. "Also, I got the report from Langley just this morning on those listening devices we found."

"Any luck in tracing the origin?"

Levi nodded. "It's a newer version of KGB technology that was used in the eighties. The analysts said the bugs had definitely been here for approximately two to three years."

"Were they still operational?"

"Yes, all but one."

"Any idea who might have planted them?"

"We're still combing through the paperwork for all of the contractors who worked here at the time. It's possible that the people behind the queen's kidnapping last month were responsible, but there's no way of knowing without a confession, and I doubt we're going to get that," Levi said.

"Is there any way we can identify who was receiving the transmissions?"

"Maybe if we can find the transmitter, but so far we haven't had any luck," Levi told her. "One of the main reasons the technology is so popular is the standard security sweeps don't usually pick them up."

"Why not?"

"Something about the type of metal alloy they're made of." Levi shrugged. "We're still looking, but with the size of this place, it's going to take some time."

"Let me know if you find anything."

"You know I will," Levi said, his eyes narrowing. "What has you so worried, Janessa? Prince Stefano's accident or the listening devices we found here?"

"Both."

Levi gave her a look of understanding. "Me too."

Chapter 6

"WHAT DO YOU MEAN THE transmissions stopped?"

"Someone in the chateau did a complete security sweep and found all of the bugs that had been planted."

"All of them?" His voice was filled with disbelief. "I thought they weren't detectable."

"They weren't before now. The new guy, Levi, used some new equipment and wiped all of them out."

"I can't believe this. They've been in place for almost three years, and now, when we need them the most, they're discovered." He shook his head. "What are the chances that the listening devices can be traced back to our supporters?"

"None, as long as they don't find the transmitter, but our latest intelligence indicates that the security team at the chateau is searching for it. If the transmitter is found, we are definitely vulnerable."

"You need to get someone in there. We need to make sure that equipment isn't discovered, and we have to find a way to know what's going on with the royal family. Everything depends on having perfect timing. If we don't know exactly where everyone is going to be on the day we strike, we can't guarantee complete success."

"I'll take care of it."

* * *

"Here you are, sir." Martino set a six-inch stack of files on the table in Stefano's sitting room.

"It looks like this should keep me occupied for a few days." Stefano lifted a file and glanced at the first page. Then he shook his head. "Make that a few weeks."

"Is there anything I can help you with, Your Highness?" Martino asked. "The auditors looked through all our financial files only three weeks ago. If there is something specific you need that isn't in their report, I'd be happy to call them for you."

"I appreciate the offer, but this is little more than my father hoping to keep me occupied for a while." Stefano granted Martino a small smile.

The phone rang, and Stefano nodded for Martino to answer it.

"Hello?" Martino listened for a moment before hitting a button to put the caller on hold. He turned to face Stefano and said, "Luigi Ovalle asked to see you. I'm sorry, sir, but he doesn't have an appointment."

"That's okay, Martino." Stefano suppressed a sigh. Luigi had been working for his family for decades, most recently as the events coordinator for both the summer chateau and the winter palace. While he was meticulous with detail, he could be relentless when he wasn't granted the attention he felt he deserved. "Please tell him I'll meet him in the parlor in five minutes."

"Yes, sir."

Stefano made his way downstairs to find the wiry man waiting for him, a file folder in his hand.

"I'm sorry to disturb you, Your Highness, but I have several documents that require a signature, and I'm afraid your brother isn't available."

"I gather we have some social events coming up," Stefano commented as he extended his good hand and took the file from Luigi.

"Yes, sir. Several dinners are coming up here at the chateau, and of course, I'm already looking forward to the Winter Ball in November."

Stefano looked over the contractor bids for several local companies and then signed in the appropriate places. "Please make sure Martino is given copies of all these contracts."

"Of course. Thank you for making time for me today."

* * *

"Come on, Janessa. It's time to go." Garrett leaned on the doorjamb of his fiancée's temporary office at the naval base in Bellamo.

Janessa pushed her hair behind her shoulders and looked up at him. "Go where? I really have to finish the security plans for next week. In case you've forgotten, construction for the new administration building is supposed to start next Thursday."

"Bring it with you. You'll have plenty of time to work on the plane."

Both elegant eyebrows lifted. "On the plane?"

"Yes, on the plane." Garrett smothered a grin and moved farther into the room. "We're taking a little trip. Get whatever files you'll need for the next few days and let's go."

"Where are we going?"

"It's a surprise."

She cocked her head to one side and looked at him skeptically. "Garrett, I have work to do. I don't have time to take off right now. Besides, Alora and her boys are arriving sometime next week. I want to be here when they get here."

"Patrice will help them get settled if they arrive before we get back."

"Tell me where we're going."

"I told you. It's a surprise." He picked up her briefcase from the chair opposite her desk and handed it to her. "Last chance. You can get your files yourself or you can go without them. We're leaving in ten minutes."

"Are you trying to be difficult?"

Humor flashed in his eyes. "Absolutely."

Janessa pressed her lips together, and Garrett could tell she was trying to fight the oncoming smile. With a shake of her head, she stood and shuffled the papers in front of her into a folder. She powered off her laptop and slid it into her briefcase, along with several files. Then she crossed to Garrett. "Okay, you win, but I really would like to know where we're going. And we'll need to swing by the chateau so I can pack."

"Patrice already packed your things for you. Your bags are in the car," Garrett told her.

"You thought of everything, didn't you?"

"I hope so." Garrett leaned down and brushed his lips against hers. "Come on. We have a flight to catch."

* * *

"Dr. Casale." Stefano shifted in his chair and looked up inquisitively as his physician entered his sitting room at the chateau. "I didn't expect to see you for a few more days. Please come in and sit down."

"How are you feeling?" The doctor lowered himself into a chair and gripped his medical bag with both hands.

"I'm fine." Stefano sensed the doctor's tension. "What's wrong? Is it my driver?"

"No. He's improving steadily, as we had hoped."

"Then what?"

"We ran some routine blood work on you when you were at the hospital."

Stefano's eyebrows went up, and an unsettled feeling pulsed through him. "And?"

"I'm sorry, Your Highness. There's no easy way to say this." He took a steadying breath and kept his eyes on Stefano. "You have Merid's syndrome."

"Merid's?" Stefano repeated. Shock came first, followed swiftly by denial. Only years of training allowed him to control the turmoil stirring inside him, to present a calm front. He knew of the stories, of the many family members who had supposedly been afflicted by the rare hereditary disease, but no one had been diagnosed with it in his family for several generations. Surely this couldn't be happening, not to him. He swallowed the lump that had formed in his throat and was surprised his voice sounded calm. "Are you sure?"

Dr. Casale nodded. "We ran the test multiple times. Since the blood test was developed to diagnose Merid's several decades ago, we have made it a policy to screen every member of the royal family. The test is unreliable until adulthood, so we typically conduct it around the age of twenty-one."

"I passed my twenty-first birthday some time ago."

"Yes, sir. According to our records, you were screened once before. After your accident, my assistant noticed the results in your file couldn't be yours. They were from someone with a different blood type. Realizing that an error had been made, we ran the test again."

Stefano tried to absorb the news, all the while praying to whatever god might be listening that this was some kind of mistake. Merid's syndrome was the reason the Fortier family had remained so small over the centuries, why there were currently only four male heirs to the throne despite the fact that his family had ruled Meridia for more than six hundred years. The effects of the disease were nearly undetectable, but the results were unmistakable: infertility.

"You're telling me that I can't have children? That I can't produce an heir to the throne?"

"I'm sorry, Your Highness, but yes, that is exactly what I'm telling you."

Stefano picked up the water glass on the table beside him and sipped slowly as his mind turned the facts over and over. He couldn't have children. Never would he know the joy of parenthood. Following that thought was the realization that his successor to the throne would not be his own child but would instead be Garrett's. "What about my brother? Has he been tested?"

"Yes, Your Highness." Dr. Casale nodded. "Prince Garrett is not affected by the disease."

"I see." Stefano pushed his emotions aside and tried to consider his country and the future of Meridia. One of his father's greatest concerns when Garrett chose to become a member of the Mormon Church was the possible upheaval that could occur if Garrett or one of his descendants ever took the throne.

Stefano let out a sigh as the full reality punched through him. No longer was there a question of whether his country would ever have a king who did not belong to the Meridian Church. If he was really afflicted with Merid's, it was now a matter of when. His grip tightened on his water glass before he set it down next to his bottle of pain medicine. "Who else knows about this?"

"Only the nurse who ran the tests. All of the documentation has been destroyed, and I have sworn her to secrecy," Dr. Casale told him. "I felt it prudent to protect your privacy considering the circumstances."

"I appreciate your efforts, Doctor," Stefano managed, even though he felt numb inside. "I trust you will allow me to share this information with my family when I feel it appropriate."

"Of course, Your Highness." The doctor held up his bag. "I thought perhaps we should run the tests one more time, just to be sure."

Stefano nodded, even though he already saw on the doctor's face that the man didn't expect different results. The doctor drew out the supplies he needed to take another blood sample. When he finished, he packed his bag, and Stefano asked, "How long will it take to get the new results?"

"I should have them for you by tomorrow."

"I'll look forward to hearing from you." Despite the pain in his side, Stefano pushed himself to a stand. "Thank you for making the time to come see me today."

The doctor's eyes narrowed. "When was the last time you took your pain medicine?"

"Sometime this morning," Stefano admitted.

"You need to take some. There's no reason you should be in pain." Dr. Casale picked up the prescription bottle on the end table. After dispensing a pill into his hand, he turned and handed it to Stefano along with his water glass.

In no mood to argue, Stefano popped the pill into his mouth and washed it down with the rest of his water.

The doctor walked to the door. "I'll be stopping back in to check on you in a couple days. In the meantime, please call me if you need anything."

"I will. Thank you." Stefano watched him leave then pressed a hand against the door to make sure it was closed. He looked down to see the now empty glass still gripped in his hand. Frustration, disappointment, denial all bubbled up inside him as he heaved the glass across the room and watched it and his future shatter against the wall.

Chapter 7

JANESSA STARTLED AWAKE WHEN THE plane touched down. She shifted in her seat, the soft leather giving beneath her as she stretched her arms above her head and tried to shake the sleep out of her brain. She glanced over at Garrett sitting beside her, a thick file open in his lap, and asked, "Are you going to tell me where we are now?"

"Andrews Air Force Base."

"We're in Maryland?" She turned toward the window and looked at the green rushing by them as King Eduard's private jet slowed and then began taxiing off the runway. "Why didn't you tell me we were coming to the DC area? If I had known we were going to be so close to CIA headquarters, I would have brought the paperwork with me that Director Palmer asked for yesterday."

"We aren't going to CIA headquarters," Garrett told her. "I have some meetings at the White House today, and then tomorrow we're going to escort your sister's family back to your parents' home in Iowa for the weekend."

"What?" Janessa stared at him wide-eyed. "Does Mary know about this?"

"Of course. She's the one who mentioned she wanted to bless her baby in Iowa so all your family could be there for it."

"Yeah, but I doubt she mentioned that in the hope that we would pick her up in your father's private plane and take her there."

"She didn't seem opposed to the idea."

Janessa had to laugh. "This is a wonderful surprise. Thank you."

"You're welcome." Garrett smiled back at her. The plane came to a stop, and he motioned toward the restroom. "Did you need to freshen up before we go to the White House?"

"Actually, I think I'd prefer to go straight to my sister's house," Janessa said. "Although I probably should swing by CIA headquarters first."

"You can't go to CIA headquarters."

"What? Why not?"

"First of all, someone might see you, and we definitely don't want the press to get wind that my fiancée is a spy."

"I'm not a spy."

"Close enough." Garrett waved away the triviality between *spies* and *intelligence officers*. "Besides, Director Palmer will be at the White House to meet with you while I meet with your president."

"You're meeting with the president?" Janessa asked. "Why?"

"Just some final details that need to be ironed out before construction starts on the new naval base next week."

"I thought the agreement was already signed."

"It was. My father just wants a few of the legal points clarified. Besides, it was the perfect excuse to be able to bring you to the U.S."

"Any idea how long our meetings are supposed to last?"

"Probably all afternoon," Garrett told her. "After we finish with our meetings, we'll have time to change for dinner with the president tonight. Then, tomorrow morning, your sister and her family will meet us at Andrews Air Force Base, and we'll fly into Des Moines."

"Aren't we staying at Mary's house tonight?"

Garrett shook his head. "We're staying at the White House tonight."

"What?" Janessa's eyes widened. She considered for a minute what an honor it was to be invited to spend the night in the president's home, but then reality set in. She didn't know the president. She hadn't even voted for him. Given the choice, she would definitely prefer to spend those precious few hours in her sister's company. "Garrett, that's very generous of the president to let us stay there, but I really would rather stay with my sister."

Garrett looked at her, apparently surprised that she wasn't excited about the prospect of sleeping at the White House. Then he let out a sigh. "I'm sorry, Janessa, but it isn't an option. It isn't safe."

"Wait a minute." She held up a hand. "You're telling me that it isn't safe for me to visit my own sister?"

"Not without a lot of advance planning." He shook his head, his expression sympathetic. "I know that being in the spotlight is still pretty new to you, but the press alone would cause too big of a security concern for you to stay anywhere that isn't secure. Besides, the police still haven't finished their investigation into Stefano's accident."

She was silent for a moment as she considered Garrett's words. "What about when we go to Iowa? We will be able to stay with my family there, won't we?"

Garrett nodded. "Our visit to your family's farm isn't on our official itinerary. Besides, we won't have as many security concerns out in the country as we would in DC."

A sigh escaped her, and she nodded. "You know, I don't think I like being the person being protected very much. I much prefer being the person doing the protecting."

"I know. It's an adjustment." Garrett stood up. "Are you ready to go smile for the cameras?"

Janessa rolled her eyes. "Maybe I will take a minute to freshen up."

* * *

He leaned back in his leather executive chair and read the single sheet of paper before looking up at his associate. "How reliable is this information?"

"Very." The other man spoke in hushed tones. "I verified it myself."

"A Mormon prince." He shook his head, the hint of a smile forming. "You realize this changes everything."

"Perhaps." He tapped a finger on the side of his chair, considering. He had waited patiently for his dues, for the position of responsibility he had trained for. For so long he had been denied that right. Now, finally, things were about to change.

"If we wait to release this until right before we follow through with our other plans, we might not need to eliminate Prince Garrett. It's possible his choices will alienate him from his subjects at the same time everyone discovers Prince Stefano can't do his duty," he said. "One or two well-placed phone calls to the media will destroy the royal family, and no one will ever know who was behind it."

"But King Eduard would still be in power, and the U.S. navy would likely maintain their presence here. Besides, we can't be certain how the public will react. We need to make sure we have a backup plan in place."

Dark eyebrows lifted over equally dark eyes. "Are you certain that once we follow through with our plans, the public will embrace everything we have to offer? You are deliberately creating chaos here in Meridia."

"Chaos is necessary before the calm." He smiled charmingly. "Patience, my friend. Everything will happen when the time is right."

* * *

Janessa clutched the strap of her briefcase with one hand as she followed a White House aide down a wide hallway in the west wing. The past several hours had been completely surreal, starting with Garrett escorting her onto his father's private jet and continuing right up to being greeted by the White House chief of staff when they arrived a few minutes ago. Then again, life for her had hardly fallen into the normal category since meeting Garrett last spring.

The young man escorting her stopped and pushed a door open for her. Then he motioned her inside.

"Thank you," Janessa said to the aide before stepping in where the director of the Central Intelligence Agency was sitting at a conference table reading through files.

Director Palmer stood and reached out to shake her hand. "Hello, Janessa."

"Director Palmer." Janessa smiled warmly at the gray-haired man in the tailored suit. "How are you, sir?"

"I'm well, thank you." Director Palmer motioned to the conference room chair beside him. "Please, sit down."

"I'm sorry I don't have those reports you asked for. I'm afraid Garrett didn't tell me where we were going until we landed."

Director Palmer nodded as a smile crossed his face. "I haven't heard of any problems in Meridia over the past few weeks. Is it safe to assume you haven't broken anyone's nose lately?"

Janessa chuckled and shook her head. An unfortunate incident in Paris a few years ago had grown into a running joke within the Agency. "No, not lately. I've been trying to control my temper."

"Good to hear. How are the security plans going for the naval base?" Director Palmer asked as he settled back into his chair. "Are we still expecting to break ground on Thursday?"

"We are." Janessa nodded. She gave him the updated timelines and took the time to discuss a few other security matters.

"You're doing a good job over there," Director Palmer told her. "Is there anything new about Prince Stefano's accident?"

"The findings are inconclusive, but the police chief still suspects foul play."

"Our analysts have expressed similar concerns," Director Palmer admitted. "We think it's possible that someone was trying to eliminate a member of the royal family and make it look like an accident."

"To what end?" Janessa asked, mulling over the information. "Stefano isn't king yet, and all indications are that Eduard will continue to rule for many more years."

"Yes, but if the attempt had been successful, the succession to the crown would be altered."

"Garrett would be next in line," Janessa said slowly. "Surely you don't think Garrett would hurt his own brother."

"No, not at all." Director Palmer shook his head.

"Have our analysts expressed any concern about Garrett's extended family?"

"Nothing of significance."

"Would it be possible for me to get copies of the dossiers on Elam, Victoria, and Philippe?"

"Has something happened to cause you concern, or do you just want to check up on your future in-laws?"

"Some comments have been made about that side of the family living beyond their means," Janessa admitted, certain this information would not be anything new to the CIA. "I would feel better if I had a clearer picture of what their situation is like in case there are any vulnerabilities that could be exploited."

"I'll make sure you get copies of our files, but there is another angle you need to consider."

"What's that?"

"Have you heard of Caspar Gazsi?"

Janessa shook her head. "Who is he?"

"He's the president of Caspian Oil."

"Isn't that the Libyan company that petitioned for the rights to drill for oil off the coast of Meridia?"

"That's right." Director Palmer nodded. "He owns a residence in Meridia just outside Medina. He is also a known supporter of Liberté, a small faction in Meridia that's showing strong anti-American tendencies." He took a photograph out of his file and slid it toward her. "We're concerned that this group might try to use the construction of our naval base and Prince Garrett's engagement to an American to trigger civil unrest in Meridia."

"In Meridia?" Janessa's eyebrows drew together. "That's crazy. Meridia is a peaceful country, full of loyal citizens, most of whom are pro-American."

"Yes, but almost 90 percent of those citizens are also loyal members of the Meridian Church," Director Palmer pointed out. "If something did happen to Prince Stefano, how do you think they would feel if they found out their future king and queen were both Mormon?"

Janessa's eyes widened. "What?"

Director Palmer gave her a knowing look. "We've known for some time that Prince Garrett was interested in your religion. I realize his baptism isn't yet public knowledge, but it's possible that someone is planning on using that information against you."

"How did you know Garrett is LDS?" Janessa asked now. "Only his immediate family and a small handful of Church members were at his baptism. Everyone there promised to keep the information confidential. Even the members of our branch don't know he's a baptized member."

"One of the locals who works at our embassy in Calene was there when he got baptized. He said something to our operative there, assuming we already knew about it," Director Palmer told her. His voice took a serious tone when he added, "Janessa, Garrett isn't the only one at risk right now. Your association with the royal family makes you a target too."

Janessa swallowed hard as she considered his words. "How credible do you think this threat is?"

"We've seen an increase in chatter in the region over the past week, but we aren't sure yet if it has anything to do with Prince Stefano's accident," Director Palmer admitted. "I promise you'll be among the first to know if we uncover anything new."

"I would appreciate it," Janessa said. "I don't know if the royal family can handle another threat like the last one."

Chapter 8

"MAMA, MAMA! LOOK!" DANTE POINTED excitedly out the window as the royal chateau came into view.

The stone structure itself was exquisite, towers and turrets spearing into the sky in a way that made Alora think of fairytales. Summer flowers contrasted with the lush green hillside and the bright blue of the Mediterranean. Her eyes shifted to the water and the pristine white beach that stretched out behind their new home.

"Are we really going to live here?"

Alora swallowed a bubble of uncertainty and managed to nod. "Yes, we're really going to live here." She glanced at her children in the rearview mirror. "Now, don't forget what we practiced. When you greet any grown-ups, you need to bow, right?"

"We remember, Mama," Giancarlo insisted.

Dante shifted excitedly beside his brother. "Can we play on the beach? And go swimming? And get a puppy?"

"Slow down." Alora chuckled at Dante's enthusiasm and his continued plea for a puppy. She slowed the car as she approached the gate at the entrance. "I'm sure you'll be able to play on the beach, but only if I'm with you. For now, we need to get settled."

"But we've been driving forever." Dante's voice came out in a whine. "Can't we go play first?"

Before she could answer, Giancarlo asked, "Are you sure they're going to let us in?"

"We're about to find out." Alora rolled down the window.

"May I help you?" the guard asked, looking first at Alora and then glancing at the two boys in the backseat.

"Yes, I'm here to see Janessa Rogers."

"I'm sorry, but Signorina Rogers is not in right now," the guard informed her. "Was she expecting you?"

"Yes. I'm Alora DeSanto." She started to fumble for a way to explain that she was moving in, but then the guard smiled warmly.

"Ah, yes, we've been expecting you. I will need to see some ID though."

"Of course." Alora rummaged through her purse and pulled her passport free. "Here you go."

"Thank you." He looked down at the passport to verify her identity. Then he motioned to a second guard to open the gate. "Follow the driveway to the front of the house. After your luggage has been unloaded, you can park your car in the garage."

"Thank you."

"Of course, Signora. Welcome to Bellamo."

* * *

The green and brown patchwork of fields stretched out for miles under the wispy white clouds that accented the brilliant blue sky. In the distance, Janessa could see the cluster of neighborhoods that made up the outskirts of Des Moines, Iowa, the closest town to her family's farm.

Idly, she fiddled with the diamond engagement ring on her left hand, twisting it back and forth as she leaned back beside the man she planned to marry, the man who was about to meet her family for the first time. Besides the obvious concerns of whether her fiancé and family would like each other, Director Palmer's revelation had pushed Janessa's already strained nerves into overdrive.

She had expected suspicions to arise about Garrett's religious preferences as time went on, especially once he became a regular member of the local congregation in Bellamo. What she hadn't anticipated was for the information to leak so quickly. She understood Garrett's need for privacy, but the fact that the CIA knew of his baptism only proved that people liked to talk and that eventually someone in the media was going to find out that Garrett had strayed from the Meridian Church.

Not willing to put a damper on their weekend with her family, Janessa had chosen to keep this new information to herself for now. Today she had enough to worry about, although she wasn't sure if she was more concerned about what Garrett would think of her family or the other way around.

"You aren't nervous, are you?" Garrett asked with a touch of amusement in his voice. "I'm the one who should be nervous."

Janessa glanced over at him. "Why should you be nervous? You're a potential father-in-law's dream."

His eyebrows winged up. "Oh really?"

"Oh yeah." Humor danced in her eyes. "A handsome prince who's also kind and generous. You're definitely a keeper."

Garrett grinned at her. "Glad you think so."

"I know so." Janessa leaned forward and pressed her lips to his. Warmth spread through her, but the kiss did little to calm the nerves fluttering in her stomach.

Garrett looked over at her, his expression becoming serious. "You really are nervous. Why?"

She shifted restlessly. "I always get nervous when I go home to see my family. They have a tendency to ask questions I'm not prepared to answer." She glanced at the back of the plane, where her sister and brother-in-law were sitting, their month-old daughter strapped into a car seat between them. Instinctively, Janessa lowered her voice. "I don't like lying to them."

"Why would you lie to them?"

Janessa looked at him, a little surprised that he didn't already understand her reasons. "Because they always want to know how work is going, and I hate not being able to tell them the truth about what I do."

"Surely they know you can't talk about your work. That's the nature of the CIA."

Understanding dawned on her, the realization that he didn't know how deep her cover ran. "Garrett, they don't know I work for the CIA."

His eyes widened. "Your own family doesn't know who you work for?"

Janessa shook her head. "Of course not. No one knows who I work for except the people I work with. Even when I was working in Venezuela, only a handful of people knew I was really an intelligence officer."

"Wait a minute." Garrett held up a hand and shook his head as though trying to clear his confusion. "You're telling me your parents don't know why you've been in Meridia all this time?"

"They believe what the tabloids have told them. They think I met you a few years ago and that I went to Meridia to visit you." She rolled her eyes. "Believe me, I've had a ton of e-mails from my family over the past few months asking why I never told them I knew you."

"Surely you can tell them the truth now."

Her eyebrows drew together as she considered the implications. Then she shook her head again. "No, I couldn't do that. Besides the fact that I signed a secrecy agreement with the CIA, I don't think either of us wants to take the chance of one of my siblings sharing my secrets. Could you imagine what would happen if the newspapers got wind of the fact that I work for the Agency?"

"Don't you trust them?"

"It's just safer if they don't know the truth," Janessa insisted. She drew a breath as though steadying herself, and he was surprised to see the raw emotion in her eyes. "A few years ago, a friend of mine was working undercover for the CIA. His brother was all bent out of shape about holiday plans, and he finally broke down and explained who he worked for and why he couldn't come home to the United States. Two weeks later a bomb went off at my friend's house. He didn't survive. Most of his family died with him."

"His brother blew his cover?" Garrett's eyes widened.

"According to the investigation, it was an inadvertent disclosure. He told his wife in confidence, who then told a friend. It didn't take long before something ended up on the Internet. That was all it took for the group my friend had infiltrated to discover his true identity."

"That's awful."

Janessa nodded, and she blinked back the tears that misted her eyes. "It really brought home how important it is to protect my cover, even from those I trust the most."

Chapter 9

STEFANO MOVED GINGERLY AS HE walked down the stairs. He knew Patrice would have a fit if she saw him up and around without his sling on, but he was already tired of wearing it, and he still wasn't convinced it was helping. Not that he'd spent the past twenty-four hours dwelling on his injuries. His thoughts instead had been consumed by the doctor's news, the news that had been confirmed only an hour ago when the doctor had called to give him the results of the second set of tests. There wasn't any doubt. He had Merid's syndrome.

He thought he'd accepted the diagnosis after his first conversation with the doctor, but the phone call had proven to him that he'd still held on to a seed of hope that there had been some mistake. That seed had been smashed beyond repair. Now, after being cooped up for the past couple days, Stefano found himself in desperate need of some fresh air and a fresh perspective.

He crossed the chateau's main entryway and moved into the main parlor. Light streamed through large windows into the enormous room and spilled onto the comfortably faded furnishings. Couches, chairs, and loveseats were arranged to create cozy conversation areas, but Stefano ignored them and headed through the room toward a set of French doors leading to the terrace.

For as long as he could remember, the chateau had been the place he was always drawn to when he needed some time to himself. He supposed it was ironic that he was here when he was forced to face an alternate reality for his future from the one he had always planned for himself.

He had never seriously considered what he wanted in his future family life. He had simply expected that he would someday marry and have children of his own. As the heir to the throne, he had been subject to the media's speculations about whom he might marry since he'd turned twenty, but now at the age of thirty-two, he still hadn't met a woman who held his interest for more than a few months.

His heart ached at the realization that he would never know what it was to have children of his own, that he would never experience the joy of being a father. Now that the duty to produce an heir could no longer be his, he wondered if marriage would even be in his future. What woman would want to wed a man and live in the spotlight while the world anticipated the children that would never come?

Still moving gingerly, he pulled open the door and stepped outside just in time to see two dark-haired bodies streak past him and head toward the gardens.

He stared after them, confused at first by the presence of children on the grounds. Then he remembered the impending arrival of Janessa's friend. He thought back to the days when he and Garrett had spent their summers playing hide and seek in the bushes and creating havoc as often as humanly possible. If these two little boys were anything like he was at their age, Stefano imagined they were more interested in the beach that lay beyond the gardens than they were in smelling the flowers.

His eyebrows lifted when he heard a woman's voice call out in Italian. "Boys, come back here!"

Both boys stopped, and Stefano could have sworn he heard their twin sighs of resignation. "Yes, Mama."

Moving much more slowly, they turned to head back the way they had come just as a delicately built woman hurried around the corner. Stefano's first impression was that this could not be the mother of two children.

She pushed her dark hair behind her shoulders, her attention so focused on the boys that she didn't notice Stefano standing in the doorway.

She gripped each of the boys by the arm as she squatted in front of them so she could look them in the eye. "Didn't I tell you two not to run off?"

"Sorry, Mama. We just wanted to look around."

"I know, but for now, we need to go find out where we're staying, and I'll need your help while I unload." She started to usher the boys back to the front of the house. Then she noticed Stefano and froze. "I . . . I'm so sorry. I didn't see you standing there."

Stefano stepped forward, oddly amused to see the blush creeping into the woman's cheeks, her dark eyes cautious. "You must be Alora."

She nodded, her blush deepening as she dipped into a curtsy. "I'm sorry if my children disturbed you. I went to knock on the front door, and when I turned around, they were gone."

Stefano looked down at the two boys, who were studying him openly. "Looking to explore the place, are you?"

Both boys looked up with wide eyes and nodded, all their mother's instructions on protocol forgotten.

The older one stared for a moment and then asked, "Are you a prince?"

Stefano's lips curved up. "As a matter of fact, I am." Stefano ignored the twinge of pain in his ribs as he reached out and shook the little boy's hand. "Prince Stefano Fortier, at your service."

Both boys giggled.

"And you are?"

"I'm Giancarlo, and this is my little brother, Dante."

"It's a pleasure to make your acquaintance," Stefano told him and then shook hands with Dante in turn. He straightened and noticed the chateau manager standing in the open doorway behind him. "Martino, our guests have arrived."

The dark-haired older man stepped outside onto the terrace, carrying with him an air of formality. "Welcome, signora. If you would like to come with me, I will show you your quarters."

"Thank you." Alora motioned to the boys. Then she bowed slightly to Stefano. "It was a pleasure meeting you, Your Highness."

"The pleasure was all mine," Stefano said, his heart lifting fractionally as he watched both boys bound up the steps toward the door.

Alora stepped back awkwardly and then, with a glance over her shoulder, followed her children inside.

* * *

Garrett climbed out of the limousine that had picked them up from the airport, gravel crunching under his shoes and the sweet aromas of hay and apple pie scenting the air. As Janessa stepped beside him, he turned to look at the fields spreading out from the large white farmhouse in front of them.

A new pickup truck and an old tractor were parked next to the faded red barn across the yard. A large silo cast its shadow over what appeared to be some kind of shed beside it. Several horses grazed in a nearby field behind split-rail fences; rows of corn dominated the fields to the west.

Janessa slipped her hand into his, giving encouragement as well, he was sure, as receiving it. He still couldn't believe what she had told him on the plane. For the past three years, she had been lying to the people closest to her about her profession.

He supposed he should have expected it. After all, he'd seen enough spy movies over the years to know that protecting one's cover was paramount for an undercover operative. He just never considered that Janessa would follow that example.

Now he was beginning to understand the source of Janessa's nervousness. Over the past few months, her photograph had been splashed all over newspapers and magazines around the world as her name had been linked to his. For media purposes, they'd announced they had been dating for two years. In reality, they had only known each other a few months.

Garrett stepped aside as Mary and Kevin exited the limo behind them, Kevin holding the car seat baby Lindsay was still strapped into. Mary hurried up the front steps onto the wide front porch and reached for the door just as it swung open and a broad shouldered man stepped out. His short, dark hair was peppered with gray, and his eyes were the same deep green as Janessa's. A smile lit his face as he scooped Mary into his arms, and Janessa rushed forward to be hugged in turn.

A moment later, an energetic blonde woman joined them on the wide front porch. They exchanged greetings, and the proud grandparents took the time to ooh and ah over their baby granddaughter. Then Janessa turned and motioned for Garrett to join them.

"Mom and Dad, this is Garrett Fortier. Garrett, these are my parents, Scott and Donna." Garrett stepped forward, amused when Donna offered something between a bow and a curtsy. Fighting a smile, Garrett shook hands with Janessa's mother. Then he turned to offer his hand to Scott and immediately sensed the man's reservation.

"I'm pleased to meet you both," Garrett said formally as Scott reluctantly shook his hand, his eyes shifting to the limousine in the driveway before focusing more fully on Garrett.

"Please come inside," Donna said, waving everyone toward the open door.

"Are your other children home?" Garrett asked as he walked into a tidy living room.

"It's the middle of the day. There's work to be done," Scott said gruffly.

Donna sent a stern look in the direction of her husband and then added, "Our son Pierce is serving a mission right now in the Philippines, so he won't be here this weekend, but everyone else is working the fields today. They should all be home by supper."

"I need to check on the cattle in the west pasture." Scott motioned toward the door. "Maybe Prince Garrett would like to ride out with me."

The way he said the word *prince*, with the hint of a sneer in his voice, suggested that while many men would be thrilled with the prospect of their daughter marrying into royalty, Scott Rogers apparently wasn't one of them.

"I would like that, thank you," Garrett said, determined to rise to whatever challenge Janessa's father had in mind. He turned to Janessa. "If you'll direct me to somewhere where I can change."

"Maybe I'll come with you," Janessa said, eying her father suspiciously.

Garrett reached for her hand and gave it a squeeze. "You should stay and visit with your mother. I'm sure your father and I will get along just fine."

* * *

The two men rode their horses in silence as they left the barnyard and skirted a field of wheat nearly ready for harvest. Garrett wasn't sure what he had done to warrant the cold welcome from Janessa's father, but he had a feeling he was about to find out.

When they came to the top of a bluff, Scott reined in his horse and waited for Garrett to stop beside him. "We keep a small herd of cattle to help hedge against a bad growing season."

"It always pays to be prepared," Garrett commented then hesitated a moment before plunging in to what had been running through his mind during their ride up the bluff. "I know this is late in coming, but I want you to know I am very much in love with your daughter. I hope you can give our marriage your blessing."

Scott shifted in his saddle to face Garrett more fully. "You know, around these parts, men ask for the young woman's hand *before* her family reads about his intentions in the newspaper."

"I'm sorry that events unfolded as they did, but I'm here, and I'm asking now." Garrett kept his eyes on Scott's as he pressed on. "Can you support Janessa and me and give me her hand in marriage? I know having your blessing would mean a lot to both of us."

Scott stared at him for a moment and gave a subtle shake of his head. "I don't know that I can support a marriage I know is a mistake."

"A mistake?" Garrett repeated, a little taken back by the man's directness, although impressed by the diligence with which he was determined to look out for his daughter.

"You've known my daughter for some time. You must know how important her religious beliefs are to her."

"I do. In fact, her strength of faith as well as her kindness and generosity are among the qualities I most admire."

"Do you understand her beliefs?"

Garrett nodded in understanding. He sat up straighter in the saddle. "Would it change things if I were Mormon?"

"Of course it would change things." Janessa's father scowled at him. "Janessa obviously loves you, or she wouldn't have agreed to marry you, but it breaks my heart that she's giving up on finding someone who can give her everything she's always dreamed of."

Garrett's eyebrows lifted slightly. "So you would give us your blessing if we were getting married in the temple."

"That's right."

"Then thank you," Garrett said, his tone matter-of-fact.

Scott's eyes narrowed. "What do you mean 'thank you'?"

"If all goes as planned, the Meridian temple will be completed within the year. That is where we hope to marry."

Confusion and a glimpse of compassion crossed Scott's face. "You know that even royalty can't go into the temple without being Mormon."

"I know. I am a member of the Church."

"What?" Scott blinked rapidly and shook his head. "My wife's been reading every article she can find about you and Janessa. No one ever mentioned you being Mormon."

"I guess you could say that this information is still classified."

"Why's that?"

"Right now, I'm second in line to the throne. Church and state have been separate for some time, but our citizens don't always perceive things as they really are. The change in my religion could cause political ramifications. So far, I've been able to keep my baptism private."

Scott was silent for a moment, and his eyebrows drew together. "Are you being private, or are you embarrassed that you've converted to the Church?"

"Private," Garrett insisted. "My decision to keep this information out of the public eye is as much for your daughter's safety as it is for my own."

"What does your religion have to do with Janessa's safety?"

"Religious freedom is relatively new to Meridia, and we have no idea how our citizens will take the news that they now have a Mormon prince," Garrett told him. "With all the media attention we're receiving right now, we're more vulnerable to security concerns than would normally be the case." Garrett hesitated and then added, "In fact, I hope you can give me your word that what I have told you will stay between us."

Scott stared down at the cattle for a moment before turning his attention back to Garrett. "My wife needs to know, but if you want to keep her brothers and sisters in the dark for now, I'll leave that up to you." He shook his head. "You sure live in a different world than we do."

"I suppose I do," Garrett conceded. "But you should be proud of how well your daughter moves between our worlds."

He chuckled. "Janessa has always been one to do things her own way, but I've always been proud of her."

Garrett managed to smile. "So what do you say? Can you give us your blessing?"

Scott nudged his mount closer to Garrett and extended his hand. "I suppose she could have done worse."

Now Garrett laughed and shook hands with his future father-in-law. "Thank you, sir."

"Welcome to the family."

Chapter 10

ALORA'S CHEEKS STILL BURNED AS she followed Martino across a tiled entryway and up a wide, sweeping staircase. She couldn't believe she hadn't even been on the grounds for two minutes before stumbling across royalty. She had realized, of course, that eventually she would meet Prince Garrett, but she hadn't really anticipated meeting anyone else from the royal family. She especially hadn't expected Prince Stefano to look even better in person than he did in his photos.

His dark hair was just long enough to curl over the collar of his shirt, and his broad-shouldered physique suggested he was active in more than just politics. His dark eyes had been almost mysterious with the way he somehow managed to keep his emotions from showing there, although she thought she had caught a glimpse of something troubling him when she had first spotted him.

He was intimidating at first glance, his posture so rigid and his manners so polished. However, after witnessing his kindness to her boys, she could admit she was no longer intimidated but intrigued.

As she walked through the wide halls behind Martino, she let her thoughts drift to her surroundings, and she couldn't help but feel the history of the chateau. The hall looked more like a living room than a functioning hallway. It was three times the width of a typical hallway, and priceless artwork and tapestries hung from the walls, an eclectic collection from some of Europe's most renowned artists.

Royals from all over Europe had visited this tiny fairytale country, and now Alora would have the chance to see history unfold in the form of her friend's wedding.

She knew, of course, that despite her friendship with Janessa, she would be little more than a glorified servant during her time here. After all, she could hardly expect that she and Janessa would socialize in the same circles. Janessa's life now included formal dinners and spending time with handsome princes. The best Alora could hope for was finding a few other moms through the boys' new school to set up some play dates.

She hoped she would last here long enough for that to happen. She thought again of how Prince Stefano hadn't looked terribly happy when she'd first seen him. He had recovered quickly, showing warmth and humor as he greeted her and her children, but she doubted he would want to cross paths with them often.

Martino pointed to a door as they passed. "Signorina Rogers' rooms are in there." He then led them farther down the hallway. "This is where you will be staying."

Martino opened the door and stepped aside as Dante and Giancarlo rushed through. Alora simply stared. Janessa had told her she would have a private living space, but she hadn't expected anything so grand. The living area to her right was as big as her entire apartment in Italy. Light spilled in through the French doors leading to a balcony, and the Mediterranean was like a picture spread out before her. A kitchenette was situated to the right, a serving bar separating it from the rest of the living area.

"Mama, look in here!" Dante called from a doorway on the far side of the room, where Alora presumed the bedrooms were located.

"I'll be right there, sweetheart," Alora managed. Then she turned to face Martino. "All of this is really for us?"

"Yes, signora." Martino, who had been every bit the stuffy butler up to now, granted her a small smile. "I will have your belongings brought up to you momentarily."

"Oh, that's not necessary." Alora shook her head, acutely aware of her lack of belongings and the ragged condition of her luggage.

Martino simply motioned inside. "Take a few minutes to get settled in. If you need anything, press zero on the house phone."

"Thank you," she managed, too awestruck by her surroundings to argue. Then he bowed and left her alone with her children.

"Mama! Come look!" Dante called to her again.

"I'm coming." She crossed the living room and followed her youngest son into the bedroom on the left. The room looked like it was straight out of a magazine. Three tall windows overlooked the front entrance, giving the boys a view of the lush hillside. Two captain-style twin beds sat on either side of the room, their bright blue bedspreads decorated with sailboats and seashells. An enormous gift-wrapped box rested on a low-lying table in the center of the room.

Giancarlo was already sitting on one of the child-sized chairs, one hand resting possessively on the present. "Can we open it, Mama? It has our names on it."

"Let me see." Alora stepped forward and read the simple white card. *Giancarlo and Dante—Welcome to your new home.* Even though the card wasn't signed, Alora had no doubt it was from Janessa. She smiled and nodded at Giancarlo. "Go ahead. Let's see what Aunt Janessa left for you."

Giancarlo didn't have to be told twice. He ripped the paper as Dante scrambled closer and started pulling at the wrappings from the other end. Both boys stared down with delight when they revealed the box that held a wooden train set.

"Oh wow." Giancarlo breathed out a sigh of delight before he looked up at his mother. "Can we play with it? We promise to share, right, Dante?"

Dante's head bobbed up and down enthusiastically, and Alora let herself get caught up in her boys' delight. "Go ahead. Just make sure you keep the pieces on the table so they don't get broken."

The box was barely open when a knock sounded at the door. For the next twenty minutes, a steady stream of uniformed servants paraded in and out of her new quarters, her shabby belongings taking residence next to elegant antiques and plush furniture.

She had turned over her keys to one of the servants, who had insisted he would park her car in the garage for her. A young woman was currently unpacking her boys' suitcases in their room.

Alora was contemplating unpacking her kitchen supplies when a smiling older woman entered. Both chubby hands gripped a serving tray laden with all the fixings for sandwiches.

"So you made it." She spoke in Italian, but her accent was definitely French. "I am Patrice Saldera, the cook here at the chateau." She walked straight into the kitchen and set the tray on the counter. "I'm sorry I haven't stocked your kitchen yet. I didn't expect you quite so soon, but this should get you through until dinnertime."

"That is so kind of you. Thank you," Alora managed, accepting Patrice's outstretched hand. "It's so good to finally meet you. You have made quite a favorable impression on Janessa."

Patrice's cheeks flushed pink with pleasure. "Our Gianessa is a good girl."

"Yes, she is definitely that."

"Now, where are those little ones of yours?"

"They're enjoying their new bedroom." Alora motioned to their room, and Patrice crossed to peek in at them.

"Oh, what handsome boys you are." Patrice didn't cross the threshold into the room, but from behind her, Alora could hear her sons introduce themselves and invite Patrice to play with their new toy. After chatting with them for a moment, Patrice turned back to Alora, a satisfied smile on her face. "They are darling. We are going to enjoy having little ones around here again. It's been far too long."

Alora immediately thought of her sons' earlier dash to the garden. "I hope you feel like that after you've gotten to know them a little better."

"Oh, I'm sure we'll get along just fine," Patrice assured her. She motioned to the young woman currently in her sons' room unpacking their suitcases. "Brenna here is available to watch your boys anytime you need so you won't have to worry about them getting into too much mischief when you're working with Gianessa."

"Oh, I didn't expect that you would provide babysitting services for me. They can tag along with me when I'm working."

"That wouldn't be any fun." Patrice waved away the suggestion. "Little boys need fresh air and sunshine. We'll make sure they get plenty."

"Well, thank you for all your hospitality. I can see why Janessa is so fond of you."

Patrice patted Alora's hand. "I'd best get back to the kitchen to start on dinner. What time do you like to eat?"

"We normally eat between five and six, but I brought a few things with me. I can fix something up here."

"Don't be silly." Patrice shook her head. "You've been driving all day, and you need the chance to settle in. Dinner will be ready for you in the dining hall at six."

Brenna emerged from the boys' room and offered Alora a warm smile. "I will come back at dinnertime to show you to the dining hall."

Alora started to refuse but then reconsidered. She imagined that her embarrassment earlier when she met Prince Stefano would pale in comparison to getting lost in the chateau in search of food. "That would be wonderful. Thank you."

"You're welcome," Brenna said as she and Patrice left Alora alone to explore her new home.

Chapter 11

"WHAT DID YOU DO TO my father?" Janessa eyed Garrett suspiciously as they stood outside on her parents' front porch. "When you left, I thought I might have to send your bodyguards with you for protection, and now you two are acting like you're best friends."

"Your dad's a good guy. You know that."

Janessa's eyebrows lifted. "And?"

"And what?"

"What did you say to him?"

"Have you ever thought about working in interrogation? I think you'd be good at it."

"Ha ha. Very funny." Janessa leaned back against the porch rail and crossed her arms. "Tell me what happened."

"Nothing happened. Your dad asked questions. I gave him answers."

"And which answer changed his mind about you?"

Garrett fought back a smile and shrugged. When Janessa continued to stare at him, he shook his head and laughed. "Okay. He might have been swayed a bit when I told him we're planning to get married in the temple."

Janessa chuckled. "I can see how that might change what he thinks of our engagement."

"I invited your parents to come visit us in Bellamo after they finish with their harvest this fall."

"Really?"

"Yes, really." Garrett nodded. "The first phase of the naval base should be well underway by then, and I thought you would enjoy showing them your new home."

"I would love that." Janessa reached for his hand and linked her fingers with his. "Thank you."

Garrett leaned down and pressed his lips to hers. "You're welcome."

* * *

"Alora's already there?" Janessa said into her cell phone as she stepped outside onto the front porch.

"Yes. They're settling in as we speak," Stefano told her.

"Stefano, I am so sorry." Janessa raked her fingers through her hair. "I hope the boys aren't bothering you. I didn't think they would get there until Tuesday at the earliest."

"Janessa, it's fine," Stefano assured her. "Brenna is getting them settled in, and Patrice has insisted on making them dinner tonight. I'll let Alora know you'll be back in a few days."

"Thanks. I appreciate it." Janessa let out a little sigh. "How are you feeling?"

Stefano hesitated for a brief moment. "I'm a bit sore, but I'm doing better. How is everything going with Garrett and your family?"

"When my dad and Garrett went out for a ride earlier, I was afraid they weren't both going to come back," Janessa admitted.

"I gather your father is the protective type?"

"Apparently so. I guess he warmed up to Garrett though when he found out he's Mormon."

"Garrett *told* him?"

Janessa's eyebrows drew together, surprised by the sudden tension in Stefano's voice. "Stefano, my father understands that this information is private."

"Look, Janessa. It's nothing against your father. It's just that every person who knows about Garrett's choice is another potential security risk. I thought he had planned to keep this information to himself."

"My parents can be trusted," Janessa said, immediately defensive. "Besides, they were bound to find out eventually since they will obviously attend our ceremony in the temple next year."

"I don't get this whole temple marriage thing."

Janessa's tone softened, but her words were matter-of-fact. "It's simple. If we get married in the temple, our marriage lasts for eternity, not just for this lifetime."

"Regardless of your beliefs, you need to make sure your father understands how sensitive this information is," Stefano insisted.

"I will," Janessa agreed. "But I promise you there's nothing to worry about. My father is better about keeping a confidence than I am."

"Considering your profession, I'll assume that's a good thing."

"It is." Janessa laughed.

* * *

Stefano hung up the phone and walked out onto his balcony. He couldn't believe his brother was being so careless in his confidences. The family had discussed his religion at length, all of them agreeing they would keep Garrett's baptism confidential as long as possible. Garrett and Janessa had agreed to that.

Movement caught his attention in the gardens below, followed by the sound of laughter.

Giancarlo ran into view, with Dante following behind him. Alora jogged after them, her long hair now pulled back into a ponytail. Stefano expected her to grab their hands to keep them close, but she simply motioned to a path that led deeper into the gardens. One of the boys said something, and her musical laughter joined with theirs.

He listened to their voices and laughter fade as they continued past the rose bushes and toward the swimming pool. A few minutes later, he glimpsed the boys rushing toward one of the twin stairways that led from the chateau grounds down to the beach. Alora's ponytail danced in the wind as she took her boys' hands now and moved with them down the stairs and out onto the sand.

Their laughter rang out again and fell over Stefano like a cloud. Had his life ever been so simple?

Stefano's phone rang again, only this time it was his brother on the other end.

"Stefano, I was hoping you could do me a favor," Garrett began.

Stefano cut him off, his voice demanding. "Did you have to tell Janessa's father you changed religions?"

"What's your problem?" Garrett asked, his own tone suddenly challenging. "My religion is my business, and it's my decision if I choose to share my beliefs."

"You know your choices affect everyone in the family, or have you forgotten your duty?"

"I understand my duty perfectly," Garrett said evenly. "And Janessa's father understands my need for privacy and the security issues that are at stake."

Stefano opened his mouth, tempted to confide in his brother that everything had changed for both of them, but the words wouldn't come. He took a deep breath and said simply, "I hope you know what you're doing."

"I do know what I'm doing," Garrett insisted. "Stop worrying so much."

"It's my job to worry."

"Sometimes you take your job a little too seriously," Garrett retorted.

Stefano was man enough to recognize the truth in his brother's statement and proud enough not to acknowledge it. He let out a resigned sigh and changed the subject. "You said you wanted a favor?"

Garrett didn't respond, and Stefano guessed he too was calming his emotions.

"What is it you need?" Stefano asked, trying to erase the tension in his voice. "I'd welcome a distraction right about now to help ward off the boredom."

"This will definitely give you a distraction," Garrett began. "What do you have planned for this evening?"

* * *

Alora held hands with both of her boys as they descended the curving staircase behind Brenna and then crossed through the wide front entryway. Antique furniture dominated everywhere she looked, and already Alora worried that her boys might break something irreplaceable.

The rooms Janessa had given her made her feel like she was living in an alternate universe. Even though she had spent the past several hours unpacking her things, she kept expecting to wake up from this dream. After spending the past two years sleeping on a couch so her children could share the single bedroom in their old apartment, she had been admittedly excited about having privacy again, but nothing could have prepared her for this new reality.

Her bedroom was incredible. Tall windows on one wall offered the same view her children enjoyed of the expansive front lawn. On the adjoining wall, French doors opened to the balcony overlooking the beach. A small sitting area separated the large walk-in closet and the private bathroom, and the sleeping area boasted an oversized, four-poster bed and elegant touches, such as a gilded mirror on the wall and silk flowers on the antique dresser.

She drew in a steadying breath, nerves dancing in her stomach as she considered that perhaps this move had been a mistake. She glanced down at her simple white button-up and pencil skirt and knew she didn't belong here. Part of her wanted to believe she could live in this fairytale, that she would be able to make a home here for herself and her children.

But another part of her dreaded the possibility that the royal family would quickly tire of having two young children running around the grounds.

Alora needed her children to have that, the opportunity to play outside and explore their surroundings. Though her apartment in Italy had been tiny, she had still managed to take the boys to the park several times a week, even though it had required a mile's walk each way.

She so wanted to encourage their inquisitive natures, yet she also knew they needed to understand that rules and boundaries were necessary in life. Her boys were simply everything to her, and she dreaded the possibility of them creating problems for Janessa. Even worse would be the moment they would have to leave this place to go back to reality.

She had agreed to come here and stay for at least a year until Janessa and Prince Garrett married. After that, Alora could decide if she wanted to continue working as Janessa's assistant. Even if she decided not to stay in Meridia after Janessa's wedding, she hoped the prestige of working for Meridia's royal family would lead to employment that would allow her to support herself and her children. Sometimes she even dared hope that she would be able to buy a little house for them, someplace they could call their own.

Alora's thoughts were interrupted when Dante tried to pull his hand free from hers as they continued through the parlor and entered the enormous dining hall.

"Wow." Giancarlo breathed the word with awe.

Alora squeezed both boys' hands automatically. Three exquisite chandeliers hung from the ceiling over a table that looked like it could easily seat fifty people. The evening sun splashed through tall windows onto the polished wooden floor.

"Please be seated." Brenna motioned to the near end of the table where four places were set. Alora barely had time to wonder why there was an extra place setting on the table when Brenna added, "Prince Stefano will join you shortly."

"I'm already here." Prince Stefano stepped into the doorway, and Alora caught the musky scent of his cologne as she fought to keep her jaw from dropping open. Her heartbeat quickened, and she found herself intimidated all over again. He was dressed in what she would normally consider church attire, but the left sleeve of his jacket hung loosely over his shoulder.

Prince Stefano continued into the dining hall, and Brenna dipped into a curtsy. "I will inform Patrice that you are ready for dinner to be served."

"Thank you, Brenna." Prince Stefano reached for a chair next to the one at the head of the table. He pulled it out and motioned for Alora to take her seat. "Please, sit down."

Bound by protocol she barely understood, Alora let go of her children's hands and took the seat Prince Stefano held for her. Never had she dreamed that she and her children would be dining with the prince, and she wasn't quite sure what to do about the fluttering in her stomach. She looked up into his dark, serious eyes and managed a smile. "Thank you."

She turned to instruct her children to sit down, but they were already scampering into their seats, Dante in the chair beside her and Giancarlo in the seat across from her.

Gingerly, Prince Stefano sat down at the head of the table.

Alora's eyebrows lifted with concern. "Are you okay? You look like you're in pain."

"I'm fine, thank you." Stefano nodded. "Just some lingering pain from a recent automobile accident."

She saw it then, a flash of white beneath his jacket that she recognized as a sling. "I'm sorry. I hadn't heard about that."

He smiled, and Alora was surprised to see humor light his face. "It's refreshing to know there are still people in this world who don't spend their days reading the tabloids."

Alora smiled despite her nerves. "I'm afraid I've never had time for that type of reading."

"What's a tabloid?" Giancarlo wanted to know.

"A kind of magazine," Alora told him, silently praying that her children would behave during dinner. "One that tells stories about famous people."

"Oh."

"Giancarlo and Dante, how do you like your new room?"

"Aunt Janessa gave us a new train set!" Dante shifted up onto his knees so he could lean forward on the table. Alora tapped him on the back and motioned for him to sit back down in his seat.

"Did she now?" Prince Stefano nodded thoughtfully. Then he turned to Alora. "That reminds me. I spoke with Janessa earlier this evening. She asked me to convey her regret that she wasn't here to greet you when you arrived. She and my brother expect to return on Wednesday."

Alora nodded. "I look forward to seeing her again."

"Might I be so bold as to ask how you two met?"

"We went to church together when we were all living in Paris," she told him, censoring her answer out of habit.

"Paris?"

"Yes." Alora reached out and caught Dante's glass before it toppled over. "That's where we lived until a few years ago."

"Then you speak French?"

She smiled now. "Yes. I served a mission for my church in the South of France before I got married."

Surprise lit his eyes. "You were a missionary?"

"I was."

"I'm going to be a missionary too," Giancarlo announced proudly.

"Me too!" Dante added.

"I see." Stefano nodded thoughtfully. "Aren't you two a bit young to be missionaries?"

Giancarlo rolled his eyes. "We aren't going to go on our missions yet. We have to turn nineteen first."

"Oh, is that how it works?"

Alora thought she sensed humor in the prince's tone, but still, she opened her mouth, an apology ready to roll off her tongue. Before she could get any words out, Brenna walked through the door.

"Dinner is served." Brenna set one plate in front of the prince and another in front of Alora. She looked down at the shrimp pasta dish colored with peppers and mushrooms. Immediately, she turned to see what her sons thought of the unfamiliar cuisine, but to her surprise, their plates were laden with spaghetti and meatballs instead.

When she glanced up at Brenna, she saw her smile of understanding. "Patrice thought your children would be more comfortable with familiar food on their first day here."

"That was very thoughtful of her. Would you please tell her thank you for me?"

"Of course. Enjoy your dinner." Brenna stepped back from the table and positioned herself unobtrusively near the door.

"Mama, is it my turn to say the prayer?" Giancarlo asked, his dark eyes lifting to meet hers.

Alora felt her cheeks color as Prince Stefano looked at her inquisitively, his fork already lifted halfway to his mouth. She briefly entertained the idea of skipping the blessing just this once, but she quickly dismissed it as she realized it would be easier to ask the prince to indulge them in their religious traditions rather than try to explain to her sons why it was sometimes easier to break them.

Still feeling terribly awkward, she shifted her gaze from Giancarlo to Prince Stefano. "Would you mind terribly if Giancarlo blesses the food before we eat?"

The prince was silent for a moment, but then he shook his head and lowered his fork to his plate.

Alora offered the prince a timid smile and turned back to her oldest son. "Go ahead, Giancarlo."

After Giancarlo offered a simple blessing, Alora turned back to look at Prince Stefano. "Thank you."

Prince Stefano nodded. "Tell me, are your accommodations to your liking?"

"Our rooms are wonderful." Alora's eyes lit up. "I have never lived anywhere so grand, and everyone here has been so kind. I feel bad that our early arrival has created a hardship on all of you."

"It's not a hardship to have you here." Prince Stefano offered her a charming smile, but a touch of sadness lit his eyes. "In fact, if anything, having children here has been a breath of fresh air already."

Alora studied the man beside her, sensing a vulnerability in him she hadn't expected. "I'm glad you feel that way. And I do appreciate you making us feel so welcome in your home."

"It has been my pleasure."

Chapter 12

Stefano stepped out onto his private balcony and stared at the moon's reflection in the Mediterranean. The pain from his injuries was barely noticeable now that his medication had taken effect. He was pleased that he had already been able to downgrade from the prescription pain killers to the over-the-counter variety. If all went as he hoped, he expected he would be able to start working from the chateau within the week.

For now, he could admit that he needed some time away from his duties and obligations, some time to adjust to his new reality. Staring out at the water, he thought back to his dinner with Janessa's guests. He hadn't expected to enjoy himself, especially knowing that he would be spending time with someone else's children only a day after discovering that he would never have any of his own.

Surprisingly, he found himself amused by the two young boys. He had never considered himself particularly good with children. He had rarely had the opportunity to associate with them, even when he had been one. Now that he had been exposed to their rare innocence and honesty, he found himself looking forward to his next encounter with Giancarlo and Dante.

The corners of his lips lifted into the beginnings of a smile when he remembered the look on Alora's face when Giancarlo had asked about the blessing on the food. She had been so flustered, yet she had handled herself well. Diplomatically, even. The tradition might not be one he was personally accustomed to, but he had been around Janessa enough that it wasn't foreign to him either.

The need for religion had never tugged at him the way it had Garrett. He was practiced in the traditions and beliefs of the Meridian Church and well schooled in the beliefs of many other religions. As the future ruler of Meridia, understanding the cultures of his allies and his enemies was often just as important as understanding their politics. Now that he faced such uncertainty in his personal life, Stefano could only ask why any god would want him to suffer this way.

From his first breath, he had been groomed to someday take over as king. He had worked hard throughout his school years and during the time he served in his country's navy, always working to establish the groundwork for the day that the burden of leadership would become his. Though his responsibilities were many, at the core, he only had two duties to his country. First was to rule justly and serve the people of Meridia. The second was to produce an heir.

In the past, he had never considered failure to be an option in any aspect of his life. Now he was faced with the reality that in this one area he had always taken for granted, success wasn't possible. Before meeting with Dr. Casale, he had naively assumed that someday he would meet a suitable woman who would be able to share the burden of leadership with him.

He thought of his dinner companions once again. A beautiful woman, two delightful children. Why had he never cared about having such things for himself until now—when he knew it could never be? His heart heavy, he turned from the water and wished for the miracle that would never come.

* * *

Alora guided her children down the hallway that appeared to lead to the kitchen. She hadn't made it out to the grocery store yesterday, and unfortunately, the boys had already polished off the food Patrice had brought them. She supposed she should have taken a trip into town before dinner, but she and her boys had needed a little downtime after their long drive and the hours of unpacking.

They had taken a walk together yesterday afternoon, and Alora could admit she had delighted in the experience as much as her sons had. The gardens were simply stunning, and the rambling paths through them were a trove of unexplored treasure.

Excitement fluttered in her stomach as Alora thought of dinner last night. The prince hadn't seemed to mind having her children there, had even made a sincere effort to speak with them. That shared meal had done more than he could possibly realize to help her believe she could stay here indefinitely like Janessa hoped.

Now if she could just find the kitchen, she hoped to fix the boys something for breakfast before heading into town for some basic supplies.

A maid turned the corner and approached them. She smiled down at Giancarlo and Dante before asking Alora, "Are you looking for the kitchen?"

"We are. Are we heading in the right direction?"

She nodded. "It's the next door down on the right."

"Thank you." Alora moved to the door and pushed it open to find a huge kitchen that looked more like it belonged in a restaurant rather than in a home. Patrice was standing at a stove frying bacon, and Alora instinctively grabbed both of her boys by their arms to keep them away from the splattering grease.

Patrice turned and smiled at them. "*Buon giorno*! Are you ready for some breakfast?"

Both boys nodded eagerly, and Alora shrugged awkwardly. "I was going to go into the store a little later for supplies, but I was hoping to feed the boys first."

"I'd be happy to show you around town after breakfast," Patrice offered. "But for now, why don't you tell me what you would all like to eat. How about waffles and bacon?"

"Anything would be fine. Thank you."

"Okay then. You go right through there into the breakfast room." Patrice motioned to the door on the far side of the room. "I'll bring your food in to you in just a minute."

"Thank you." Alora followed the boys into the breakfast room, where a dozen chairs surrounded a large, square table. Her eyes widened when she saw Prince Stefano sitting in one of them, trying to butter a croissant one-handed.

He looked up, a brief moment of surprise registering on his face. Alora froze in place, not sure whether to continue to the table as Patrice had instructed or to usher her children back out of the room so they could leave the prince alone. The surprise on his face melted away, replaced by an unexpected look of frustration.

"I don't suppose I can get you to help me with this? I'm afraid I'm not very good one-handed." He looked unexpectedly sheepish as he held out the croissant and motioned to the butter dish.

"Of course." A smile tugged at her mouth as she considered the absurdity of the situation. Here she was about to dine with a prince for the second time in less than a day while others prepared her food and waited on her and her children. Alora motioned for her boys to sit down as she slid into the seat next to Prince Stefano. She took the croissant from him, sliced it in half, and spread butter inside before handing it back. "Here you go."

"Thank you." He passed her a basket filled with croissants and offered her a wry grin. "This injury is making me feel like I'm their age again."

Alora's smile broke free. "I imagine it isn't an easy adjustment."

"A loss of independence is never easy," he agreed.

Alora buttered another croissant, broke it in half, and handed a piece to each of her boys. She caught the amused look on the prince's face when both boys set their food down on the table in front of them and folded their arms. A little flustered, Alora instructed Dante to say the blessing. As expected, his prayer was short and sweet, and the boys quickly busied themselves with the food she had given them.

Before serving herself, Alora gathered her courage to ask, "How long do you have to wear the sling?"

"About six weeks." He lifted his eyebrows as though remembering she hadn't read about the details of his accident. He touched his right hand to his shoulder. "Broken collar bone."

Alora's voice was sympathetic. "That must be incredibly painful."

"Only when I refuse to wear the sling and don't take my pain medication." He started to reach for a pitcher of orange juice and winced. "Or forget how short my reach has become."

"Here. Let me get that." Alora stood up and poured him a glass. She then turned to serve her children. "Were you wearing a sling when I first met you yesterday?"

He shook his head. "I was doing great until I sat down at my desk and reached for my keyboard. Apparently I need the sling to remind me not to do simple tasks."

"I'd be happy to help out if there's anything I can do for you."

"I may take you up on that."

Patrice and another servant walked in, each holding two plates. Alora's eyes widened when she saw the huge Belgian waffles garnished with peach slices, a dollop of fresh whipped cream, and three slices of bacon.

"Oh wow," Giancarlo said, edging forward in his seat.

Alora looked up at Patrice. "This looks wonderful. Thank you."

"You're welcome. Enjoy your breakfast."

"Mama, will you cut mine up?" Dante asked as Patrice left the room.

Alora nodded. She slid his plate closer and cut the waffle into bite-size pieces. Then she repeated the process with Giancarlo. When she looked up, Prince Stefano edged his plate toward her and looked at her expectantly. Her eyes lowered to his plate to see his breakfast was still untouched. With a laugh, she reached for his plate and then took her knife to his waffle as well.

Chapter 13

STEFANO STARED AT THE EIGHTEEN file boxes stacked along the wall in his office. He knew analyzing the latest environmental studies was a necessary step to ensure that the new U.S. naval base wouldn't create any significant impact on Meridia's local waters or wildlife, but he had hoped the newest batch would be sent to him in summary report form instead of boxes of raw data.

He had requested that the reports be redone only to find that the engineers responsible for gathering the data were already conducting the next set of soil and water tests off the coast of Bellamo. Resigned to the reality that he would have to sort through these boxes himself, he looked down at his sling and considered having his personal secretary join him from the palace in Calene.

As he thought of all the scheduling details Lorenzo was juggling for him because of his accident, he shook his head. If he had someone to help search through the boxes, he knew he could get everything done within a few days. Immediately he thought of Alora's offer to help.

Turning away from the boxes, he picked up his phone. "Martino, I need a favor."

* * *

Alora unpacked the last of her clothes into her dresser and slid the top drawer closed. She nested her smaller suitcase inside her larger one and then moved to her walk-in closet to store them. Even though all her clothes were now hanging neatly, half of the closet was still completely empty. Maybe with the steady income Janessa had promised her, she would finally be able to improve her wardrobe as well as buy her children a few new things for their upcoming school year.

Patrice had pointed out the school when they had ventured into town earlier that morning. The building itself had been neat and tidy, the grounds impressive. Alora smiled as she remembered Dante and Giancarlo's excitement about exploring the playground. Since returning from town, her children had been unbelievably quiet, playing in their bedroom as they continued to discover toys that had previously been buried in the bottom of their toy box.

Alora padded quietly across the thick carpet to peek into their room. She grinned when she saw both boys leaning against their new play table, the train set Janessa had given them surrounded by little green army men. Giancarlo was busily arranging his troops while Dante perched a ratty stuffed dog on the edge of the table, where it could supervise the coming battle. "How are you boys doing?"

"Good," both boys echoed without looking up.

"Are you about ready to take a break and have some lunch?"

Giancarlo shook his head. "Not yet, Mama."

"You need to eat something," Alora told him. "Tell you what. You keep playing, and I'll make you both a sandwich."

"Okay." Giancarlo reached into a plastic bucket and pulled out another handful of army men.

Alora left them to their toys and walked into the kitchen to fix lunch. She started gathering her supplies, wondering if she could convince the boys to leave their toys for a while after lunch to go outside. She prepared the sandwiches as she enjoyed the picturesque view of the Mediterranean through the window. Another walk on the beach would do them all some good, she thought.

Alora put two plates on the table and called out, "Boys! Lunch is ready." She turned to fix herself something to eat when a knock came at the door.

"I'll get it!" Dante rushed to the door and pulled it open to reveal Brenna standing outside.

"Well, hello there, Master Dante. How are you today?"

"We've been playing with our new train." He lowered his voice as though sharing a secret. "An army's about to attack it!"

"Oh my. That sounds pretty scary," Brenna said in a completely serious tone. "Are you going to let me see?"

"Okay."

"Dante, you need to eat first," Alora told him and waved at Brenna to come in. "Hello, Brenna."

"Prince Stefano asked if you would be willing to assist him with some work in his office this afternoon." Brenna motioned to the children. "I can watch the boys for you here in your suite, or I can take them outside to play."

Alora nodded automatically. She wasn't sure what to think of Prince Stefano requesting her help, but if she was going to work here, she supposed she should do what was asked of her. "I guess that will be okay." She glanced down at her cotton pants and T-shirt. "I should probably change."

"Oh, you don't have to do that." Brenna shook her head. Then she stepped closer and lowered her voice. "By the way, is it okay if I take the boys swimming?"

"They don't know how to swim yet," Alora told her quickly. "They would probably enjoy playing on the beach though."

"I'll make sure they're entertained," Brenna assured her. "And that they stay safe."

"Thank you." Alora glanced toward the kitchen, considering if she might have time for a quick lunch. Afraid to keep the prince waiting, she turned back to Brenna. "Where is the prince's office?"

"Just go past the main staircase. His office is the third door on the right."

"Okay." Alora leaned down and kissed each of her boys on the forehead. "You boys be good for Brenna."

"We will," Giancarlo told her around a mouthful of sandwich.

"And don't talk with your mouth full." Alora laughed and leaned down to kiss him again. She looked at Brenna. "Let me know if you have any problems."

"We'll be fine. I'll plan on having them all washed up and ready for dinner. We'll meet you in the dining hall at six if you don't finish before then."

"Thank you." With a last glance at her children, Alora walked into the hall and closed the door behind her.

* * *

Stefano looked up, relief and gratitude showing on his face when Alora walked through his open office door. She was dressed casually, her hair pulled back in a ponytail, making her eyes look more exotic somehow. Her T-shirt looked like it was designed to be fitted, but it was several sizes too large and hung loosely past the waistband of her khaki colored pants.

Her eyes were wary as they had been when she first spotted him in the breakfast room that morning, but she offered him a timid smile.

"Thank you for coming." He motioned to the stack of boxes and returned her smile. "I'm afraid I'm in a bit over my head."

"What's all this?" Alora moved closer.

"Environmental impact studies for the expansion of the military base. I need to review them before construction begins on Thursday, but sorting through these files one-handed . . ."

"Is painful," Alora finished for him, her smile widening.

"I was going to say difficult, but painful is probably a more accurate statement."

"Tell me where you want me to start."

"Let's start with box number one. It should contain a summary of where everything is filed."

Alora shifted boxes until she could access the correct box and pulled off the lid. "Okay, here it is."

"Great." Stefano reached out with his good hand and took the stack of papers she handed him. He moved over to his desk and lowered himself into his chair. "It's going to take me a minute to get organized. Would you mind calling Patrice and having her send up some lunch? You haven't eaten yet, have you?"

"Actually, I haven't."

"Good. I hate to eat alone." He motioned to the phone on the corner of his desk. "Just dial five for the kitchen. Patrice said she was fixing roast beef sandwiches for lunch, but if you want something else just let her know."

"Whatever she's fixing is fine," Alora said. She picked up the phone and called in Stefano's request.

He listened halfheartedly to Alora's side of the conversation. When she laughed in response to something Patrice said, he looked up inquisitively. She grinned at him and spoke again into the phone. "No, that's not the reason. I'm actually helping him with something else."

After she ended the call, he asked, "What was that all about?"

"Patrice thought you asked me to have lunch with you so I could cut up your food."

Stefano's laughter joined hers, and he shook his head in amusement. "I can't say her logic is flawed." He glanced down at his sling and considered for a minute. Humor lit his eyes when he added, "Maybe I should plan my meals to coincide with yours while I'm here."

Her smile didn't fade, and Stefano felt a sense of satisfaction when she spoke as she might to a friend. "I'm happy to help with whatever I can."

Chapter 14

To Alora's amazement, she was given free run of the chateau and treated more like a guest than an employee. She and her children started each day in the breakfast room with Prince Stefano. Her original plan to fix breakfast for her family in their quarters had been overruled by both Patrice and the prince. He had teased that he would go hungry without her help, and Patrice had insisted that it was no trouble to cook for three more.

Alora gave in as soon as Patrice promised to let the boys help with a few simple chores so they wouldn't get too accustomed to being waited on. After their chores were done each morning, Brenna stepped in to oversee the boys' activities. And Alora's concern that they would miss her during the day was completely unfounded.

A swimming instructor arrived every morning to teach her children, after which they played in the pool or on the beach under Brenna's watchful eye. Alora still wasn't sure who had arranged for the swimming lessons. When she had asked Brenna about it, her answer had been simple. The boys needed to know how to swim to make sure they were safe around the pool. The conversation had ended there, and Alora had been too grateful to argue.

Dinner was served each night at six in the dining hall, where Giancarlo and Dante reveled in sharing their adventures of the day. Alora was touched by how patient Prince Stefano was with their stories. He acted like he was interested, whether they were telling him about the toad they found in the garden or the battle they were waging in their bedroom.

When he arrived at their door on Saturday night, Alora thought perhaps he needed her help for something, but to her surprise he asked to see the boys. He looked at her hesitantly when he said, "I brought them something. I hope that's okay."

"Of course. Please come in."

He barely made it through the door before both boys rushed out of their room to greet him. They both remembered to bow, and the prince watched them with a combination of amusement and an unexpected trace of sadness. "I have presents for both of you." He lifted his good hand to reveal two small gift bags dangling from his fingers. "The red one is for Giancarlo, and the blue one is for Dante."

"For us?" Giancarlo asked, even as Dante reached for his.

Prince Stefano nodded. "I thought these might help with the battle you were telling me about."

The boys dumped out the contents of their bags, both of them grinning when they saw the assortment of miniature tanks and army jeeps tumble out onto the carpet. "These are great!"

"What do you boys say?" Alora asked gently.

Both boys looked up and echoed, "Thank you!"

"You're welcome."

"Do you want to come see our army?" Dante broke protocol and grabbed Prince Stefano's hand.

Stefano looked over at Alora as though silently asking her permission. A little self-conscious, Alora looked at him helplessly and shrugged.

"Sure, I'll come take a look."

Alora watched Dante pull him into their room. As soon as they were inside, she could hear the prince making the appropriate comments about what a great job they were doing. When he emerged from their room alone a minute later, he was grinning.

"They're deciding where to put the new vehicles."

"That was very sweet of you."

"It wasn't any trouble." Stefano nodded toward the door. "They've been good sports about letting me borrow their mother this week. I thought they deserved a little token."

Emotions tangled within her as Alora considered that this was the first time since the bombing that her children had received a gift from anyone besides her or Janessa. She managed to push aside the grief that threatened and focus on her gratitude. "Was it you who arranged for them to have swimming lessons too?"

"Brenna mentioned that they didn't know how to swim," Stefano said in the way of an answer. "I thought you would feel more comfortable here once they were water safe."

"That was very astute of you. Thank you."

"You're welcome." Stefano stared at her a moment, his eyes dark. Then he drew a folded piece of paper out of his pocket. "I thought you might need this." He gave an awkward shrug when he added, "It's directions to your church. Last time I saw Janessa and Garrett go to Sunday services, they left around eight-thirty, so my guess is that services begin at nine."

Touched by his thoughtfulness, she stared up at him. "Thank you. I was going to ask for directions in the morning."

"You are still going to have breakfast with me before you leave, aren't you?"

"Of course." Alora smiled. "I'll see you downstairs at eight just like always."

Stefano returned her smile and gave her a satisfied nod. "Good. I'll see you then."

* * *

Stefano checked the caller ID on his phone before pressing the talk button. "Hey, Garrett. Is everything still going okay with the future in-laws?"

"So far, so good; I'm quickly gaining a strong appreciation for people who grow the food Patrice puts on our table."

"I gather they're putting you to work out there." Stefano chuckled.

"Something like that," Garrett agreed easily. "I was actually calling to see if you can do me another favor."

"Possibly. What do you need?"

"I was hoping you could speak with Martino about setting up an office in the chateau for Janessa," Garrett told him.

"I thought she was working over at the naval base."

"She is, but she's also doing a lot of work in her private quarters. We both know how difficult it can be to try to relax when your work is staring at you from across the room."

Stefano stared across his office at the stack of files and nodded to the empty room. "Did you have a preference of where you want her office to be?"

"I thought Uncle Elam's old office would work well," Garrett suggested. "He hasn't used it since the new offices were built for the Meridian Church in Calene two years ago. The layout is perfect, since Alora could use the adjoining office for herself."

"That's a good idea. It shouldn't take much effort to modernize the equipment," Stefano considered. "Although we should probably speak to Uncle Elam before we make any significant changes."

"I already did," Garrett told him. "In fact, that's why I didn't ask you about this sooner. I left a message for Uncle Elam last week, and he didn't respond until this morning."

"What was his reaction?"

"He thought we had taken over his office months ago." Humor laced Garrett's tone. "If it's okay with you, I thought perhaps Alora could help you. After all, she'll be spending a good amount of her time there."

Stefano considered the prospect of working with Alora for a while longer, and he found himself looking forward to it. "Don't worry. I'll take care of everything."

"Thanks, Stefano."

* * *

"Prince Stefano knows." He breathed the words, his voice filled with angst.

Dark eyebrows drew together. "The prince knows?"

Frustration and impatience surfaced now. "Blood work was done when he was in the hospital after the accident. The test was ordered for Merid's syndrome. The results would have been processed days ago. He must know by now."

"How did you find this out?"

"I had one of the orderlies at the hospital check the prince's chart. A series of blood tests was run before he was released from the hospital. The one for Merid's syndrome was among the blood tests ordered, but the results were missing from the file."

"It's possible that someone else stole the results . . . just as we did when the test was run years ago."

"But how can we be sure?" Anxiety hummed through his voice. "If the royal family knows the truth, they may realize that Prince Stefano wasn't the only one we were after in that car accident."

"You're overthinking this. They still believe it was only an accident." He tapped a finger against his chin, his confidence never wavering. He would gain the power he was entitled to, and he was prepared to destroy anyone who dared deny him. "Did Prince Stefano's medical record show who ran the blood tests?"

"I believe so." He flipped through the file he held. "Name was Belinda Parnelli. Why would that matter?"

"Because if she ran the tests, she knows who received the information."

Awareness filled his eyes. "Perhaps I should have a talk with her."

"I agree. I'm sure we will both feel a lot better if we can gain a more complete understanding of the current situation." He nodded, evil shining from his eyes. "And of course, we don't want to take the chance that she might be starting any unfortunate rumors we aren't prepared to handle."

Chapter 15

Janessa felt the stares the moment she walked into the chapel. She automatically reached for Garrett's hand in search of comfort.

Over the past several months, she had grown accustomed to the curious looks when she and Garrett entered a room. She hadn't expected those looks today though, now that she was among her family and friends.

Self-consciously, she followed her brother Jake down the aisle and sat on the same pew her family had been sharing for years, the fourth one from the back. When the time came for Lindsay's blessing, Janessa watched all of the men in her family stand and walk up to the front of the chapel where the baby would be blessed, leaving only Garrett behind. Since Garrett was a new convert to the Church, he hadn't yet received the Melchizedek priesthood, which would have allowed him to participate in the blessing.

Even if Garrett had been able to participate, the moment he exercised his priesthood in public, he would be acknowledging that he had joined the Church.

As her brother-in-law began the blessing, Janessa tried to focus on his encouraging words about Lindsay's future rather than the sinking feeling in her stomach as she realized that such precious moments would never be simple for her in Meridia.

* * *

Alora parked her car in her assigned spot at the far end of the twelve-car garage. Most of the spaces were occupied, the structure deep enough to accommodate two stretch limousines on the side farthest from her.

"Can we go for a walk now, Mama?" Dante asked, tugging at his clip-on tie. "We were good in church."

"You were good in church," she agreed with a smile. "Let me hang up my keys, and then we can go explore a bit."

"Yes!" Giancarlo grinned.

Alora couldn't help but smile at her son's enthusiasm. They all climbed out of the car and crossed to the cabinet where she had been instructed to leave her keys. Martino had explained that the chateau drivers preferred to have the ability to move cars if it was necessary. She didn't see why anyone would want to bother with her car, since it was tucked away in the last space, but she didn't see a reason to argue the point either.

"Can we go down to the beach again?" Giancarlo asked as he trotted along behind her.

"We'll see," Alora said in the tone that made her sons know that if they were good they would get what they wanted.

She hung up her keys in the appropriate spot then turned toward the door. Stepping to the side, she waited for Giancarlo to pull the door open for her. She stepped through the doorway and smiled down at her older son. "Thank you, Giancarlo. You are such a gentleman."

A deep voice sounded behind her. "I see you are training them early."

Alora whirled around and lifted a hand to her rapidly beating heart. Remembering herself, she dipped into a curtsy. "Prince Stefano, you startled me."

"I do apologize." He was dressed casually, at least she guessed he would think of the camel colored slacks and white button-down shirt as casual. He looked down at the two boys as they followed their mother outside, and Alora could have sworn he was fighting back a grin when both boys bowed to him. He greeted them both by name before turning his attention back to Alora. "I gather you found your church building okay?"

"We did. Thank you for giving me such good directions."

"It was no trouble." He motioned toward the path leading to the chateau and then fell into step beside her as the boys scrambled along ahead of them. "I forgot to mention at breakfast this morning that my brother asked a favor of us."

"Oh?" Alora's eyebrows lifted in surprise. "What favor is that?"

Stefano explained Prince Garrett's request, surprising Alora with the fact that she too would be provided with office space outside her private quarters.

"I would love to help," Alora agreed eagerly.

Prince Stefano motioned to the chateau. "Shall we go look at what needs to be done?"

Alora hesitated, glancing down at her boys before lifting her eyes to look at him once more. How could she explain to a prince, one who had allowed her to move into his home, that she didn't work on Sundays?

"Is something wrong?"

"I'm sorry, but I try to reserve Sundays to spend with my children." She looked at him apologetically. "We always go for a walk after church."

"Of course," Prince Stefano said, his tone more formal than Alora had expected.

"Would you mind terribly if we started first thing tomorrow morning?"

He nodded to her and stepped back stiffly. "Tomorrow morning, then."

She hesitated for a moment before giving in to her instincts. "If you feel up to it, we would love for you to join us for our walk."

Surprise and something else flashed in his eyes and then was quickly gone. "I wouldn't want to intrude."

"You wouldn't be intruding," Alora said. The boys began speaking over one another as they echoed their mother's invitation.

"Please?" Dante crossed to the prince to grab his hand excitedly.

Prince Stefano stared down at him for a moment, and Alora watched with amazement as he smiled down at her son and his formal air melted away. "Well, Master Dante, how could I refuse such an enthusiastic invitation?"

Dante grinned excitedly. "So you'll come with us?"

"Yes, I would be happy to accompany you." Prince Stefano glanced up at Alora and offered her a smile. "And where are we walking to on this fine day?"

"The boys mentioned walking down to the beach, but we're open to suggestions."

"You can never go wrong with a walk on the beach," he agreed easily, motioning toward the path that led through the garden, past the swimming pool, and then to the stairs leading down to the sand. "Shall we?"

"Yes!" Giancarlo didn't have to be told twice, and he dashed toward the gardens. Dante abandoned Prince Stefano and raced to catch up with his brother.

"Stay where I can see you!" Alora called after them as they continued down the path.

"I think they're a little excited about the beach."

"Yes, very much so." Alora nodded, her eyes shining with humor. "I walked with them down to the beach the afternoon we arrived. They loved every second of it."

Prince Stefano smiled as they followed behind the boys. "My brother and I always loved it here when we were children."

Alora noticed a bodyguard stationed by the seawall a short distance away. "What was your life like growing up, if you don't mind my asking?" She nodded toward the guard. "I imagine it wasn't easy having guards following you around everywhere."

"The guards have always been there. I guess I'm used to them, and they don't really follow me around unless I'm away from home." He looked at her as though he sensed her unasked questions. "You want to know what it was like to be both a child and a prince?"

"I'm curious, but I don't want to pry." She pointed at her boys who were impatiently waiting for them to catch up. "I look at my sons and see how hard it is for them to stay within the safety net I try to give them. I can't imagine how restrictive your childhood must have been."

"It wasn't as bad as you might think," Prince Stefano told her. "Security was always tight enough here and at the palace for us to feel like we had our freedom even if it was more illusion than reality. More than once the guards gave us enough rope to hang ourselves."

Her eyebrows lifted, and humor lit her eyes. "Oh really?"

He chuckled. "You have two sons. I don't have to explain to you what kind of mischief little boys are capable of."

"No." Alora shook her head, and laughter escaped. "No, you don't."

They continued to the top of the stairs, where the boys were waiting anxiously.

"Go ahead," Alora told them. "But don't go near the water."

"Okay!" Both boys shouted in unison before scrambling down the dozen steps to reach the sand.

Alora caught the scent of his aftershave when Prince Stefano moved closer and took her arm to escort her down the stairs. Nerves fluttered in her stomach as his fingers touched her arm.

He didn't speak until they reached the sand. Then he released her arm and asked, "What about you? What was your childhood like?"

"I grew up on a little farm outside of Zena, Italy. It was as close to a perfect childhood as anyone could ask for," Alora said a little wistfully as she thought of her family. She caught herself before she let her memories go beyond her childhood. Instead, she motioned to her children who had stopped to stare out at a sailboat in the distance. "Now I'm doing my best to give my sons what my parents gave me."

"I'm certainly no expert on children, but from what I've seen, you are doing an excellent job."

Alora smiled fully. "Thank you."

Chapter 16

STEFANO WALKED INTO JANESSA'S NEW offices and surveyed what needed to be done. The windowless reception area was painted stark white, a single painting of a stormy sea hanging on the wall. With a shake of his head, Stefano continued into the inner office. He couldn't say that he had ever had much interest in interior decorating, but he liked to think he had a good eye for what worked and what didn't. Although he would never admit it to his uncle, the dark, hunter-green paint, the dark shelves, and matching shutters definitely did not work.

He pulled the shutters open now. The wide window overlooked the fountain in front of the chateau and the lush foliage beyond. If he had to guess, he imagined that his uncle had chosen to hide the view as part of his temper tantrum for not getting the ocean view he felt he deserved.

His lips curved when he thought of the contrast between his uncle and the two women who would now call these offices their own. Even though Janessa had been officially associated with the royal family for only a few short months, she was already well thought of by those who knew her. Stefano could admit that he already had a fondness for his future sister-in-law, especially for her lack of arrogance. In contrast, his uncle had turned arrogance into an art form.

Although he admittedly didn't know Alora well, he expected that she too was more likely to look out the window and appreciate the view rather than complain about what wasn't there.

When Stefano heard a familiar aloof tone, he turned to see Elam standing in the doorway. As always, Elam's voice was tainted with disdain. "That will be all, Martino."

"Very well, Your Highness." Martino's tone was respectful, but Stefano didn't miss the way the chateau manager's lips tightened as he bowed and then left them alone.

"Uncle Elam," Stefano said in the way of greeting. "What brings you to Bellamo?"

"I came to make sure you were recovering well," Elam told him. "I'm glad to see that you are up and moving around."

"I'm getting there." Stefano waved him into the office that Elam had once called his own. "Come sit down and tell me how things are with you."

"Busy as always." Elam lowered himself into a leather chair the color of deep burgundy. "I had hoped my schedule would open up a bit more after Philippe's wedding, but that hasn't been the case."

"I understand you are still actively involved with the Meridian Church."

Elam nodded. "My involvement there has become somewhat consuming. I try to limit my time in the office to once a month, but lately it seems I find myself in my office twice that often."

Only years of training kept Stefano from pointing out that one or two days a month was hardly a full-time job. He managed to smile, and his voice was diplomatic. "I'm sure the archbishop appreciates all your efforts."

"One would hope," Elam agreed. He motioned to the bookcases lining the far wall. "Garrett mentioned you were preparing my old offices for his fiancée. I remembered I left some things here I have been missing for some time. I thought perhaps you would give me the opportunity to pack up a few of my personal items before you start your redecorating."

"Of course. I have a few phone calls to make, so I will leave you to it." Stefano stood and moved toward the door. "If you need any help, I'm sure Martino can send someone to assist."

Elam simply nodded, apparently content to search his office alone.

* * *

"That didn't take long." Garrett tried to bank down his frustration as he stared at the front page of the local newspaper. A photograph of him and Janessa walking out of the LDS chapel was centered on the page, the caption stating simply, "Prince Garrett of Meridia attends Mormon Church with bride-to-be Janessa Rogers."

"Someone at the airport must have tipped off the paparazzi that we were here in Iowa." Janessa lowered herself onto the porch swing beside him and laid a hand on his arm. Her voice was gentle as she added, "We both knew it was only a matter of time before the press saw you attending church with me."

"I know, but I had hoped it would take at least a few more weeks before this came to light." Garrett skimmed the article, his stomach churning when he reached the second paragraph in which the reporter speculated whether the prince was considering joining The Church of Jesus Christ of Latter-day Saints. He pointed down at it. "Look at this."

Janessa took the time to read the article before looking up at him. "It will all die down," she assured him. "You've said before that the press has the attention span of a two-year-old. Within a couple weeks, the idea of you going to church with me will be old news."

"You're probably right." Garrett let out a sigh. "I guess as long as I don't do anything to draw attention to the fact that I'm already a member, the attention will fade."

She shifted to face him more fully. "What are you going to do when you're asked to serve in a calling?"

Garrett's eyebrows drew together. "I don't know. I hadn't really thought about it."

Janessa hesitated a moment as though gathering her courage. "It was hard for me yesterday to watch my niece being blessed and know that even if you could have been in the circle, you might have chosen not to because of what others might think."

Garrett didn't deny the truth of her statement. Hadn't he considered himself lucky that the choice hadn't been his to make? "It won't always be like this."

"When is it going to change? Garrett, how long is it going to take before you're comfortable with people knowing you're LDS?" Janessa pushed off the swing and walked across the porch. She turned back to face him, crossing her arms as she leaned back against the railing. "Are you planning on sneaking into the temple on our wedding day? What about when we have children? Are you going to be afraid to bless them in front of the congregation?"

"It wouldn't be like that," Garrett said gently. "I don't know if we can keep it to ourselves until we get married, but I would like to try. It's safer for both of us."

"People will know you're LDS the minute you walk into the temple."

"The Mormons will know, but most people in Meridia don't understand what is required to enter the temple," Garrett told her. "We'll make it work."

Janessa was silent for a moment. Then she took a deep breath, and her eyes met his. "The CIA knows you were baptized."

"*What?*" Garrett's eyes widened. "How did they find out?"

"Someone at your baptism was an employee at the embassy and mentioned it. Director Palmer believes the information is still contained, but the fact remains that at some point the news is bound to get out."

Garrett dragged a hand through his dark hair. "I can't believe this."

Janessa let out a sigh. "Assuming by some miracle we're able to get sealed in the temple without the press getting wind of your religion, then what?"

"We'll have to issue a formal press release eventually, but I know my family is hoping we can put it off until after we get back from our honeymoon." Garrett closed the distance between them. "Whenever we release the information, we're just going to have to pray for the best. Hopefully the public will come to accept the fact that you are Mormon during our engagement, and it won't be such a difficult transition to know that I am no longer a member of the Meridian Church."

"I didn't expect this to all be so complicated." She stared out at the fields in the distance before turning her attention back to him. "Every time I think I finally understand what it's like to be royal, I realize how wrong I am."

"What do you mean?"

"Up until a few months ago, the public didn't have any idea who I was, didn't care to know. Now I'm faced with the fact that personal decisions we make can impact people we've never even met."

Garrett shifted. "I know this is an adjustment, but you need to trust that I've prayed about this and that I'm trying my best to do what feels right. Please don't make this any harder than it already is."

"I'm not trying to make any of this more difficult for you, but you have to understand that I don't want the kind of happily ever after that people read about in storybooks. I want the one that ends with a happy, eternal marriage."

He took her hand and nodded. "Believe me. That's what I want too."

* * *

Alora stepped into the outer office and tried to focus on the work to be done rather than on the man beside her. She looked up, appreciating the ten-foot ceilings and open space. A single antique desk was the only furniture left in the room. Whatever chair might have once accompanied it was missing, but the polished honey oak would be easy enough to match.

Prince Stefano led the way into the inner office, where a workman was patching some holes in the wall by the window, presumably from where shutters had once been. The man fumbled with the small plastic tub of spackling when he saw Prince Stefano. He bowed and then quickly gathered his supplies.

"I'm all done in here, Your Highness." He snapped the lid onto the spackling bucket and motioned to the smears of white against the dark green paint. "It should be dry within three hours."

"Thank you." The prince nodded his approval as the workman placed his tools into a box and left the room. His eyebrows drew together as he focused on a side wall where another thick patch of spackling was visible. Based on the size of it, Alora guessed that someone had knocked a hole in the wall that had needed to be repaired.

"Is something wrong?"

"I just don't remember there being a hole in the wall there." He shook his head. "It was probably from one of the workmen who was taking out the shutters." He turned and picked up a stack of papers off an ugly mahogany desk. "This is the list Martino put together for you of approved contractors and suppliers. If there is anything you need beyond what is here, give him a call, and I'm sure he can offer you some guidance."

"Are you sure your brother doesn't want Janessa to have a say in the decorating of her own office?"

"He said he wanted it to be a surprise. I think he's trying to prove that he's capable of surprising her twice in one week."

Humor lit her eyes. "In that case, I'd better see how soon we can get painters in here."

"Remember that you are representing the royal house of Meridia now. You should expect your wishes to be met without resistance," Prince Stefano told her before stepping toward the door. "I have a few things I need to see to this morning, but I should be able to come back in about an hour to help. If you run into any problems, let me know. I'll be across the hall in my office."

"Thank you." Alora nodded. "I'll see what I can get done before my children wear Brenna out."

"I wouldn't worry too much about that. If they're anything like my brother and me, they'll spend half the day playing on the beach and the other half tracking sand through the gardens while they play hide and seek," he said knowingly. "Besides, I heard Patrice talking about making cookies today. The promise of a treat should make them easy enough to handle."

"It sounds like you understand children better than you admit."

The light in his eyes dimmed, and his voice became stiff. "I don't know about that, but I do remember my own childhood well enough." He stepped toward the door. "I'll see you back here in about an hour."

Alora nodded and watched him leave, wondering what she could have said to cause his mood to shift so suddenly.

Chapter 17

STEFANO'S CELL PHONE RANG AS he entered his office. He answered it to find his father on the other end. "I didn't expect to hear from you until this afternoon."

"I wanted to let you know I received the final accident report this morning," King Eduard began. "The police found no evidence of foul play."

"You don't sound convinced."

"I'm not. I am adding an additional guard to everyone in the family for the time being, but I think it's time we try to return to our normal schedules."

"When did you want me to come back to the palace?"

"There isn't anything pressing here that can't wait a few weeks," Eduard told him. "I did, however, want to see if you would still be able to attend the opening for the new exhibit at the museum in Bellamo tonight. After the problems at the gallery last month, I think it is important that we have a representative there."

Even though it was phrased as a simple request, Stefano heard the underlying command. "Of course."

"It is a social event," Eduard reminded him. "Perhaps you should take an escort."

"Father." Stefano let out a sigh as he moved farther into his office and dropped down into his chair.

"I know the social aspects can be a challenge at times, but it would be best if you didn't attend alone, especially since Marguerite Galleau will be there."

The mention of the currently unattached heiress from Marseille was all that was required for Stefano to change his tune. "I'll take a date."

Stefano could imagine the smile on his father's face as he said simply, "I think that will be best."

As soon as he hung up, Stefano ran a hand over his face and then leaned back in his chair. Generally he didn't mind attending social events. In fact, he usually enjoyed them, but he was already dreading tonight. Marguerite invariably brought with her a large contingent of paparazzi and a fully operational rumor mill. The last time they had attended the same event, rumors of a secret engagement between her and Stefano had surfaced within hours despite the fact that they had merely shared a single dance. Undoubtedly, Marguerite had fueled those false reports.

His eyes lifted when a knock sounded on his still-open door. Alora stood awkwardly in the doorway. "I'm sorry to bother you, but I wondered if you might know where I can find a receipt book or an expense ledger to track the costs of this renovation."

Stefano stood and waved her inside. "Yes, of course." He opened a drawer in his desk and retrieved a pad of ledger paper. "You can use this, but if it's easier you can simply track the expenses on your phone or laptop, and we can print them out later."

"I'm sure this will work fine," Alora said a little too quickly.

Stefano glanced down at his phone and considered the dozens of women's phone numbers it held. Then he studied the woman standing across from him, and he deliberated a new option for the evening. "I wonder if I could ask a huge favor of you."

"Of course." Alora nodded automatically. "What do you need?"

"I need a date for tonight."

She looked at him skeptically. "A date?"

Stefano fought back the urge to smile. "Yes. The museum in town is hosting a new exhibit tonight, and it would be best if I didn't attend alone."

"Forgive me, Your Highness, but there must be any number of women who would love to accompany you. Why would you want me to go?"

"For purely selfish reasons," Stefano admitted with a grin. "I enjoy your company, and I would prefer to go with someone who doesn't list becoming a princess as one of her priorities."

Alora gave him a wry smile. "I can honestly say I've never considered that as a possibility."

"Please come," Stefano said. He could tell she was wavering, and he dreaded the possibility of going with someone else. "I imagine it's been some time since you've gone anywhere without your children."

"That's true, but I don't think I'm suited to high society events." Alora looked up at him with dark eyes. Stefano couldn't say why it pleased him to see the nervousness shining there.

"Alora, this isn't a formal state dinner. It's just an exhibit," he assured her. "Please say you'll join me."

She stared at him a moment longer before reluctantly nodding. "Okay."

"Wonderful." Stefano smiled. "The event doesn't start until seven thirty. If you like, we can eat an early dinner with your children before we go."

"I would appreciate that. Thank you." She started to leave and then turned back to face Stefano once more. "I meant to ask if there's another phone I can use besides the ones in Janessa's offices. Neither one of them is working."

"That's odd," Stefano said, but he waved in the direction of his outer office. "My secretary is still working out of my office in the palace. You can use his desk."

"Thank you," Alora said and moved quickly through the door.

* * *

Belinda headed for the hospital exit, her heart still heavy as she considered Prince Stefano's situation. As a nurse, she understood a patient's right to confidentiality, but this secret was burning her up inside. Rarely did a day go by when someone didn't comment on the royal family and speculate about the future king.

Just the night before, her mother had mentioned an upcoming visit from a princess from Monaco and expressed her opinion that she would make a fine match for Prince Stefano. After all, he was already thirty-two years old, and it was high time he settled down and gave his country an heir. *If only that were possible.*

Dr. Casale hadn't spoken of the test results since returning from speaking with Prince Stefano several days before. Even then, he had only asked for her reassurance that she had not discussed the findings with anyone and had insisted once more that she continue to keep the confidence.

She stepped outside and headed to the side of the building where her car was parked. She didn't take notice of the tall man standing at the edge of the parking lot until he spoke to her.

"Belinda Parnelli?"

"Yes?" Her eyebrows rose inquisitively. "Can I help you?"

"I believe you can."

* * *

"You look pretty, Mama." Dante bounced up and down on her bed as Alora fastened a simple strand of pearls around her neck.

"Thank you." Alora pointed at his reflection in the mirror and added, "Stop jumping on the bed. You need to go get your shoes on. It's time to go down for dinner."

She watched him bounce one more time before he slid down to the floor and headed into the living room. With a steadying breath, Alora ran her hand over the rich gold fabric of her gown and then pressed a hand to her stomach. All day her thoughts had been on Prince Stefano, and she had frequently reminded herself that his request for her to accompany him was a gesture of friendship and nothing more.

The realization that she had nothing to wear hadn't surfaced until lunchtime, but thankfully that problem had been solved when she returned to her room to find the gown hanging from her bedpost along with a matching pair of shoes. A note from Patrice told her the gown and matching handbag were on loan from Janessa but that the shoes were for her to keep.

Alora felt a bit awkward with the idea that Prince Stefano had arranged for her evening attire, but the simple fact remained that evening gowns were not a part of her wardrobe and hadn't been for some time. She looked down at the wedding band on her finger and debated for a long moment. Prince Stefano hadn't seemed to notice that she still wore a ring, but then, Janessa had probably told him she was single.

She rubbed a finger over the simple gold band, memories tumbling over each other: her wedding day, when Carlo had slipped it on her finger that first time; the way his eyes had misted when he'd held each of their sons right after they were born; that moment when she had kissed him good-bye on their last Christmas Eve, so sure that they would have a lifetime filled with more holidays together.

The unbearable desolation that followed the bombing had nearly destroyed her. She and her children had been left alone in the world, and those first few months were now merely a blur of days running together as she had tried to function through the most basic tasks. She doubted she would have survived her grief had she not had to focus on caring for her children. At first, her ring had provided her a sense of comfort, reminding her that her marriage was eternal. She supposed she wore it now as much out of habit as to remember the life she was still so reluctant to let go.

She knew Carlo wouldn't want her to cling to the past, that he would want her to find happiness in her life until they could be together again. Her heart squeezing a little, she reached down and gently slipped the ring from her finger. She opened her jewelry box, set it inside, and whispered, "I still miss you, Carlo."

She closed the lid softly and drew a deep breath. She and her children were beginning a new life, and she needed to start living in the present. Trying to shake off her melancholy mood, she picked up her handbag. Then, feeling a bit like Cinderella, she straightened her shoulders and walked into the living room to find Prince Stefano sitting on the couch talking to Dante and Giancarlo.

"Prince Stefano." Alora nodded to him in greeting. "I thought we were dining together downstairs."

He stood, his eyes sweeping down to take in the full effect of her in the formal gown, the shimmering fabric that accented her waist before flowing sleekly to the floor. "You look stunning."

Her lips curved automatically. "Thank you."

He crossed to her, took her hand in his, and lifted it to his lips with a great deal of charm. "I am going to be the envy of every man there tonight."

She managed to keep her smile in place even though her heartbeat had quickened. "I seriously doubt that."

Before she could say anything further, a knock sounded at the door. Prince Stefano motioned to Giancarlo. "Would you get that, Giancarlo? That should be dinner." He turned back to Alora and added, "I thought it might be easier on you if we dined up here tonight."

"That would be wonderful. Thank you." Alora smiled as Giancarlo opened the door and two servants entered. Once the table was set, the servants curtsied to the prince and then left them alone.

Prince Stefano pulled out a chair for Alora and turned to the boys. "Are you two ready to eat?"

Both boys scampered into their chairs and folded their arms. Alora saw Prince Stefano fight back a grin as she asked, "Whose turn is it to say the blessing tonight?"

"Can I say it?" Dante asked eagerly.

"Absolutely." Alora nodded and struggled against a grin of her own.

After the blessing, the boys regaled them with their adventures of the day. Alora gave the prince the news that the painters expected to finish the next day and that Martino had helped her replace several pieces of furniture, as well as the outdated phones. When the prince suggested they all take a walk on the beach the next morning, Alora was struck with the surprising reality that this man had become a friend.

After dinner, Prince Stefano looked down at his watch. "Brenna and Marie should be here in about five minutes. Marie will take care of the dishes while Brenna tends to the boys."

"Can you read us a story before you leave?" Giancarlo asked eagerly.

"Maybe just a short one." Alora looked to Stefano for approval.

"I want Prince Stefano to read to us."

"We don't want to impose on the prince."

He waved away her concern. "That's okay. Go pick out a book and bring it here."

"Okay!" Giancarlo raced into his room, returning a minute later with a popular children's book written in English.

The boys settled on either side of him as Stefano opened the book and began reading in an animated voice that made the boys giggle and Alora smile. His English was perfect, with a smooth European accent, and despite his formal attire, he didn't seem to mind the boys snuggling up next to him as he read.

Her heart warmed as she considered what a precious gift he was giving her children right now. So often she had wished Carlo had lived for moments like these, always regretting that Giancarlo and Dante didn't have a male role model in their lives. Not that Prince Stefano was likely to be around much once he had healed from his injuries, but for the moment, Alora let herself be grateful for this brief glimpse of normalcy.

Chapter 18

"Your guards are in position, Your Highness."

Stefano nodded to his driver before turning to Alora. She was a vision in the borrowed gown, her dark hair piled artistically on top of her head, her features enhanced with a light dusting of make-up. While he could admit to himself that he always enjoyed having a beautiful woman on his arm, for the first time in years, he was actually looking forward to spending time with his date. He was struck with the realization that the woman beside him had the potential of becoming a real friend. At least he thought this was what friendship was supposed to feel like. "Are you ready?"

She shook her head and pushed a hairpin more securely into place. "Probably not."

Stefano's eyes lit with amusement. "Don't worry. If it's too boring, we won't stay long."

"I may hold you to that," Alora murmured as the back door of the limousine opened.

The moment they stepped from the limousine, cameras started flashing. As expected, the paparazzi were out in full force. Stefano took Alora's hand and tucked it into the crook of his arm before starting toward the museum entrance. Though outwardly she looked composed, she gripped his arm tightly as they walked leisurely from the car to the front entrance.

She scanned the crowd as though searching for someone, and he heard her sigh of relief the moment they walked through the doors and left the spotlight behind them.

A little surprised by his desire to put her at ease, Stefano leaned down and whispered in her ear, "Don't worry. The worst part is over."

She glanced at the crowded room and arched her eyebrows. They only made it a few steps before Marguerite Galleau was at their side. Well versed in her publicity stunts, Stefano deliberately pulled Alora closer before Marguerite could greet him with her typical kiss. "Marguerite, what an honor it is for Meridia that you were able to come tonight," Stefano said formally. "May I introduce my date, Alora DeSanto."

Marguerite nodded a greeting to Alora without actually looking at her. Instead her eyes stayed fixed on Stefano. "Darling, I heard of your accident. I am so pleased to see you have recovered."

"Thank you." Stefano knew what was coming next, the inevitable request to spend time with him alone. He caught sight of the museum director and took a step in his direction. "I hope you'll excuse us, but I see someone Alora needs to meet. It was good seeing you again."

Ignoring the pout on Marguerite's lips, Stefano nudged Alora toward the director. As expected, the museum director approached as soon as he saw them.

"Your Highness. I'm so glad you were able to come."

"Thank you, Pierre." Stefano motioned to Alora. "This is Alora DeSanto. Alora, Pierre Dumond is the director of the museum."

Some of Alora's nerves seemed to ease as she shook Pierre's hand. "It's so nice to meet you. I believe we spoke earlier today on the phone about a painting I wanted to acquire for the chateau."

"Oh, of course." He smiled more fully. "It's nice to be able to match the name to the face."

"Yes, it is." Alora glanced at the artwork on display around the room. "You certainly did a wonderful job on the exhibit. It is very impressive."

"Thank you." Pierre's cheeks flushed with pleasure. "I hope you enjoy yourselves."

"I'm sure we will." Stefano shook his hand before moving on to make the next set of introductions.

As they worked their way around the room, Alora seemed content to stay on the fringes of the conversations taking place around her, as though she were afraid she might say something wrong. Outwardly her posture and manners were polished, despite the nerves that seemed to be thrumming just beneath the surface. As the evening wore on, Stefano found himself wondering if perhaps she too had been trained for social events such as this.

After more than two hours of constant conversation and a second confrontation with Marguerite, Stefano leaned down and spoke softly in her ear. "Are you about ready to go?"

She gave him a subtle nod, and a short time later his guards escorted them out the rear entrance so they could avoid the press.

"Was it as bad as you thought it would be?" Stefano asked as he settled back onto the seat beside her.

"Actually, no." Alora smiled up at him. "Thank you for asking me to come. I had forgotten how nice it is to talk to adults without having children constantly interrupting."

"It was truly my pleasure."

"And thank you for reading to my boys tonight. They have become quite fond of you."

"I have to admit, I have enjoyed having them around." He shifted to face her more fully. "I didn't realize you and your children speak English."

"The boys are still learning, especially Dante. He hasn't had as much exposure to the language as Giancarlo."

His eyebrows lifted inquisitively. "Oh?"

Alora's eyes darkened, and she hesitated as though she had said too much. She took a steadying breath, and her voice was thick with emotion when she spoke. "My husband was American. It was his idea to read them stories in different languages so they would be able to communicate with their different family members." She looked down and spoke quietly. "Dante was just a baby when Carlo died."

"I'm sorry." He reached for her hand. "Do you mind me asking how he died?"

"It was a house fire." She glanced out the window, and Stefano guessed she was fighting back her emotions. Then she looked back at him with an expression of vulnerability that pulled at him. "It's hard knowing that Dante doesn't remember his father, but in a lot of ways, it's been easier on him than on Giancarlo."

"What do you mean?"

"Giancarlo wanted to stay home with Carlo the day of the fire. He wasn't quite three yet, but he remembers coming home to find nothing left, to find out from the police that his father hadn't survived." Alora let out a little sigh. "I think this move has been good for him though. He hasn't had a single nightmare since we got here."

Stefano rubbed his thumb over the back of her hand as he considered what she must have suffered. His voice was soothing as he said simply, "Such a young child shouldn't be haunted by nightmares."

"I agree," Alora said softly. "No one should."

* * *

"This is a potential nightmare," Janessa said as she read the papers in her hand. Only ten minutes ago she had been saying good-bye to her sister, brother-in-law, and baby niece and felt like everything was right with her world. Then a courier from the CIA had arrived and had succeeded in shocking her back to reality. "Garrett, you need to take a look at this."

"What is it?" Garrett shifted in the seat that he typically used to work from when he was on his father's jet.

"The CIA believes that Hector Ambrose is in Meridia." Janessa managed to keep her voice steady, but her stomach twisted uncomfortably.

Garrett reached out and took the report from Janessa. He skimmed through the first few pages, and his jaw clenched. Ambrose was suspected in nearly a dozen bombings, but no one had ever been able to get a jury to convict him. "How confident is Director Palmer in this intel?"

"Apparently the CIA has confirmed that Ambrose is currently living in Medina. He is the one person suspected of being involved in planning the bombing of the *U.S.S. Kohl* who wasn't convicted."

"Medina is only thirty miles from Bellamo." Garrett's voice was tight. "Do you think he's planning a similar attack at our naval base?"

"It's possible." Janessa shrugged. "This information is a courtesy so your family is aware of the potential threat, but they don't know if Ambrose might be targeting the U.S. base or something else in Meridia. All they know is he is living in Medina."

"Theoretically, he could just be hiding out there."

"I doubt it." Janessa shook her head. "Director Palmer mentioned last week that they've been picking up a lot of chatter in the region. That makes me think he's involved in something."

"It sounds like we should have him picked up and deported before it's too late."

"We might want to wait on that." Janessa sat down beside him. "The CIA has offered to send over a few operatives to help track him. The U.S. government is also planning on sending over another complement of Marines to help guard the naval base during construction."

"What does that have to do with anything? If a terrorist is in Meridia, he poses a potential threat to our citizens. We can't just ignore the fact that he's there."

"I agree, but if you get rid of the bomb maker, whoever hired him will likely go hire someone else. We need to know who he's working for and make sure we get everyone involved," Janessa said gently. "Besides, no one is exactly sure where Ambrose is staying. We only know he's been seen in Medina. I think the CIA would also appreciate the chance to identify his target."

"I would think the target would be obvious."

"Not necessarily." Janessa shook her head. "Meridia is 99 percent Christian. One hypothesis is that an attack may occur against the citizens of Meridia, possibly some kind of religious target."

"That doesn't make sense." Garrett shook his head, clearly hoping and praying that this hypothesis was unfounded. "Meridia is a small country and only a minor part of the war on terrorism."

"Yes, but your naval forces have nearly doubled over the past decade." Janessa motioned to the report. "The fact that your country has become a significant supplier of oil at a time when the Middle East has faced so much unrest would also put Meridia on the radar, especially since your main customers are western Europe and the United States."

"That may be true to some extent, but since my father has prohibited offshore drilling, we don't expect our oil production to change significantly any time soon," Garrett commented. "We aren't any more of a player than we were five or ten years ago."

"At this point, we have no way of knowing if the person behind this is motivated by profit, power, or hatred. According to this report, Ambrose will make anyone a bomb for a price. Until we figure out who's paying him to be in Meridia, we aren't going to be able to identify the potential targets. For now, it's best to be prepared for anything."

Garrett considered for a moment. "I'll talk to my father about allowing your CIA friends to track him, but I don't think he's going to be willing to let Ambrose operate in our backyard for long."

"Believe me, everyone will be relieved to see him behind bars. We just need to find a reason to put him there."

Chapter 19

STEFANO PUT HIS LAPTOP DOWN on a small table situated on his balcony and then sat on a cushioned wicker chair. A thin layer of clouds scattered the sun's early rays, and a light breeze brought some relief from the already warm temperatures. Stefano looked out over the horizon as his computer warmed up, and he thought of the night before.

After Alora's initial reaction when he'd asked her to be his date, he had expected her to be out of her element as they socialized with many of the region's most prominent citizens. He had sensed her nerves throughout the evening, and she had been somewhat withdrawn, but he doubted that many of the other attendees had noticed her discomfort.

Though he typically didn't bother looking at the social pages, today he tapped on his computer keyboard until he found the first of many articles about the exhibit from the night before. As expected, a photograph of Alora and him filled up most of the screen.

Stefano indulged his curiosity and skimmed several articles. The press didn't offer any information about Alora except for her name. One even dubbed her *Prince Stefano's mystery woman* because of the lack of background information available on her. He supposed there was some accuracy to the statement. After all, he didn't know much about her either except that she was a dedicated, caring mother and a trusted friend to Janessa.

It was easy to see why the two women were friends. They were both genuine and kind and tended to look for the good in everything around them. The fact that Alora had lost her husband so suddenly without becoming bitter was a miracle in itself, but even more amazing was how she had helped him look past his own situation. It wasn't until he was alone in his room last night that he had remembered his future wasn't what everyone thought it to be.

A knock sounded at his door, and Stefano called out, "Come in."

Martino entered the sitting room and then crossed to the balcony, where Stefano was still sitting. "Good morning, Your Highness. I have some paperwork that needs your attention if you have a moment."

"What is it?"

"The approval forms for Signorina Rogers' new assistant." Martino handed him the single folder he carried.

"Thank you, Martino. I'll take a look at it and get it back to you this afternoon."

"Very good, sir." Martino bowed and then turned and left the way he had come.

Casually, Stefano opened the file. He flipped past the standard employment forms until he reached the routine background check. He expected a basic work summary and perhaps a quick background on Alora's family. Instead, he found himself staring down at a photograph of Alora's late husband. He flipped past the photo of the dark-haired man with the crooked grin to find the report on the fire that had claimed Carlo DeSanto's life.

His stomach clutched when he realized the fire hadn't been an accident as he had assumed. Alora's husband had died when a bomb had detonated at his house. He read further, his jaw dropping when he discovered that Alora's parents, her older brother, and her in-laws had also died in the explosion.

A glance at the financial records revealed why Alora had shown up with so few belongings. Not only had she lost everything she owned in the fire, but she had also been forced to sell her childhood home when she was unable to pay off the mortgage. Left with only the proceeds of a modest life insurance policy, Alora had opted to live frugally so she could stay home with her children.

When he noticed her previous work experience, he looked up and stared once more at the horizon. Perhaps Alora and Janessa had even more in common than he'd thought.

* * *

Alora walked into her living room, her eyes immediately drawn to the children's book resting on the coffee table. Prince Stefano had been so kind to her the night before, first spending time with her children and then allowing her to talk about the loss of her husband in a way that hadn't made her feel self-conscious. She hadn't told him everything, of course.

Some things could never be spoken of, but for the first time since that dreadful day, she felt a weight easing off her shoulders.

Even their time at the exhibit had been more enjoyable than she had expected. She had been admittedly nervous at first, especially when she had seen all the photographers and reporters outside the museum, but Prince Stefano had stayed by her side, and she had drawn comfort from his presence.

She wondered if any of the photographs taken of them the night before had made it into the local newspapers, and she was torn on whether she should let the evening fade into memory or if she should try to search out a souvenir of her night out with royalty. Since she didn't have a computer of her own, she couldn't take the easy route and do an Internet search, but she might be able to pick up a newspaper when she went into town later.

She couldn't say why she wanted a memento of the night. Perhaps it was her lack of photos from her past that made her want to have something to hold on to. Except for the few photos she had salvaged from her parents' house, all of her old scrapbooks had been lost in the fire.

A sigh escaped her. She knew from Janessa that Prince Stefano typically lived in Calene and that their night out was likely a one-time event, but the fact remained that he had opened her eyes to possibilities she hadn't previously wanted to consider.

As much as she didn't want to admit it, the prince had made her *feel* again. He made her want things she had never thought possible. Carlo was gone, but maybe someday she would find a man who could love her children enough to want to take the time to sit down and read bedtime stories or take them for a walk on the beach. Maybe she could even find someone she could love who would remind her that there was life outside of her sons' little world.

"Good morning, Mama," Giancarlo said from his bedroom doorway. He balled up his hands and rubbed at his eyes as he crossed to her.

"Good morning." Alora motioned for him to join her on the couch. She smiled when he snuggled onto her lap, his body still heavy from sleep. "Were you and your brother good for Brenna last night?"

"Yes, Mama." Giancarlo nodded and then burrowed his head just beneath her chin. "Brenna said we can have ice cream after lunch today because we were so good."

A smile crept across her face. "She did, did she?"

"Uh huh."

Alora heard a knock, but before she could move, Dante raced into the room and headed straight for the door. "I'll get it!"

"Okay." She turned her head, expecting to see Brenna standing in the hall. To her surprise, Prince Stefano filled the doorway. Her eyes lowered to the clutch of yellow roses in his hand, and her heartbeat quickened.

His eyes turned dark and unreadable as he stared at her. She started to rise despite the weight of Giancarlo on her lap, but he motioned for her to stay seated. "I hope I'm not disturbing you."

"Of course not. Please come in."

"We were good last night, and we get ice cream," Dante announced as Prince Stefano stepped over the threshold.

"Were you, now?" Though there was a touch of humor in his voice, his expression remained serious. "Well, I was going to give these to your mom as a thank you present for coming with me last night, but maybe I should give them to you and your brother instead."

"Nah." Dante shook his head. "Flowers are for girls."

The corner of his mouth lifted. "I guess they are."

Alora smiled as Giancarlo finally shifted off her. She stood up and stepped toward Prince Stefano. "Thank you. They're beautiful."

"You're welcome." He handed the blooms to her and then linked his hands together, watching her intently as she walked into the kitchen and retrieved a vase. When she set the flowers on the kitchen counter, he continued, "I wanted to let you know the painters have arrived. I thought perhaps you and the boys would like to go into town for some breakfast, and we could do some shopping afterward."

"Can we, Mama?" Dante grabbed at her hand and bounced up and down.

Alora looked at Stefano hesitantly. "Are you sure you want to brave going into town with these two?"

"I am certain that Giancarlo and Dante will be perfect gentlemen." Prince Stefano looked expectantly at the boys, who both nodded in agreement.

"Okay, if you're sure." She motioned her boys to their bedroom. "Let me help them find something to wear. Please make yourself comfortable. I'll be right back."

When she emerged from the boys' room a minute later, he was sitting on the couch holding the book he had read to the children the night before.

"They should be ready in just a minute."

"There's no hurry." He held up the book. "You mentioned that you're teaching the boys both English and French?"

"I'm trying." Alora nodded. "We've been working more on English since I need the practice too, and I don't want Giancarlo to lose what he already knows."

"I was just thinking that you might want to mention to Patrice that your boys speak some French. She taught me more of the language than my tutors ever did."

"Really?"

"It's amazing how much you pick up when someone's yelling at you while holding a frying pan."

Alora's laughter rang out. "I can imagine."

* * *

Stefano fell into step beside Alora as they strolled down the sidewalk in the main shopping district in Bellamo. A few enterprising photographers followed behind them, snapping photographs, and a few pedestrians greeted him as they passed. Stefano responded automatically, but his attention was on the woman beside him.

Alora seemed content to walk aimlessly down the street, although she kept Dante's hand firmly in hers while Giancarlo trotted along in front of them. They stopped occasionally to look through the windows, but Stefano was surprised that the boys never asked to go inside any of the stores, nor did they ask their mother to buy them anything.

They lingered at the toy store window a bit longer than the others, but the boys happily moved forward when Alora nudged them along. It wasn't until they reached the pet store window that Dante pulled free of her grasp and both boys pled with their mother to make a purchase.

"Please, can we get a puppy? Please, Mama?" Giancarlo looked up at her, his dark eyes filled with hope.

"You know that's not something we can get right now," Alora said firmly. Then she motioned to the door. "I'll let you go inside for a closer look though."

"All right!"

The boys darted through the open door.

Alora turned to Stefano with an apologetic look on her face. "I hope you don't mind if they look for a minute."

"That's fine," Stefano assured her and followed her inside.

Alora stopped just inside the door, watching as the boys greeted each of the puppies in the various cages that lined the far wall. She let out a small sigh, just loud enough for Stefano to hear it. He looked over at her, a bit surprised to see the look of disappointment on her face.

"Are you okay?"

Alora's shoulders lifted. "It's difficult to see your child want and not be in a position to give."

"I gather they have been asking for a puppy for some time."

She nodded. "It broke Giancarlo's heart when his last dog died. He's been after me to give him a new puppy ever since."

"Why didn't you get a new one?"

"We couldn't have it in our apartment."

"I'm sorry."

She shrugged, and her voice was matter-of-fact when she spoke. "Disappointment is a part of life. We all have to go through it eventually."

Chapter 20

ALORA STARTLED WHEN THE PHONE on the end table rang. She tried not to think about the last time she had answered the phone or the reason she had refused to own one for the past three years. She glanced at the boys' bedroom, reminding herself that they were safely tucked in bed and that she didn't have anything to worry about.

She cleared her throat and picked up the receiver. "Hello?"

"Alora, it's Stefano. I wanted to let you know the furniture you ordered has arrived."

"I was hoping it would get here before Janessa got back. How does it look?"

"Why don't you come down and see for yourself?"

"I'd love to, but I just put the kids to bed. I wouldn't feel comfortable leaving them alone, especially if they don't know where to find me."

"I'll send Brenna up to sit with them," Prince Stefano offered. "If the boys wake up, she can call down and let you know."

He was right, of course, and if she could get Brenna to stay for an hour or two, she would be able to get a few things done before the workers arrived tomorrow to hang drapes and set up computers. "That would be great. Thank you."

"I'll meet you in your office in ten minutes."

* * *

Alora walked into the room and ran a finger over the aged cherry desk she had chosen for Janessa. "This is perfect."

Stefano nodded in agreement. The desk was smaller and sleeker than the monstrosity his uncle had left behind. "I can't tell you how glad I am that you decided to replace the furniture in here."

Alora turned to him and smiled. "I gather you don't share your uncle's taste in furniture either."

"Not at all."

Alora motioned to the empty space in front of the window. "Would you mind helping me move this? I think it will look better over there."

A combination of humor and surprise lit his face. He couldn't remember the last time someone had asked him to do something so casually, and he didn't know if anyone had asked him to perform menial labor since he had reached adulthood.

She looked up at him and seemed to catch herself. "I'm sorry. I forgot who I was talking to."

He couldn't say why that simple comment made him feel like he was being challenged. "Do you think I'm incapable of moving a desk because I'm royalty?"

"No, but I think your broken collarbone would cause you some trouble."

"It's more annoying now than painful." Stefano tugged on the sling that still held his left arm in place. "Besides, you shouldn't be moving furniture around anyway. You might hurt yourself."

She stared up at him with a look of disbelief on her face. "I hate to break it to you, but for most people, if they want something done, they have to do it themselves."

"I am well aware of that," Stefano said as he watched Alora slide a chair into place beside a work table. "But I don't see any reason why rearranging furniture can't wait until tomorrow since we do have workers who are available to assist you."

"I suppose you're right." Alora looked around the room, and Stefano could almost see her making a mental checklist of what still needed to be done. "I guess I'm just anxious to make sure it's all finished before Janessa gets back."

"She won't be back until tomorrow afternoon at the earliest, and you don't have much left to do," Stefano assured her. "If you want, I can make sure Martino calls you as soon as they arrive."

"Actually, that would be great."

Stefano's eyes narrowed. "You know, I don't think I have your cell number."

"Oh, you can just have Martino call me on the office phone," Alora told him. "A technician came in yesterday and fixed the phones in here."

"Did he say what was wrong with them?"

She nodded. "Apparently some of the wiring was messed up. All the calls to these phones were going to Martino's office next door."

"That's odd."

"That's what the repairman said," Alora told him. "He never did figure out how it could have happened."

"As long as it's fixed now," Stefano said, ignoring the uneasy feeling that something wasn't quite right. He noticed a small box of toys in the corner of the room. "Have the boys been helping you out in here?"

"Not yet, but I was planning on having them help me finish up tomorrow. I'm letting them keep a few toys in my office for when they need to tag along with me."

"I'm sure they'll love that." He nodded and then motioned to the door. "It's a beautiful night out. Let's go for a walk in the gardens."

She seemed to consider before nodding. "That would be nice, thank you, but I need to make sure Brenna doesn't mind sitting with the boys a little longer."

He led her into the hall. "Don't worry about that. She isn't expecting you back until ten."

Her eyebrows drew together. "Why did you tell her I'd be gone for so long?"

"Because I thought you could use some downtime," Stefano said simply. Before she could protest, he added, "You've been working incredibly long hours for the past two days. It won't hurt for you to stop and smell the flowers, so to speak."

"I suppose you're right." She walked outside with him and looked up at the night sky before motioning to the gardens. "It's so beautiful here. Everything looks too perfect to be real."

"I will convey your compliments to our gardeners." He turned down a path that ran parallel to the water. They walked in companionable silence until the path curved around a three-tiered fountain and they reached the stone wall that separated the gardens from the Mediterranean. Stefano rested a hand on the wall and stared out at the water. "So tell me, Alora, how do you like your new home?"

Alora stepped beside him and mirrored his stance. "Before I moved here, I didn't believe people really lived like this."

"Like what?"

"Like this." She waved her arm and motioned to the gardens and the chateau beyond them. "A beautiful home in a stunning setting, people who are kind and generous with their time and are always so willing to help with every possible need. You must have lived a very blessed life."

Stefano understood what most people believed life was like for a prince. He also knew that those same people would be shocked to know how many hours he worked in a typical day. Rarely did he sleep past six, and his social obligations typically kept him occupied well into the night. Realizing that Alora had only been around him while he was basically on a holiday, he kept his comment neutral. "Being royal brings both advantages and restrictions."

"I'm sure there are many things that are more difficult for you than they are for the rest of us," Alora said softly. "I can't imagine what it's like having the public so aware of every move you make or having so many guards following you every time you go out. Still, you can't deny the advantage of having gardens like these to play hide and seek in."

"That is true."

Stefano shifted to face her. A strand of her hair caught in the wind, and he reached out to tuck it behind her ear. Time froze for an instant when his hand skimmed across her cheek. Alora's dark eyes lifted to meet his, her lovely features silhouetted in the moonlight. His heartbeat quickened, and his eyes lingered on her lips.

It would have been so easy to lean forward for a kiss, to see if their blooming friendship had the potential of becoming something more. Then he thought of her children, of the fact that he could never offer her the opportunity to have more. Why his thoughts jumped from simply kissing her to making a life with her he couldn't say, but something tightened in his stomach and then sank like a ball of lead.

With a great deal of regret, he motioned back the way they had come. "I'll walk you back."

* * *

"Aunt Janessa!" Giancarlo and Dante raced down the curved staircase as though they had been doing so their whole lives.

Alora followed behind them and bit back a smile when Janessa winked at her before focusing on the boys, her eyes widening in mock surprise. "Who are these two handsome boys? They can't be Giancarlo and Dante. They're much too tall."

"It's us, Aunt Janessa!" Dante squealed with delight and grabbed on to her hand.

Janessa leaned down so they were eye to eye. "Dante? Is that really you?"

"You're just being silly." Dante giggled.

"Oh, I am, am I?" Janessa pulled him close for a hug and then turned to give Giancarlo a hug. She stood and glanced back at Prince Garrett, who was watching with amusement. "Garrett, these are the friends I was telling you about."

Alora immediately caught herself comparing Prince Garrett to his older brother. They both had classic good looks—tall with dark hair and dark eyes—although Prince Garrett was an inch or two taller than his brother and not as broad through the shoulders.

When her boys bowed to the prince, Alora noticed the amusement in his eyes that was very much like the expression she had come to expect from Stefano. She caught herself, realizing she no longer put Stefano's title in front of his name when she thought of him. Not quite sure what to think of this unexpected familiarity, she focused on exchanging greetings with Prince Garrett.

He chatted with them for a moment before he excused himself. He gave Janessa's hand a squeeze before heading upstairs.

Janessa turned her attention back to Alora and reached out to embrace her friend. "I'm so sorry I wasn't here when you arrived. I hope everyone has made you feel welcome."

"I'm not sure if *welcome* is the word I would use. *Spoiled* is more like it."

Janessa smiled. "Let's go for a walk, and we can catch up."

"Can we come too?" Giancarlo asked.

"Absolutely."

* * *

"Come in," Stefano called out in response to the knock on his office door. He smiled when he saw his brother walk in looking both content and rested. "Welcome back. I hope you had a successful trip."

"I did, thank you." Garrett closed the door behind him and then folded his long, lanky frame into the seat across from his brother. He shot Stefano a boyish grin. "I see you aren't taking the doctor's orders too seriously."

Stefano's eyes darkened as he thought of his last conversation with the doctor. He planned to confide the recent diagnosis to his brother, to explain that everything had changed for both of them. He opened his mouth to say the words, but once again they wouldn't come. "Dr. Casale's orders are a bit strict considering how minor my injuries are." Stefano shifted in his seat. "Besides, I don't think I'm going to be able to stay out of the game for much longer. Things are starting to pile up."

"I'm sure it didn't help that I've been out of town for the past few days," Garrett admitted. "Any chance that you were able to get anything done on Janessa's new offices?"

"Alora was a bit hesitant to decorate them without Janessa's knowledge, but once I told her you wanted it to be a surprise, she jumped right in."

"How much longer do you think it will take before everything will be ready?"

"It already is," Stefano said, delighting in his brother's surprise. "Alora started first thing Monday morning, and the painters finished up yesterday afternoon," Stefano told him with a hint of pride in his voice. His mind turned briefly to his and Alora's time together the night before, but he quickly pushed past it. "She's been working with the staff all day, moving furniture and taking care of the final touches."

"It sounds like she's every bit as organized as Janessa said," Garrett commented. "I have to head to the base for a couple hours, but I thought we could show Janessa her new space after dinner."

"Sounds good." Stefano nodded. "Is six o'clock okay for dinner?"

"I should be back by then." His eyebrows drew together. "Why so early?"

"Seven is a bit late to eat for Alora's children."

"Ah. How has that been so far, having little ones underfoot?"

Stefano smiled now. "They remind me of the two of us when we were young."

Garrett chuckled. "Heaven help us."

Chapter 21

"Tell me what you've seen so far," Janessa said to Alora as they walked out of Janessa's rooms with the boys trotting along behind them.

Alora immediately thought of her walk in the garden with Stefano the night before. She still wasn't quite sure what to think of that moment when he had reached out, his fingers skimming her cheek. At first she had thought the gesture had simply been one of familiarity and friendship. Then she had seen something in his eyes, some window that let her see beyond his typical polished exterior. She felt the change between them, an intimacy that left her yearning to discover the man behind the princely exterior.

Impatient with herself, she pushed the image aside and tried to focus on the intent behind her friend's question. "Patrice showed us around the chateau a few days ago, and we've been through the gardens and down to the beach."

"Have you been out to the stables yet?"

She shook her head. "They have horses here?"

"Yes." Janessa nodded, laughing as Giancarlo and Dante both rushed in front of them with pleas to see the horses.

"Can we ride one?" Giancarlo asked eagerly.

"I want to ride a pony!" Dante announced.

Janessa grinned down at the boys and winked. "We'll see if we can talk your mom into it."

Alora leaned closer to her and whispered, "They don't know how to ride."

"Yet," Janessa corrected. "Come on."

Together they walked past the gardens and up a dirt path that snaked through the trees and up a small rise. At the top of the hill, split-rail fences sectioned off the open fields, a long white building situated in the center of the paddocks. A trio of horses gathered in a far pasture under a large cyprus tree. The bay mare grazing in the field closest to them lifted her head and stared for a moment before slowly moving closer to the fence.

"She's hoping I have an apple for her." Janessa reached out and stroked her neck as she spoke gently. "Sorry, girl. I don't have anything for you today."

"Can I pet her?" Dante asked eagerly.

"Sure. Come here." Janessa lifted him up so he could reach the mare more easily. "Just move slowly so you don't scare her."

"Okay." Dante reached out and rubbed her long nose. The mare snorted and tossed her head. Dante giggled, and Giancarlo took a step back and gripped his mother's hand.

"Who do we have here?" The stable manager stepped out of the stables and grinned at the boys. His husky build nearly disguised the fact that he had already seen his seventieth birthday come and go, but what little hair he had left was snow white. His dark eyes twinkled mischievously at Janessa as he asked, "Did you bring me some new stable hands?"

"Oh, I think you might be able to put them to work," Janessa said and then introduced the older man as Paolo Saldera.

Never one to think of anyone as a stranger, Dante stepped forward. "Can I ride a pony?"

"Well . . ." Paolo scratched at his chin as though deep in thought. "I don't know that we have any ponies here, but maybe I can interest you in riding a horse."

"Oh, they've never ridden before," Alora said quickly.

Paolo's eyebrows lifted, and he spoke to Alora now. "Is it okay with you if they learn?"

"I would love for them to learn, but . . ."

Before she could continue, Paolo nodded and reached out for Dante's hand. "Well, let's get started on your first lesson." He offered his other hand to Giancarlo, who glanced up at his mother for a brief moment before abandoning her for Paolo. "Did you know I taught Prince Stefano and Prince Garrett to ride?"

"Really?" both boys asked in unison.

"Absolutely." Paolo started toward the stables, leaving Alora feeling somewhat overwhelmed.

"Don't worry. He won't let anything happen to them."

Alora watched the boys disappear into the stable before turning to Janessa. "Janessa, you know I can't afford to pay for lessons."

"Paolo wouldn't want you to pay him." Janessa shook her head. "In fact, this will be great for everyone. Paolo will expect them to help out with the horses if they want to ride, and I know he'll enjoy their company."

Alora let out a nervous laugh. "I just can't get over how great everyone is here. I feel like we're living in a fairytale."

Janessa simply grinned. "Don't look now, but I think we are."

* * *

"I can't tell," the young nurse said, repeating the words like a chant. "I can't tell. I can't tell."

Caspar Gazsi stepped away from where Belinda Parnelli was bound to a chair, bright lights shining overhead. The sleeves of his dress shirt were rolled up to his elbows, and a trickle of sweat beaded on his brow. He rubbed a hand idly over his neatly trimmed beard and considered his options. He turned to the man standing in the corner and lowered his voice. "We may have to resort to more drastic measures."

"I already told you we can't leave any evidence that she was being pressed for information."

"Are you sure you really need this information?" He glanced over his shoulder, staring at the woman. She was slumped forward, her head hung low, her hair disheveled and curtaining part of her face. Turning his attention back to the man beside him, he continued. "What difference does it make if the prince knows? Certainly he'll keep it quiet."

"He will, but we need to know if anyone else might have gotten ahold of it. If someone sells it to the press, it could throw the timing off for all our other plans."

Caspar lowered his voice even further. "If it's that important, we can always dispose of the body so she won't be found."

He shook his head. "Bodies have a tendency of popping up at the worst possible time. Besides, I think we're going to want hers to be found."

"Then you'd better get your hands on a pentothal agent."

"Wouldn't an autopsy be able to reveal that?"

Caspar shook his head. "Not if we keep her alive long enough for it to get out of her system."

* * *

Janessa sat between Garrett and Giancarlo in the dining hall and reveled in the knowledge that, for the first time in a week, she wouldn't be expected to help with the after-dinner dishes.

When Marie walked in carrying cannelloni, she grinned across the table at Alora. "Have you had Patrice's cannelloni yet?"

Alora shook her head. "No, but everything I've had here has been incredible. We've been so spoiled already that I'm afraid the boys won't want to eat my cooking anymore."

Dante patted her arm. "I still like your raisin cookies the best, Mama."

Alora chuckled and leaned down to kiss his forehead. "Thank you, Dante."

"What can I get you to drink, Your Highness?" Marie asked Stefano. "Would you care for a glass of wine?"

Stefano nodded his assent only to have Giancarlo shake his head disapprovingly at him. "Mama says we aren't supposed to drink wine."

"Oh really?" Stefano glanced briefly at Alora, and Janessa was sure he couldn't miss the color rising to her friend's cheeks. Before Alora could fumble over an explanation, Stefano gave Giancarlo his full attention once more. "Well, then. What do you suggest I drink with dinner instead?"

"Apple juice," Giancarlo announced with conviction.

"Okay." Stefano nodded thoughtfully. Then he looked up at Marie, who was struggling to keep a straight face. "I'll have some apple juice."

"Yes, Your Highness." Marie took everyone else's drink orders and left to fill them.

Alora leaned toward Stefano, probably to apologize, but he merely shook his head and offered her a smile filled with humor. Janessa watched the silent exchange, pleased to see her friend and her future brother-in-law appeared to have developed a friendship over the past week.

Janessa took a roll out of the bread basket Garrett handed her and passed it to Giancarlo. He took out one for himself and immediately climbed onto his knees so he could reach across the table to give it to his mother. Alora took it from him, buttered it, and then handed it back. Janessa's eyes widened when Alora then reached her hand out to Stefano, who passed his roll to her. Alora buttered it and passed it back before proceeding to butter another roll for Dante.

Janessa looked over at Garrett, who was already so focused on his dinner that he had apparently missed the unexpected familiarity between

Alora and Stefano. Curious now if perhaps more had been happening over the past week than she had realized, Janessa looked at her friend. "Alora, I didn't get a chance to ask you how you've been spending your days since you arrived. Have you and the boys spent much time on the beach?"

"The boys have," Alora began.

"I'm afraid I've been dominating her time," Stefano interrupted before Alora could continue. "She's been helping me sort through all of those environmental reports. We were able to send the final summaries out yesterday."

"Did anything concerning pop up?" Garrett asked.

"Everything was pretty much what we expected," Stefano told him. "I sent you an electronic version, but I'm sure it'll take you a few days to sort through all of your e-mail."

Conversation over dinner centered on the upcoming construction at the naval base, mixed with a few stories from the children about their adventures on the beach that day.

When the meal concluded, Garrett reached for Janessa's hand. "If everyone is finished, we have something to show you upstairs."

"What's going on?" Janessa looked at him quizzically and then caught Alora's blank stare, the one she always wore when she was trying to hide her emotions.

Rather than answer her, Alora spoke to her boys as she stood up. "Come on, boys. It's about time we head to our rooms."

"Do we have to?" Giancarlo asked, disappointment in his voice.

"If it's okay with you, Alora, I would love for you all to join us," Garrett invited.

"Can we, Mama?" Dante jumped out of his chair and looked up at her hopefully.

Alora hesitated a moment before nodding at Garrett. "We would love to join you."

"Is anyone going to tell me where we're going?" Janessa asked as Garrett started leading everyone out of the room.

"You'll see soon enough," Garrett told her.

Janessa narrowed her eyes as they left the dining hall and walked through the parlor. "What is it with you and surprises lately?"

Garrett grinned down at her. "I love a challenge."

"He always has," Stefano agreed as he followed behind them.

They walked up the stairs and then started down the main hallway that led to the chateau offices. Janessa expected him to stop at his office or even the security office, but he continued past them both, not stopping until he reached another office, one she knew to be unoccupied.

"The family decided that you should have your own work space here at the chateau." Garrett pushed the door open, and Janessa's eyes widened as she looked inside and caught the scent of fresh paint.

She stepped through the doorway and turned in a circle. The chair railing and crown molding were painted the same cream color as the upper part of the wall, contrasting with the warm beige below the chair rail. A large ceramic vase held three miniature palm trees, and on the walls an original Monet hung opposite a modern seascape. The furnishings were a mixture of old and new: a new office chair behind a polished antique desk, a sleek laptop and a wireless printer resting on an aged credenza in the same honey oak as the desk.

"This is incredible. It looks nothing like it did before."

"Can we play for a minute, Mama?"

"Just for a minute," Alora agreed. Both boys raced across the office to an armoire on the far side of the room. They opened the bottom section and pulled a bin of toys out onto the thick carpet.

"We thought Alora could work in here," Garrett said and then motioned to the door leading to the interior office. "Your office is in there."

Janessa followed him through the doorway, and her breath caught. "Oh wow."

"Do you like it?" Alora asked as she and Stefano joined them in the inner office.

"Did you do all this?" Janessa asked with wonder in her voice. The room had been completely transformed. Like the exterior office, the walls had been repainted in warm neutral tones, and the artwork had been replaced with a tasteful combination of classic and contemporary.

Alora motioned to Stefano and Garrett. "They spearheaded the remodeling. I only helped a bit with the decorating."

"She's being too modest," Stefano insisted. "I just gave her a list of contractors and then stayed out of her way."

Janessa looked around the room once more in admiration, and she didn't miss the way Alora's cheeks flushed at Stefano's compliment or the way Stefano's eyes lingered on her a bit longer than usual. She reached out and ran a finger over a round cherry table and continued through the room until she reached the exquisite Chippendale desk positioned near the window. "Thank you all so much. This is a wonderful surprise."

Alora let out a sigh of relief and stepped closer to the window. "Can you believe this view?"

Janessa turned and looked out the window, which was now framed by elegant lace curtains. Her smile came quickly. "It appears I have the best of both worlds. I can see the Mediterranean from my room when I wake up in the morning, and we can see the country landscape from here."

She noticed Stefano's quick smile, and her eyebrows drew together. "What?"

"Nothing." Stefano shook his head, his eyes shifting to Alora before he spoke to Janessa once more. "I'm just pleased that you're happy with your new space."

Chapter 22

HIS EYES NARROWED AS HE studied the piece of equipment on the table and then looked up at Prince Elam. "You told me days ago that you recovered the transmitter. Where is the other half?"

"That's all there was."

He shook his head. "There were two pieces."

"No one told me that." Elam's voice tightened. "I had to break a hole in the wall to get that one. By now the renovations must be complete. There's no way I can retrieve the other piece without raising suspicions."

"If the other half was discovered, we need to know about it." His voice darkened as he added, "If your intelligence service is able to trace it back to my supporters, all of us will be exposed."

"This is already getting out of hand. I didn't sign up for this."

"No, but we have an agreement. You don't want to find out what will happen if you break your end of it." The unspoken threat hung in the air.

Elam swallowed hard. "I already told you, my brother doesn't confide in me about security matters. There's no way I can get that information."

"Perhaps there's another way. With the right technology, you would be able to scan the wall in your old office, and no one will ever be the wiser."

"No one will know?" Elam asked.

"Your secrets will stay safe with us," he promised, a slow smile spreading across his face. "But there is one more thing we need."

Elam drew a deep breath. "What do you want me to do?"

* * *

After getting a glimpse of Janessa's ever-changing schedule, Alora expected her own routine to be turned upside down. To her surprise, her days played out very much like they had before Janessa arrived home. She and her children still started their day in the breakfast room with Stefano. More often than not, Janessa and Prince Garrett joined them, and Alora was pleased to see the strong bond between her friend and the man she intended to marry.

Patrice still supervised the boys as they did their chores each morning, simple tasks that typically included helping take out the trash and clearing the table. More and more, Alora noticed that Patrice was also letting them help when she baked. She also now insisted that Giancarlo and Dante speak to her in French so they could practice.

With their newfound interest in the horses, the boys spent the rest of their mornings helping Paolo in the stables, followed by riding lessons. As soon as they were finished at the stables each morning, Brenna stepped in to oversee the rest of their activities. The swimming lessons had been rescheduled for after lunch, following which they played in the pool or on the beach.

Every night when she knelt to pray, Alora was amazed that this life was really hers. She had hoped this move would help her children gain more exposure to the world and give them the opportunity for a better education. Never had she expected private lessons and regular meals with royalty to be part of the experience.

Since Janessa was typically at the naval base in the middle of the day, Alora often still ate lunch with Stefano. She found it a bit unreal that for the past three years she had eaten nearly every meal sitting at a wobbly table in a tiny apartment, and now she was living in a place where each meal was served in a corresponding dining room.

Despite the summer heat, the boys had taken to eating their lunch on the shaded portion of the terrace. They were just close enough to the beach to feel the breeze stir and cool the air, and the scents from the garden always made Alora feel like she was dining on some secluded tropical island. Although Stefano's schedule now included a steady stream of meetings during the day, typically he arrived to eat lunch with them, often lingering with Alora long enough for them to watch the boys splash in the pool before walking back upstairs to their respective offices.

Somehow Janessa had managed to get Alora's CIA security clearances reinstated so she could help manage some of the workload on the naval base as well as at the chateau. Besides setting up their new offices, Alora had also been tasked with coordinating the travel arrangements for the

CIA's personnel who had arrived to monitor a suspected bomb maker in Meridia.

The idea of terrorists in this small, picturesque country seemed surreal, but finally the CIA had their people in place, and Alora was free to concentrate on Janessa's schedules and obligations. Now that she had been living at the chateau for nearly a month, she felt like she had a handle on what was expected of her. She had even learned her way around this structure that she already considered her home.

When a man opened her office door, Alora looked up from her desk inquisitively. He was older, his beard and mustache neatly trimmed, and arrogance hung heavily over him. Her voice was professional when she asked, "May I help you?"

"No, I'll only be a minute." The man started for the door leading to Janessa's office.

Instinctively, Alora stood and moved to block his path. "I'm sorry, sir, but Signorina Rogers isn't in right now."

Irritation and disdain hung thick in his voice. "Don't you know who I am?"

"No, sir." Alora shook her head, her feet firmly planted in front of the doorway.

"I am Prince Elam. This is my old office."

"I see." Alora couldn't say why his announcement only strengthened her resolve to hold her ground. "Is there something I can help you with?"

"I left some things here I need to pick up. Now if you'll move aside."

She shook her head. "I'm sorry, but everything that was in there has been replaced. If there is anything you need, I believe Martino can direct you to where your things are being stored."

"I will see for myself."

Alora didn't budge. "I'm sure Signorina Rogers would be happy to show you her new office. Would you like to make an appointment?"

Fury lit his eyes. "Are you trying to get yourself fired?"

"On the contrary. I'm trying to do my job."

"Move aside." Prince Elam reached out to put his hand on her shoulder to shove her out of the way just as another man stepped into the office.

"Is there a problem here?"

Elam turned and looked derisively at the new arrival. "Who are you?"

"Levi Marin. I'm with security here."

Elam's jaw clenched, and he appeared to be struggling to keep his temper in check. "She won't let me into my old office."

"Sir, she's just doing her job. If you need something, I would be happy to show you to the storage room where your belongings are currently being housed. Otherwise, you're welcome to take up your complaint with Prince Stefano. I believe he is in his office across the hall."

Elam's jaw clenched, and his face flushed with frustration. "This is an outrage!"

"I'm sorry, sir, but Signorina Rogers' office is off limits to anyone besides her staff."

Elam stalked to the door until he was eye to eye with Levi. "It appears everyone wants to lose their jobs today."

Alora could feel her face pale at the thought, but she kept her head up high as the prince stormed into the hall. She'd been here barely a month, and already she'd managed to alienate herself from a member of the royal family.

Levi stepped farther into her office and closed the door behind him. He waved dismissively toward the door. "Don't worry about him. He doesn't have the authority to fire either one of us."

"Are you sure?" She eyed him doubtfully.

"Positive." Levi stepped closer and held out an oversized manila envelope heavily sealed with clear tape. "This is a pouch from Langley. The reports Janessa requested are in there."

Her eyebrows lifted. "Langley?"

He glanced behind him at the closed door before turning back and nodding. "I was brought in to help with security a few months ago. My assignment's been extended for another six months."

Alora smiled. "I guess you're right that Prince Elam can't fire you."

"Or you."

Her smile faded. "But I'm not on the Agency's payroll. Janessa said the royal family is paying my salary to be her assistant."

"Even if that's the case, I seriously doubt the royal family would bow to Prince Elam's wishes. Except for the most public events, he and his family are rarely on the guest lists for social functions."

Alora lowered into her chair with a sigh. "I can't tell you what a relief it is to hear you say that."

Chapter 23

JANESSA SET THE LATEST CIA intel report on her new desk and looked at Levi, who was sitting opposite her. "Our agents have been in place for more than two weeks, and they still don't have anything?"

Levi shook his head. "We've had a constant tail on our suspect, and so far, no abnormalities have popped up in his purchases, and we haven't seen any evidence of him receiving shipments."

"It's possible he already has everything he would need to make a bomb, if that's what he's planning," Janessa pointed out. "Our records show he arrived in Meridia at least three weeks before our operatives arrived."

"Yes, but why wait for so long?" Levi asked. "It isn't like Ambrose to stay in one place for so long, at least not in a Western country."

"You think he's waiting for something?"

"Something or someone." Levi shrugged. "Do you know of any high-profile targets scheduled to visit Meridia any time soon?"

"The secretary of the navy is supposed to come for the official opening of the new naval base, but that won't be until next year." Janessa thought for a minute. "I know Garrett has mentioned Meridia is a favorite vacation spot for many members of Europe's ruling class. I can see if he might have any idea of anyone who will be visiting in the next few months."

"It's an angle worth pursuing. No one in the Agency believes Ambrose is just here for a vacation."

"I know."

"There's one more thing." Levi slid a folder onto her desk. "This arrived in today's pouch."

Janessa opened the file, studied the schematics, and then looked up at Levi with an astonished look on her face. "Does this say what I think it does?"

"I'm afraid so."

"I need to talk to Garrett." Janessa stood up. "You'll let me know if you hear anything else from our people in the field?"

"Definitely." Levi motioned to the file. "I assume you want me to get the equipment we'll need to do a more thorough search."

"Yeah." She nodded. "That would be great. Thanks."

"Good luck explaining this to the royals."

* * *

Hector Ambrose steered the rented houseboat away from land and the few other boats on the water. He waited until they were out of sight of the local boat traffic before he motioned for the man beside him to take over. Then he went below deck, where his current employers had been hiding since before he had arrived at the pier to take possession of the boat.

"What is so important that you had to meet in person?" Caspar Gazsi asked in French. "Surely you realize how risky this is."

"We need a new target," Ambrose said simply. "The CIA has been tracking me for weeks, and they don't look like they are going to leave any time soon."

He shook his head. "There isn't another target that can serve all our purposes."

"I understand that, but the CIA knows I'm here for some reason. We need to detonate a bomb somewhere so they think I have completed my job here. Otherwise I won't be able to gain access to the building you want me to destroy."

"You're saying we need to plant a bomb now so you'll be able to plant the other bombs later?"

"Exactly." He nodded. "And I have an idea of where."

* * *

Stefano stared down at the spreadsheet in front of him, feeling like he was looking for a needle in a haystack. All the expenses for the annual gala celebration last month were in line with the previous year, and the receipts matched the ledgers. Even the two hundred thousand euros listed for security matched the corresponding receipts from the security company.

As much as he agreed with his father that it would be best not to bring in outside auditors for fear of alerting a potential embezzler of their suspicions, he doubted he was going to be able to find any evidence by himself. He heard a door open across the hall, followed by footsteps.

Remembering that Alora had an accounting background, he stared down at the reports again and considered. Perhaps he could borrow her from Janessa for a day or two. Then if she wasn't able to find any evidence of foul play either, he would recommend that his father bring in another auditing team.

Pushing back from his desk, he ignored the little tug of anticipation as he walked across the hall, rapping on the closed door twice before pushing it open.

Alora looked up at him apprehensively and immediately stood up. Her eyes dropped to the floor as she curtsied. "Your Highness."

Stefano stopped midstep and studied her demure expression. "Is something wrong?"

"That depends." Her lips pressed together as though she were fighting to keep her emotions in check. Then she took a deep breath and asked, "Did you come in here to fire me?"

His eyebrows shot up. "Where would you get an idea like that?"

"Your uncle."

"Elam?" Stefano let out an exasperated sigh. "He was here?"

She nodded, her eyes dark and wary. "He was angry that I wouldn't let him into Janessa's office."

"Why did he want to go in there?"

"He said he came to get some of his things."

"That's odd. He went through his old office right before we started the renovations."

"He didn't mention that to me."

"Well, rest assured, I am not here to fire you. My uncle has no authority here." Stefano saw the relief on Alora's face and fought to stem his disgust with his uncle. "I'm here to ask for your help if Janessa can spare you for a day or two. I have some financial records I would like you to help me analyze."

Dutifully, Alora looked down at the calendar on her desk before nodding. "It looks like Janessa is working on the base for the rest of the week. I'm sure she wouldn't mind if I helped you. When did you want to start?"

"There's no time like the present."

She looked down at the package on her desk and then stood. "Let me just lock up, and then I'll come right over."

"Excellent. I'll see you in a few minutes." Stefano started to leave, and then something Alora had said echoed in his mind. "When my uncle came in, did he tell you what he was looking for?"

"No. He was quite upset that I wouldn't let him into Janessa's office," she admitted. "I told him that everything had been cleared out of there, but he was insistent that he be able to see for himself."

"I apologize for my uncle's behavior. Quite frankly, I'm surprised he took no for an answer."

"I don't think he was going to, but Levi came in before he could push past me."

"I'll talk to Martino to make sure he doesn't show up unannounced again."

Alora's shoulders relaxed. "Thank you. I appreciate it."

"I'll go get the financial reports organized." Stefano crossed back into his office and picked up his phone. A moment later his father's voice came on the line. "Father, I think we may have a problem."

"What kind of problem?"

Stefano related what Alora had told him and mentioned his uncle's previous visit. "Do you have any idea what he might be looking for?"

King Eduard's tone was serious. "I don't. Did you find anything in those financial reports?"

"Not so far. Everything is well documented, but we both know the fees are more than they should have been, at least for security. It's possible that the private security company simply overbilled us, and it wasn't caught," Stefano suggested. "I've asked Alora to help me go through the records again in case I missed something."

Eduard's tone became cautionary. "I trust you will keep in mind how sensitive this information is."

Stefano's shoulders stiffened, but his voice remained calm. "Of course I will."

Chapter 24

"I HOPE I'M NOT INTERRUPTING," Janessa said from the doorway of Stefano's inner office.

"Not at all." Stefano stood up and motioned to Alora, who was sitting beside him at the worktable in the corner of the room. "We've been staring at these ledgers all day, and I think we're both ready for a break."

"I'm sure if there are any problems in the books, Alora will find them. She's a whiz when it comes to finances."

Alora shook her head. "I don't know about that."

"She's always been modest too." Janessa motioned to the hall. "Stefano, Garrett and I need to speak to you for a minute."

"I'll be right back," Stefano told Alora and then followed Janessa to his brother's office. As soon as they were inside, he asked, "What's going on?"

"You're going to want to sit down for this." Garrett settled back into his chair as soon as Janessa sat beside him. "First of all, Ambrose has disappeared."

"What do you mean *disappeared*?" Stefano looked at Janessa. "I thought the CIA was tailing him."

"They were." Janessa looked at him apologetically. "Ambrose rented a boat earlier today. When the boat returned, he wasn't on it."

"What?"

"We think he spotted one of his tails," she told him. "The agents did a thorough search of Medina and weren't able to reacquire him. Our best guess is that he has left town, but there's no way to be sure if he is getting ready to strike or if he has left the country."

"Great," Stefano muttered.

"There's one more thing." Janessa passed a copy of a simple floor plan of the chateau to him.

Stefano noticed the various marks on the page and shook his head in confusion. "What am I looking at?"

"All of these red dots indicate where listening devices were found here in the chateau," Janessa told him. "According to the report that arrived in this morning's pouch from the CIA, this technology requires some kind of transmitter to send the signals."

"We already knew that."

"Yes, but now we also know the range of how close the transmitter needs to be to the listening devices," Garrett interjected. He tapped a finger on the floor plan where several rooms and sections of the hallway were shaded. "This is the only area in the chateau where the transmitter could have been hidden based on the range compared to the location of the bugs."

Stefano studied the four rooms that were shaded and looked up at his brother. "Am I reading this right? These two are Janessa's and Alora's offices, and the other two are the security offices?"

"That's right." Garrett nodded. "Our best guess is that it was concealed somewhere in one of the hallway walls, probably during the renovations we did before the gala a few years ago."

Stefano's eyes narrowed. "Who was in charge of those renovations?"

"I'm not sure. Mother would probably know. Why?"

"Uncle Elam came by right before we started the renovations on his old office. Then when I came back to check on the workmen, there was a hole in the wall that I didn't remember seeing before."

Janessa looked from Stefano to Garrett and then back again. "Surely you don't think your uncle could have been involved in spying on your family."

"I wouldn't think so, but something's going on with him. He showed up and tried to barge into your office again this morning." The muscle in Stefano's jaw twitched when he thought of the look on Alora's face earlier. "He even threatened to have Alora fired when she wouldn't let him in."

"What?"

"She was pretty shaken up, but apparently Levi showed up before anything came of it," Stefano told them. "Uncle Elam has always been arrogant, but it never ceases to amaze me how rude he can be."

Janessa tapped a finger on the file in front of her. "The CIA report I read on him didn't show anything unexpected. I can ask the Agency to help me do some more digging, but I would need your father's permission first."

"I'll talk to him," Garrett offered. "I should be able to get an answer from him before our guests start arriving for dinner tonight."

Stefano's eyes narrowed. "What's going on tonight?"

"The dinner party for the Italian ambassador. Don't you remember?"

He shook his head. "I wasn't originally supposed to be here this week."

"Well, I suggest you dig out your tux because there's no way you're getting out of it."

"Great," Stefano muttered, oddly disappointed.

"What's the problem? You always like these things. Dinner, conversation, and the chance to sweep some girl off her feet," Garrett teased.

An image of Alora flashed in his mind. He ignored his brother and spoke to Janessa instead. "Do you think you might have something suitable that Alora could borrow for tonight?"

"She wasn't planning on going. She said she was just going to have dinner in her room with the boys."

Stefano considered the idea of Alora up in her rooms while he was stuck downstairs entertaining a bunch of strangers. "I'll see if I can change her mind." Stefano stood up and asked Janessa, "Would you mind making sure she has a gown for tonight? If you want, have something sent in from town. Also, could you let Brenna know we'll need her to babysit this evening?"

Janessa nodded, but Stefano didn't miss the speculation in her eyes.

"I just think it's good for her to spend some time socializing with adults. She's obviously made her children her whole world over the past few years."

Janessa nodded slowly. "Of course."

* * *

Alora shifted another receipt to the pile beside her and looked up at Stefano. "We're going to need the detailed bank records if we want to see where all of this money really went."

"The statements are around here somewhere." Stefano searched through a stack of papers and then lifted the bank printouts. "Here they are."

"Those are just summary sheets. I want to see the actual codes used to transfer the money so we can see how it was drawn and where it ended up," Alora explained. "If you can authorize me to see everything on the accounts, I can go into the bank and start researching it first thing tomorrow."

"Is there any way you can look at it from here?"

"Sure, with a computer and the right kind of encryption keys, but we would need the proper equipment and the access codes."

"I'll ask Martino and Levi if they can get those for you." Stefano glanced at his watch, adding casually, "I almost forgot to tell you that I made arrangements for you to join us tonight for dinner with the Italian ambassador. I thought you should meet some of the leaders from your country."

She looked up at him, not certain why the arrogance of his tone set her on edge. When Janessa had mentioned the dinner earlier, hadn't she secretly wanted Stefano to ask her to join them? Hadn't she been disappointed that he hadn't asked her to accompany him? Of course, he wasn't asking now. He was ordering.

Logically she knew she shouldn't let such a minor distinction feed into the fact that she didn't like being told what to do, but annoyance overshadowed logic. That annoyance quickly turned to indignation when he turned his attention back to the work in front of him, clearly not willing to consider that she might not wish to go with him. Her voice was even when she spoke, her eyes dark. "You made arrangements?"

He shifted the paperwork in front of him back into their appropriate folders. His eyes were carefully guarded when he nodded and said, "Brenna will make sure the children's needs are met. I'll come by at seven to escort you downstairs."

Rarely did she let her temper loose. She knew too well how quickly she could lose control, and she wasn't going to let that happen now. Clamping down on her emotions, she managed to keep her voice calm. "Thank you for the offer, but I think I'll pass."

"Are you sure?" He looked up at her now. "I thought you would be more comfortable going with me so you wouldn't have to arrive by yourself."

Her stomach knotted as she realized she was letting pride get in the way of what she really wanted. Her voice was cool when she said, "You misunderstand, Your Highness. I'm not going at all."

His eyebrows lifted, and he apparently recognized the temper in her eyes. "I think it's time you call me by my name, especially if you're about to argue with me."

"I'm not arguing. I'm simply pointing out that a gentleman doesn't order a woman to dinner. He asks." She pushed back from the table and stood. "I appreciate that Brenna has tended to my children while I've been working, but I prefer when possible to take care of them myself. I didn't have them just so I could pass them off to someone else any time it was convenient for me or for you."

Stefano stood as well. "What's the difference between tonight and when I took you to the exhibit?"

"Besides the fact that you didn't even ask me about tonight?"

He moved closer until they were standing only a breath apart. His eyes were dark and avid, but his voice remained calm. "Yes, besides that."

Something streaked through her, an awakening of feelings she had long since buried. Had she really thought she was ready to date again, that she might be ready to love again? She knew now that she was wrong. She wasn't ready to have these feelings, especially not for this man who was staring down at her, a man whose world she barely understood.

She took a deep breath and let it out in a frustrated sigh. Suddenly uncertain, she fell back on her standard response. "My children are still adjusting to our new schedule. They need time to spend with me, time to tell me about their day, time that they know they can turn to me for anything they need."

"Alora, our guests aren't expected to arrive until seven thirty. It's only four now. You would have plenty of time to spend with them this evening before the dinner. You could even put them to bed before Brenna takes over. I doubt we'll dine before eight."

"It's not that easy." She knew what he said was logical, but still she dug her heels in and refused to budge. "I don't expect you to understand. You're not a parent."

Stefano's jaw tightened, and he took a sudden step back. "No, you're right. I'm not a parent."

Alora blinked at the sudden transformation as Stefano's eyes went flat and emotionless. He crossed to the door and opened it, his voice taking on a formal tone. "It seems we are done here for the day. I will make arrangements with the bank to get you the information you need."

She stared at him as her anger faded and was replaced by confusion and a strange sense of loss. Without a word, she left the room and refused to look back.

Chapter 25

ALORA STEPPED ONTO THE BALCONY and sank down into a chair. Certainly she was justified in turning Stefano down on his offer to join the party tonight. Still, it bothered her that she couldn't figure out what she had said that had affected his mood so suddenly. One minute he was insistent that she join him, and the next he was cool and aloof, as though he didn't care in the least how she chose to spend her evening.

She knew she should call downstairs to let Brenna know she was done working for the day, but first she needed a few minutes to herself. She thought back over her conversation with Stefano and recognized that she had let her temper get to her. She had been childish and petty to refuse for no reason other than that Stefano had annoyed her. Her family had always joked about how much she hated being told what to do, and that characteristic certainly hadn't faded over the years.

Her heart squeezed a bit as the memory of her family formed, and she fought to remember only the good. It didn't matter anymore why they were gone. They simply were, and nothing she could do would change that or the loneliness that had followed. Her lips curved a little as she remembered Stefano asking for her phone number. She had sidestepped the question, but it made her wonder how many people even realized she hadn't had a phone for more than three years. After all, who did she have left to call?

Before Stefano had asked for her number, the last person she could remember asking had been Janessa. Of course, Janessa hadn't let herself get sidetracked, and Alora had admitted that she simply couldn't justify the cost when keeping her children clothed and fed was such a challenge. She could also admit to herself that she still struggled with that last phone call with Carlo, the one she knew now had ended at the same time a bomb had taken his life.

She stared out at a little yellow sailboat on the water, still not exactly sure how she had ended up here. So much of her energy over the past few years had been spent trying to overcome the loss of her family. Now, instead of trying to figure out where the next rent payment was coming from, she was sitting here worrying about an argument with a prince. Everything had changed so quickly, and she wasn't sure she could keep up.

When someone knocked on the door, her stomach jumped in anticipation at the thought that perhaps Stefano had come to make peace. She ignored the tug of disappointment when she opened the door to find Janessa standing on the other side, a gown wrapped in a long sleeve of plastic in one hand and a shopping bag in the other.

Alora managed to suppress a sigh as she stepped aside. "Come on in."

"I'm sorry I didn't get this to you sooner," Janessa told her as she draped the gown over the back of the couch. "I got caught up in town."

"I hope you didn't go to too much trouble to get this since I'm not going tonight."

"You aren't going?" Janessa settled on the arm of the couch. She didn't look so much surprised as curious when she asked, "Do you mind if I ask why?"

"I want to spend more time with the kids."

Janessa stared at her for a moment and then shook her head. "I don't want to know the excuse you gave Stefano. I want to know the real reason you're not going."

Alora sighed. "I hate it when you do that."

Janessa fought back a smile. "Do what?"

"You know perfectly well what I'm talking about." Alora paced across the room and then turned back to face her. "I give you an excuse and then you insist that I'm not telling you everything."

"Which is why you should just tell me everything so I'll know what's going on," Janessa suggested. "I know that technically you're working for me now, but that doesn't change the fact that I'm your friend."

Alora lifted her hands out to the side and then let them fall with a frustrated sigh. "I don't know what it is."

"Could it have anything to do with Stefano?"

"Maybe." She dropped onto a chair across from Janessa and shrugged. "I don't know."

"I know this is none of my business, but I've been wondering since I got back if something was going on between you two."

"No, it's nothing like that," Alora said a little too quickly. "I guess we've started to become friends, and I'm not handling it well. He's used to being able to do what he wants when he wants. I haven't had that luxury for a long time."

"Whether you realize it or not, he doesn't often have much say in his duties either," Janessa said gently. "The past few weeks here at the chateau have given him a lot more flexibility in his schedule, but from what I've seen since I've lived in Meridia, he works long hours and rarely has much time to himself. I'm sure you understand how difficult that can be."

"Yeah, I do."

"I hope you like the gown I picked up for you. If not, feel free to exchange it."

"Janessa, I already told you I'm not going tonight. The gown and shoes can be returned."

"Keep them. Living here, you might as well start building up your wardrobe now. You'll need it," she insisted. "I do hope you change your mind about tonight, but if not, I hope you know you'll be missed."

Alora shook her head. "I doubt that."

"I would think that by now you would know better than to doubt my instincts." Janessa laughed. "I'd better go check on Patrice and make sure everything is all set for tonight. I'll see you later."

* * *

Stefano stared down at the photograph, the twin metal boxes with wire antennas that could have been miniature versions of old-fashioned radios. "This is what the transmitter is supposed to look like?"

"Yes, sir." Levi nodded. "Janessa said you mentioned a hole in the wall in her new office. I thought you might be able to help us determine whether someone had retrieved one of them from there."

"You're telling me there are actually two transmitters, not one?"

"It's really two halves. They are positioned between six and ten feet apart. One would typically be near the listening devices to capture the information they are sending. The other is usually near an exterior wall to transmit the signal to whoever is trying to listen."

"How big are they supposed to be?"

Levi held his hands out. "About six inches wide, and with the wires, they're maybe ten inches tall."

"I'd like for you or Martino to check with the contractors who worked in Janessa's new office. We need to know how that hole got in the wall."

"Martino already checked with everyone who worked in there. The hole was there when the man arrived to take down the shutters."

Awareness swamped through Stefano. He had gone over the details in his head dozens of times. He was certain the hole wasn't there when his uncle had appeared unexpectedly to gather his things. Assuming that no one else had entered the office before the workers arrived the next morning, the only explanation was that Elam had made the hole. Since Elam wasn't known for being a klutz, Stefano could only assume his uncle had been retrieving something hidden there.

"Sir, would you be willing to show me where the hole was located?" Levi asked.

Stefano nodded and led the way from his office into Janessa's. He walked past her desk and put his hand on the side wall near the window. "It was right about here."

"That would be a logical placement for the piece that would send the outgoing signals."

Stefano studied the wall and then estimated the distance and motioned to the center part of the wall. "From what you told me, that would put the other half of the transmitter around here."

Levi nodded. "With your permission, I would like to bring some equipment up here to check out the wall."

"I thought you said this equipment is hard to find with standard security sweeps."

"It is, but we can use X-ray technology to scan the inside of the wall," Levi told him. "The question is, what do you want us to do if we find what we're looking for?"

"Remove it, and then call the contractors back in." Stefano glanced at his watch. "I need to go get ready for dinner. How soon can you get this checked out?"

"The equipment and personnel I need are over at the naval base. Since you're expecting guests tonight, I can wait until tomorrow if you want."

"No. Let's not take the chance that someone will try to take a walk and punch another hole in the wall." Stefano shook his head. "Get your guys over here now. No one from the party would have any reason to come up here tonight, so there won't be anything to get in the way of the search."

Levi nodded. "I'll take care of it."

* * *

Alora bit back her frustration as she watched Giancarlo race from the bedroom and slam the door behind him. After arguing with Stefano about how she needed to spend more time with her children, she had spent the past hour breaking up petty arguments and wishing that it was already time for them to go to bed.

Gritting her teeth together, she shook her head and gathered Dante close as big alligator tears slid down his cheeks. "I'm sorry your brother yelled at you, but both of you need to learn to share."

Dante snuggled closer, and his voice was muffled. "I was sharing, but Giancarlo kept taking everything I wanted to play with."

"Did you stop to think that maybe you were taking what he wanted to play with too?"

He let out a longsuffering sigh.

"Come on now. Let's dry those tears." Alora shifted so she could brush her thumb over his cheek, and then she stood up. "Let's go find your brother. Dinner is almost ready."

"Okay." Dante put his hand in his mother's, and together they walked into the living room to find it empty and the door leading to the main hall hanging open.

Chapter 26

STEFANO HEARD THE FOOTSTEPS WHEN he reached the main entryway. When he looked up, he was surprised to see Giancarlo running down the stairs by himself.

Giancarlo stopped on the bottom step when he saw Stefano, and immediately his eyes dropped to the floor.

"Where are you off to in such a hurry?"

He shrugged without looking up.

Recognizing the gesture, Stefano guessed at the reason behind it. "I gather you got into some trouble with your mom."

His eyes lifted and were dark with indignation. "Mama always makes me share my toys with Dante, even when I want to play with them by myself."

"I remember what that was like," Stefano said sympathetically.

"How? You're a grown-up. You don't play with toys."

"No, but I do know a bit about being an older brother." Stefano smiled wryly.

"But you're a prince."

"Yes, I am. And so is my little brother, Garrett."

Giancarlo looked at him skeptically. "Prince Garrett doesn't look very little to me."

"Maybe not now, but he was once." Stefano reached out his hand to Giancarlo. "How about if I show you where Prince Garrett and I used to play when we were your age?"

"Do you have a swing set?"

"Not exactly." Stefano looked up to see Alora rushing to the top of the stairs. He didn't miss the worry on her face, followed by the expression of relief and exasperation. He waited for her and Dante to come down the stairs before speaking. "Is it okay if Giancarlo takes a little walk with me? I have something I want to show him."

"Can I come too?" Dante asked eagerly.

"Tell you what." Stefano considered how to balance the desires of both boys. "Why don't you let me take Giancarlo with me now, and then tomorrow before dinner, you and I can go for a walk together." He looked up at Alora and realized belatedly that he should have asked for her permission. He wasn't used to asking for permission. "That is, if it's okay with your mom."

Alora looked at him skeptically. "You don't have to do that."

"I don't mind. Besides, wouldn't it be nice to have a little one-on-one time with Dante?" He saw the surprise on her face when he reached down and took Giancarlo by the hand. "Don't worry. We'll be back in a few minutes."

She stared at him for a moment and then nodded in agreement. "Giancarlo, be good for Prince Stefano."

Giancarlo didn't quite manage to look his mother in the eye, but he nodded and spoke quietly. "I will."

Stefano was surprised by the sense of satisfaction that came with Alora's permission. He quickly realized it wasn't her permission he sought but her trust. Hoping her annoyance with him from earlier was fading, he led the way out the front entrance and headed for a path that curved away from the gardens.

"Where are we going?"

"You'll see." Stefano pushed aside some foliage where part of the path was overgrown. Twenty yards later, he pointed up at the tree house he and his brother had played in when they were children. An old tire swing hung from a wide branch of the same tree.

Giancarlo looked up with awe. "Wow!"

"I used to hide out up there when I needed some time to myself."

"Can we go up there now?"

"I don't think your mom wants us to be gone for very long, but we can come back another time."

"Did you ever get lost when you played in the woods?"

He shook his head and pointed to where the path continued through the trees. "That path there leads to the stables. When you get older, you'll be able to ride through here, and you'll get to know your way around better."

"Mama said we have to start school soon, so we won't be able to ride horses every day."

"You might not have time to ride every day, but you won't have to go to school on the weekends."

"I guess." Giancarlo let out a sigh and looked up at Stefano with dark eyes. "I don't want to go to school. I won't have any friends."

"Not yet, but I bet you'll meet all sorts of friends on your very first day."

"No, I won't."

"Tell you what. I'll make sure I'm here at the chateau on your first day of school. That way, when you get home you can come tell me all about it. Okay?"

He considered for a minute and then nodded. "Okay."

"Come on. We'd better get you back for dinner."

"Prince Stefano?"

"Yes, Giancarlo?"

Giancarlo slipped his hand into Stefano's. "I'm glad you're my friend."

Stefano felt the little tug on his heartstrings, and he looked down at the boy's earnest face. "I'm glad I'm your friend too."

* * *

I shouldn't be doing this, Alora told herself for the umpteenth time as she stepped into her shoes and slipped out the door. She only took three steps before stopping and considering going back to her room. What if Stefano had asked someone else? Or if he didn't still want her to join him? Surely her time would be better served reading a book or watching television instead of spending it with a bunch of people she didn't know. With a shake of her head, she continued forward.

Maybe she could have resisted going tonight if she hadn't witnessed Stefano's kindness to her son. Giancarlo had returned from his walk with the prince a different kid from the one who had run out of his room earlier that evening. The fighting with his brother had stopped completely, and he had helped her clean up after dinner without complaining. Even Dante's behavior had improved, although Alora didn't know if it was the extra time alone with her that had helped or if he had simply needed a little time away from his brother.

She thought she still might have been able to resist giving in if she hadn't made the mistake of trying on the gown Janessa had delivered to her. The cream-colored silk fell gracefully to the floor and fit as though it had been designed specifically for her. A month ago, she wouldn't have considered owning such a dress or having anything new for herself. She also wouldn't have had any place to wear something so elegant.

A combination of stubbornness and practicality had caused her to spend her evening with the boys as she had originally planned. She could hardly arrive on time to the party after insisting she wanted to tend to her children herself, and Brenna had been needed in the kitchen to help prepare for the party until a few minutes ago anyway.

Alora pressed a hand to her stomach and then walked down the stairs to where she could hear voices mingling in the parlor. She stopped when she reached the archway and stared. The room was much more crowded than she had anticipated, nearly fifty people milling around the room, some sitting on the numerous couches, chairs, and loveseats while others stood and sipped champagne.

Her eyes swept over the crowd in search of a familiar face or at least a glimpse of Janessa's red hair. When she didn't see either, she took a step back, fully intending to disappear back upstairs before anyone noticed her. Then she saw the terrace doors open, and Stefano stepped inside followed by another man who also appeared to be in his early thirties.

She could have sworn she felt something in the air change when Stefano looked up and saw her. His mouth was firm, only a hint of a smile showing in his eyes as he said something to the man beside him and started toward her. She noticed immediately that the sling was gone, and she wondered if he had discarded it for vanity's sake or if his collarbone was fully healed. When she noticed the way he kept his arm tucked close to him as though the brace were still in place, she guessed that it was the former.

He slipped through the crowd easily, exchanging greetings and casual comments as he moved past one group and then another. Moments later, he reached her and took her hand in his.

"I can't tell you how delighted I am that you decided to join us." His voice was calm and assured, but his eyes sparked with surprising uncertainty as he lifted her hand to his lips in an annoyingly charming gesture.

"I didn't get the chance to thank you earlier for spending time with Giancarlo," Alora said formally. "He very much enjoyed it."

"I should be the one thanking you for allowing me the privilege." He lifted his left hand in greeting when someone called out to him as they passed by. Alora didn't miss the pain that registered on his face with the movement.

"Why aren't you wearing your sling?"

He smirked at her. "I wasn't sure I would have anyone to help me cut up my dinner."

"That's hardly an excuse. You're still in pain."

"Not really. The doctor said I should be able to stop wearing it within a couple days anyway. I thought I would use tonight as a test run," Stefano told her. "Besides, I would prefer that my injury not be the topic of tonight's dinner conversation."

He tucked her hand into the crook of his arm and gestured with his free hand to the parlor. "Since you're here, I was hoping you would let me introduce you to a few people."

Butterflies fluttered in her stomach, but she nodded. "All right."

Stefano led her toward the man he had entered the room with a few moments earlier. "Alora DeSanto, this is Mario Petruzzi. Mario works for the Italian ambassador. The ambassador and most of his senior staff are vacationing for a few days at the resort in Bellamo."

"I hope you are enjoying your stay," Alora said as Mario shook her hand.

"Very much so, thank you." Mario smiled charmingly and then spoke to Stefano. "How is it that you always manage to find the most beautiful women in the countryside?"

Alora could feel her cheeks heat, but Stefano simply patted her hand. "In this case, I owe the credit to my brother's fiancée. Alora and Janessa are old friends."

He turned to Alora. "You are American?"

"I'm from Italy."

"I see." Mario gave Stefano an amused look. "So you have exhausted the supply of beautiful women in your own country, and now you are stealing from mine."

Stefano merely smiled and shrugged. "Can you blame me?"

"Not at all." Mario chuckled.

"I'm sure we'll talk to you later." Stefano shook Mario's hand and led Alora through the crowd toward an older man who appeared to be in his sixties. "Alora, this is Bernardo Campesi. He is the president of the ruling council here in Meridia. He was kind enough to drive over from Calene to join us tonight."

The man greeted her in the form of a nod and then spoke to Stefano. "Your Highness, I hoped I might steal a few moments of your time while I am here. Perhaps we can meet in your office after your guests leave."

"I'm sorry, Bernardo, but tonight doesn't work for me."

"It will only take a minute," the older man pressed. "I have to return to Calene tonight."

"I'm sorry, but I really can't." Stefano shook his head. "But I would be happy to call you tomorrow."

"Very well." He nodded stiffly as Stefano led Alora farther into the room.

Stefano introduced her to several more people from the Italian embassy before dinner was served.

When they walked into the dining hall, Alora noticed the place cards on the table. Her stomach clutched at the thought of searching for her name, of the possibility that a place hadn't been set for her. To her relief, Stefano walked her to her chair before taking his place at the head of the table. She hadn't originally considered that she would not be seated beside Stefano and was a little uncomfortable when she saw that Janessa and Garrett were sitting at the far end of the table.

Then Mario took the seat beside her and started his harmless flirting once more. He introduced her to those seated closest to them, and Alora found herself fascinated by tales of embassy life and the latest political ventures of her homeland.

After the last course was cleared and the first guests began to say their good-byes, Janessa approached Alora. "I'm glad you changed your mind about coming tonight."

"Me too." Alora glanced over to where Stefano was speaking with several people, including two young women who appeared to be vying for his attention. "Do you ever feel out of place at these dinners?"

"All the time." She glanced across the room at Stefano. "Although I do have to admit that life has been a lot easier for me since our engagement was announced. I remember what it was like to have most of the single women in the room stare at you like you're the competition."

"Yes, but you were dating Prince Garrett. Stefano and I are just friends."

"Are you sure?" Janessa let the question dangle as Garrett stepped beside her.

Alora nodded but still felt her cheeks flush.

"Alora, you look stunning tonight." Garrett shook her hand before slipping his arm around Janessa.

"Thank you." Alora managed to smile. "You look rather dashing tonight yourself."

Garrett simply grinned. "I'm sorry to steal Janessa away, but I think we have a few guests who would like to say good-bye to us before they leave."

Janessa reached out to give Alora's hand a squeeze. "I'll talk to you later."

"Okay." Alora watched them cross the room to position themselves near the front entrance, where they could chat with everyone as they left. She turned to scan the room for Stefano, surprised to see him excuse himself from his current conversation and head toward her.

"I'm sorry we weren't seated together at dinner."

"That's okay." She smiled up at him. "Your friend Mario was quite entertaining."

His eyebrows lifted. "Not too entertaining, I hope."

"Let's just say he helped pass the time."

Stefano glanced around the room. "It looks like everyone is heading out. Can I convince you to take a walk with me?"

She hesitated, Janessa's suspicions rattling through her mind. "It's getting late."

"Please, Alora?" Stefano looked down at her, and she felt like they were the only two people in the room.

She hesitated again, not sure she trusted herself to be alone with him in the moonlight. As she opened her mouth to say no, the word *yes* tumbled out.

Without a word, Stefano took her hand and led her through the terrace doors.

Chapter 27

WITH HER HAND STILL IN his, Stefano led Alora down a lit path that wove through a maze of blooming flowers and ivy-covered trellises. He heard muffled voices coming from the chateau's entrance and turned away from them. Though he had spent several hours working beside Alora earlier, he wanted time alone with her away from work and family.

He studied her for a moment, trying to gauge her mood. She seemed to have gotten past her anger from earlier. Her words still stung because they were true, both the fact that he had been less than a gentleman in demanding that she come to dinner and the reality that he was not a parent. She couldn't know, of course, why the second comment had hit him so hard, but he could address the first.

"I suppose I should apologize to you for this afternoon. It appears my manners are a bit rusty when it comes to dating."

"I think you made up for that when you talked to Giancarlo," Alora said quietly. "I don't know what you said to him, but he was an angel tonight when you brought him back."

"He's just nervous about starting at a new school."

Alora stopped beside a climbing rose bush and turned to face him. "He told you that?"

Stefano nodded, noting the surprise on her face and the way the moonlight shimmered on her gown.

"That's amazing. He rarely confides in anyone besides me."

"It sounds like he hasn't had a lot of opportunities before now."

"I suppose that's true."

"Is that why you changed your mind about dinner? Because you felt grateful?"

"I came because I wanted to, but my gratitude helped overshadow my anger."

He rubbed his thumb over the back of her hand. "I really didn't mean to make you angry."

"I know." She granted him a smile. "I'm afraid my temper can get the best of me, especially when someone tells me what to do."

His eyes lit with amusement. "I'll have to remember that."

"I don't know if that's something I want you to remember about me."

"Maybe I want to remember everything about you," Stefano said, his voice lowering so it was barely louder than a whisper. He stepped closer, his hand releasing hers so it was free to trail up her arm and rest on her shoulder. He saw the alarm in her eyes. He might have been able to keep his distance if he hadn't also seen the flash of wonder.

"We should go back in." Alora whispered the words, her eyes fixed on his.

"Not just yet." Stefano cupped her shoulders as he lowered his lips to hers. The kiss was whisper soft, but it vibrated with comfort, belonging, and a hint of passion. He breathed in her scent, the exotic aroma of her perfume combined with the flavor of the sea. Something clicked inside him, a sense of rightness that he had been searching for without even knowing it. When he broke the kiss, he found clarity, but he saw confusion in her eyes.

"Stefano . . ." Her voice trailed off as though she were at a loss for words.

He smiled, amazed that her simple use of his name could feel so right. "I have to try that again."

She shook her head. "I don't think it's a good idea to complicate things between us."

"This doesn't have to be complicated." He drew her closer, and his lips met hers once more. He felt her put a hand on his chest as if to resist whatever emotions were flowing through her. Then slowly that hand slid up to his shoulder, and she simply held on. In that moment, everything he was, everything he would become, was wrapped up in her.

As if she felt the change in him, she stepped back and looked up at him with wide eyes. She shook her head. "This is wrong. We can't do this."

His eyes narrowed as he tried to understand her words. Surely her feelings had mirrored his own. Even in the heat of the moment, he understood that this whirl of emotions wasn't just the result of a kiss but the culmination of weeks of developing friendship and the underlying connection between them. He ran a finger lightly down her arm, his eyes remaining fixed on hers. "We can't do what, exactly?"

"Get involved." She took a steadying breath, and he was amazed to see her mask her emotions behind a blank stare. Her voice was calm when she spoke now, almost professional. "I have my children to think about, and it wouldn't be wise for me to start dating right now, especially when they are going through so many changes."

"Don't do that." Stefano's voice was low and even, but it vibrated with frustration. "Don't use Giancarlo and Dante as an excuse to stop living your life."

"I'm not." She snapped out the words, and part of the calm façade chipped away. "Can't you understand? I don't want this kind of complication right now."

"With me or with anyone?"

"With anyone," she said vehemently. Her voice softened fractionally when she added, "but especially not with you."

"Why not?" Stefano reached out and gripped her arms, both to keep her from backing away and to satisfy his need to touch. "I care for you, and no matter what the tabloids might say, I haven't cared for anyone in a very long time."

A spark of hope flashed in her eyes before she controlled it. Once again, her voice was unsteady when she spoke. "It could never work."

Temper and impatience snapped inside him. When he would have pulled her closer, she stepped back.

"Stefano, I'm not trying to play games with you. I'm trying to keep both of us from getting hurt." She turned and took several steps before turning back to face him. "You know my children are everything to me. The greatest gift I can give them is a sure knowledge of the gospel of Jesus Christ. It would be too confusing for them to get attached to someone who doesn't share that understanding."

He stared blankly at her for a moment. "You're telling me you won't spend time with me because I'm not Mormon?"

"I'm telling you that this can't go any further because you're not Mormon." She looked skyward as though offering some silent prayer. When she looked back at him, she pressed her lips together, and he could see her determination. "The first day I met you, my children told you they want to be missionaries someday."

"So?"

"I want to see that happen, and I'm afraid that if I fall for someone who isn't a Latter-day Saint, my boys will lose their focus on what's really important." She swallowed hard. "I already worry about what Janessa will face when she and your brother have children."

It took a moment for Stefano to realize that Alora didn't know of his brother's conversion to the Mormon Church. Shamelessly, he tried to spin the misconception to his advantage. "Let me get this straight. You won't even go out with me, but you're willing to support Janessa's choice. Why?"

"Because she said when she prayed about marrying Prince Garrett, it felt right. It isn't my place to say that she's making a mistake when the Lord already told her she isn't."

He hadn't ever considered that anyone would pray about such a personal decision and get an answer, but obviously Alora believed it was possible. He nodded, considering. "Okay, then. Why don't you pray about spending time with me?"

She shook her head immediately. "That's hardly necessary."

"If you believe God can give you guidance in such personal matters, it is completely necessary."

"Stefano, we both know you have plenty of women who would be thrilled to go out with you. I don't understand why you're wasting your time with me."

"I have feelings for you. Is that so hard to understand?"

"We're friends. That's all."

Frustration bubbled inside him. "Don't tell me you didn't feel anything when I kissed you, that you aren't interested."

Her shoulders straightened, and anger flashed in her eyes. "I'm starting to think you aren't accustomed to someone telling you no."

The truth of her statement stung, but Stefano stepped forward and took her hand. "You keep giving me excuses, but I think the only reason you don't want to be with me is you're afraid."

Tears threatened, and she blinked them back. "Maybe you're right. Maybe I don't want to feel anything for you because I know what it's like to have everything and then have it all ripped away. I'm not willing to go through that again. I can't."

"Alora . . ."

Her eyes still bright, she shook her head and took a step toward the chateau. "I'm going inside. Good night."

He started to follow, but the defiant look on her face told him that nothing he said would change her mind. Not tonight anyway.

Turning away from the chateau, he walked deeper into the gardens. She would change her mind, he told himself. This attraction between them was too strong to ignore. It demanded to be explored and developed. Neither of them would be able to leave it alone until they knew where it could take them.

He wavered between giving her some time to herself to come to terms with her feelings and putting his efforts into changing her mind. Though his pride favored the first option, his heart edged him toward the second. He could rearrange his schedule to stay at the chateau a bit longer, or perhaps he could convince Janessa that Alora should spend some time at the palace as they began working on the initial wedding plans.

Possibilities rolled through his mind until a thought struck him and overshadowed all others. Did it really matter if Alora changed her mind? She had pointed out herself that there were plenty of other women who were willing to spend time with him, women who didn't have children to tend to or religious beliefs that got in the way. Other women wouldn't scrape at his pride or point out his weaknesses.

Then again, before he met Alora, he couldn't remember anyone ever expecting more of him than what they could see on the surface. He had been photographed countless times with dozens of beautiful women, but only once had he saved the resulting newspaper clipping. His stomach clenched as he faced the simple truth. He didn't want any other woman. He wanted Alora.

His cell phone rang, and he instantly thought of her. Then he remembered he had never given Alora his phone number, that he still didn't have hers. He pulled the phone from his pocket and saw his brother's number illuminated on the screen. "What is it, Garrett?"

"They found it, Stefano. They found the other half of the transmitter."

Chapter 28

STEFANO DIDN'T MINCE WORDS WHEN he arrived in Janessa's office, where he found her and Garrett. "Where was it?"

"Exactly where Levi thought it would be," Janessa told him.

Stefano thought back to his encounter with his uncle earlier in the month and Alora's report that he had returned a second time. "I didn't want to think it possible, but I have to wonder if Uncle Elam could somehow be involved in this."

"We were wondering the same thing," Garrett admitted.

Janessa nodded in agreement. "There's no way to know if he was involved in planting the devices originally or if someone persuaded him to come retrieve the transmitter for them, but either way, his sudden visits this month are definitely suspicious."

"But why would he spy on our family?" Stefano asked with a hint of annoyance. "He had no reason to."

"Maybe he did," Janessa said gently. "According to the CIA's file on your uncle, he stopped using his offices here about two years ago. There was some speculation among my colleagues at the Agency that your father asked him to leave." Janessa looked from Stefano to Garrett. "I'm still new to Meridian politics, but can you think of anything that happened here around that time that might have caused a falling out between your father and your uncle?"

"I know he moved to his new offices right around the time the United States started negotiating for a new naval base," Garrett told her. "Uncle Elam was one of the people opposed to allowing your country access to our waters."

"He was also in favor of allowing offshore drilling," Stefano added.

"Any chance he's been associating with Liberté?" Janessa asked now.

"I don't see any reason why he would. Even if his views are anti-American, he wouldn't have any reason to support a group that is also against the monarchy."

"You're probably right. Maybe he just felt threatened when he realized he was being pushed out of your father's inner circle and planted the listening devices here so he'd know what was going on after he lost access to the chateau," Janessa suggested. "Although I still don't understand why they were planted here and not in the palace. Levi said they conducted security sweeps at the palace with the enhanced scanning equipment and didn't find any problems."

"The majority of the meetings about the new U.S. naval base were held here at the chateau because the security is so good at the naval base here in town," Garrett offered. "If whoever is behind this was trying to stop the U.S. from gaining a foothold in Meridia, that could explain why the equipment was planted here."

"It could also be a matter of access," Stefano suggested. "Elam had offices here in the chateau, but his access to the palace was limited after he married and moved out. That access was restricted further after my grandfather died and our father ascended the throne."

"What is the relationship like between your father and your uncle?"

"Apparently they got along okay when they were younger. I know as they grew older, our grandfather was impatient with the way Uncle Elam spent his time." Stefano hesitated and tried to find a way to explain his uncle tactfully. "I guess you could say he was more interested in enjoying what life has to offer than in participating in the duties expected of a member of the royal family."

"And your father mentioned when we saw him last that Elam's family is prone to living beyond their means."

Stefano's eyes narrowed. "What does that have to do with anything?"

"I'm simply trying to figure out why your uncle would betray his family," Janessa said gently. "Financial weakness is one area that is often exploited, especially in the area of espionage."

"We can't be sure that Elam was the person behind it," Garrett interjected. "For all we know, some contractor may have planted the equipment during the renovations."

"Am I correct in assuming that your family would want proof before accusing him of being involved?"

"I believe so." Stefano nodded. He considered his earlier plan of trying to spend more time with Alora and decided that perhaps a few days apart would help both of them gain some perspective. Going with instinct, he announced, "I am going to leave for Calene in the morning. I have some business I need to tend to, and I would prefer to discuss our theories with Father in person."

"What can we do to help?" Garrett asked.

Stefano ignored his brother's question and the concerned look on Janessa's face. He motioned to the hole in her office wall where the transmitting equipment had been discovered. "We'll need to have workers come in tomorrow to patch that hole. Janessa, if you want, you and Alora can use my offices until the repairs are done."

Janessa's voice held compassion when she spoke. "Stefano, I don't mean to pry, but is everything okay?"

"Everything's fine," he said abruptly. "I'll talk to you both later."

Stefano turned and left the room with the intent of packing a few things and then driving to Calene tonight. Then he remembered he had promised to take Dante for a walk tomorrow night. Although he tried to convince himself that Dante would understand if he had to postpone their time together, he remembered too well his disappointment as a child when his father's duties had interfered with personal plans.

As much as he needed to put some distance between himself and Alora, he knew he couldn't disappoint her son. Resigned to stay one more day, he crossed to his office and packed everything he would need to work from his quarters the next day. He glanced at the files he and Alora had been working on together for the past several days and wondered if she would miss him half as much as he expected to miss her.

She had feelings for him. He'd felt it when he'd kissed her, and he'd seen it on her face when she'd turned him away. Now he had to find a way to overcome the obstacles she was placing between them.

* * *

Alora knew she should have felt relieved when it was Levi who brought her the bank access codes on Tuesday morning instead of Stefano, but she couldn't deny that she was disappointed. She also couldn't deny that she didn't want to be.

Her words the night before had been the truth, at least as much of the truth as she had been able to give. She didn't want to be involved with Stefano for all of the reasons she had offered him, but most of all, she was afraid.

Earlier that morning she had mustered all her energy to be cheerful as she and her children headed down to breakfast. She had been prepared to act like nothing had happened between them, only to find that Stefano had come and gone long before their arrival.

The explanation Patrice had offered was simply that he had some early calls to make, but Alora didn't miss the disappointment on her children's faces. It was too late, she realized suddenly. Despite all her concerns that her children might get too attached to Stefano, that they might see him as the male role model they had been lacking for so long, she could see now that the connection had been made. Her boys not only looked up to the prince, but they also already depended on him in many ways.

When she walked into his office that morning, she had been braced to face this new reality. Then she had opened the door only to find his office empty.

When Levi arrived with the access codes, Alora resigned herself to working alone and tried to focus on the task at hand. She spent nearly an hour organizing the files Stefano had left on his worktable. When she tried to access the computer in Stefano's outer office, she found it lacked the security protocols necessary to link with the bank's systems. With her office once again under construction, she reluctantly moved back into Stefano's office.

She stared at the computer on Stefano's desk but couldn't bring herself to use it without permission. Just as she was considering calling Janessa's cell phone, she looked up to see Janessa walk in.

"Oh, I'm glad you're back." Alora motioned to the files on the table. "I'm afraid I can't do any more without a computer that has a high enough security level. The secretary's computer wouldn't let me access the bank files."

"Stefano's computer should work. I'm sure he won't mind if you use it."

"I don't know . . ."

"Alora, it will be fine," Janessa insisted. "He's probably already left for Calene anyway."

Her heart sank. "He left the chateau?"

"He mentioned last night that he was going to drive to the palace today to take care of a few things." Janessa's eyes narrowed. "He didn't tell you?"

"No, but there isn't any reason why he would need to check in with me."

Janessa lowered herself into a chair and leaned back. Her eyes lifted to meet Alora's. "Do you want to talk about it?"

Alora gave her a deliberately innocent stare. "Talk about what?"

"What's going on between you and Stefano." She held up a hand in anticipation. "And don't tell me 'nothing.' Let's skip to the part of this conversation where you tell me what's really going on in your mind."

Alora's shoulders drooped, and she leaned back against Stefano's desk. "Janessa, I don't know what to do." She fisted her hand and pressed it against her heart. "I feel something I'm not ready to feel. He makes me want to dream about a future I can never have."

"Alora, you're only thirty years old. You have considered that someday you would start dating again, maybe even remarry, right?"

"I guess. Maybe." Her shoulders lifted. "But I never thought I would have feelings for someone so soon—and definitely not someone who isn't LDS." Alora caught herself, remembering that Janessa had chosen to marry outside of their religion. "I'm sorry. Please don't think I'm judging you for your decisions."

"Don't worry about me," Janessa insisted, not looking the least bit offended. "I know I'm making the right decision, and I already told you my prayers were answered about marrying Garrett." She hesitated a moment. "How serious are things between you and Stefano? Maybe you need to get down on your knees and ask for some guidance."

Alora paled. "Things aren't serious. I hardly know him."

Janessa gave her a look of disbelief. "You've been eating breakfast with the man every day for a month. You worked with him on renovating our offices for the better part of a week, not to mention the financial reports you've been analyzing together. You definitely know him. In fact, I think you know him better than I do."

Alora shook her head as tears welled up in her eyes. "It hurts, Janessa. I look at him and I see this incredible man who makes my heart beat faster just by walking into the room, a man who goes out of his way to be kind to my children, and then I think of Carlo and what I used to have."

"Do you feel like you're betraying Carlo by having feelings for Stefano?" Janessa asked gently. "I know Carlo would want you to be happy."

"You're right. He would want me to be happy, but he would also want me to raise our sons in the gospel. I don't know if I can do that if I end up with someone who isn't a Latter-day Saint. Besides, I miss having the priesthood in my home." She shook her head and let out a short laugh. "Listen to me. I start having feelings for a man and all of a sudden I'm acting like he's asked me to marry him."

"We both know that dating can lead to marriage." Janessa gave her a wry smile. "I'm living proof of that."

"I guess so." Alora sighed. "So let me ask you this: If you could go back to the place I'm in right now, would you have done anything differently?"

Janessa shook her head. "All I can tell you is I have been in your shoes before, and the only thing that helped me get through it was to pray about it. I suggest you do the same thing. The Lord will have the answers even if you don't."

The corner of Alora's mouth lifted. "You know, Stefano told me to pray about him too. Isn't that odd?"

"Maybe he already understands you better than you think."

"That's what I'm worried about."

Chapter 29

"Can't we ride longer?" Dante pleaded from on top of the bay gelding. "Please?"

"These horses need to be fed," Paolo told him. "Besides, your mother is going to wonder where you are if we don't get you cleaned up in time for supper."

Stefano smiled as he approached the stables. He remembered having the same conversation so many times when he was a boy. "I thought I would find you two here."

"Good evening, Your Highness." Paolo bowed slightly. Then he grinned and motioned to Dante. "This one is just like you. He would stay on a horse all day if I let him."

"There's nothing wrong with that, is there Dante?"

"No, sir."

Stefano glanced over at Giancarlo, who had already dismounted and was obediently holding onto his horse's reins. "Are you done riding for the day, Giancarlo?"

He nodded.

"Well, Dante, maybe you and I can take that walk we talked about on horseback."

Dante's eyes widened excitedly. "Really?"

"You wait there with Paolo and let me saddle my horse." Stefano turned to face Giancarlo. "Can you help Paolo while we're gone?"

Again he nodded. "I'm a good helper."

A smile tugged at Stefano's mouth. "I'm sure you are." He turned to face Paolo and saw the older man grinning. "I'll be right back."

Stefano went inside the stables, bypassing his stallion's stall, instead choosing a mare with a milder temperament. After he saddled the horse, he led her into the yard, where Dante was waiting anxiously. "Are you ready?"

Dante nodded.

Paolo stepped beside Giancarlo. "I'll take Giancarlo to his mother when we're finished here."

"Thank you, Paolo. We should be back in a half hour."

"Keep a good eye on the little one."

"I will."

* * *

Alora headed toward the kitchen, hoping to find her children eating their afternoon snack. She had been staring at bank codes all day, making lists of money transfers and following them through various accounts. She was nearly done gathering the information on the charges Stefano had seemed most concerned about. Tomorrow she would begin analyzing the data to try to make some sense of it.

She pushed open the door to the kitchen, smiling when she saw Patrice supervising Giancarlo at the kitchen table as he stirred something in a large bowl. Her smile faded when she looked around the room and didn't see Dante anywhere. She crossed to Giancarlo and kissed him on the cheek. "Hey there, handsome. Where's your brother?"

"He's still riding."

"Oh." Alora wasn't sure what to think of Dante staying with Paolo without Giancarlo. She tried to push aside a seed of discomfort and put a hand on her son's shoulder. "Do you want to go on a walk with me?"

"No thanks." Giancarlo looked up at his mother, his eyes bright with excitement. "We're making cookies." He lowered his voice to a whisper. "It's a secret recipe."

Alora caught Patrice's amused grin, but she managed to keep her voice serious. "Oh, it is, is it?"

Giancarlo nodded and turned his attention back to the cookie dough.

"Go ahead and walk down to the stables," Patrice offered. "We're fine here."

"Thanks." Alora nodded.

She walked out of the kitchen and made her way to the terrace doors. The late afternoon sun was just beginning to dip in the sky, but the August heat had yet to dissipate. Automatically, she looked out to the water. Then she saw the two horses walking leisurely down the beach. Her heart squeezed in her chest when she realized the riders were Dante and Stefano.

The mother in her immediately worried. She had seen her boys ride in the riding ring near the stables under Paolo's watchful eye, but this was the first time she had seen either of them outside the safety net of those split-rail fences.

She took several hurried steps in their direction before she caught herself. Stefano was riding right beside Dante, and even from this distance she could see her son talking animatedly to the prince, their horses calm and controlled.

They were a picture, man and boy riding across the sand. She wished she had a camera to capture the image and then immediately wondered if the event might be repeated.

She remembered what she had told Janessa, her concerns that developing a relationship with someone who wasn't Mormon would have a negative impact on her children's testimonies. Watching Stefano with Dante, she now wondered which would be more detrimental, growing up without a father figure in their lives or growing up with a father figure who didn't hold the priesthood.

With a sigh, she was forced to admit that the more she thought about Stefano, the more confused she became. Perhaps Janessa was right. Maybe it was time she got down on her knees and prayed for guidance.

* * *

Stefano answered the knock at his door to find Janessa standing on the other side.

"Do you have a minute?" Janessa asked him.

"Sure, come on in." Stefano stepped aside and motioned her into the large sitting room. "Would you like to sit down?"

"No thanks. I'm meeting Garrett downstairs in a few minutes." She ran a hand over the small blue book she held. "I wanted to let you know Garrett talked to your father about letting the CIA do some digging into your uncle's background. Since we're talking about such a long period of time, it will probably take several weeks to get the complete report, but they'll let us know if anything concerning pops up before then."

"I'll talk to my mother when I'm at the palace to see if she can give me the dates of the different renovations here. With the placement of the transmitters, they had to have been planted when construction was going on."

"I agree," Janessa said. "If you can get me those dates, I'll send them over to CIA so they know when to concentrate their search."

"I'll ask my mother to forward the information to you."

"Thanks." She glanced over at his suitcases near the door. "Do you have any idea when you'll be coming back?"

"A few days. A week." He shrugged. "I haven't decided yet."

"Are you leaving because of work or to put some distance between you and Alora?"

Stefano's back stiffened. "I appreciate you trying to help, but Alora and I will work through this on our own. She needs time to adjust to some changes in our relationship, and I have duties I need to tend to in Calene. I'll call and check in on her in a few days if I get hung up at the palace."

The realization that he and Alora had yet to exchange phone numbers struck him, and he slipped his hand into his pocket to retrieve his cell phone. "What is Alora's number? I only have the number to your office."

Janessa's eyes met his, and slowly she shook her head. "She doesn't have a cell phone."

"What?" His own eyes narrowed. "Everyone has a cell phone."

"Alora doesn't." She seemed to debate with herself over how much information to reveal but then remained silent.

"I see." Stefano thought back to when he had asked for her phone number. She had sidestepped the question smoothly—smoothly enough that any doubts he had about her being former CIA melted away. "Well, in that case, would you mind giving Alora my number in case she needs to contact me?"

"Of course." She took a step toward the door before turning to face him once more.

"Was there something else?"

"Actually, yes." She seemed to muster her courage before continuing. "I know you've never completely understood Garrett's reason for becoming a Latter-day Saint, but I thought you should have this." She pushed the book she carried into his hands. He looked down to see the gold lettering that read simply BOOK OF MORMON. "It might help you understand Alora a little better."

Stefano started to hand it back, to insist that he didn't have a need for it. Then a knock sounded at his door, and he dropped the book into his briefcase before he crossed to answer it.

His eyebrows lifted when he saw his physician standing in the hall. "Dr. Casale. This is an unexpected surprise."

"Your Highness."

He motioned to Janessa. "I believe you have met Janessa Rogers."

Dr. Casale nodded. "It is good to see you again."

"You too, Doctor." Janessa shook his outstretched hand.

The doctor shifted his attention back to Stefano. "Your Highness, could I speak with you privately, please? It's important."

"Yes, of course." For an instant, Stefano had the fleeting hope that the doctor was here to tell him his previous diagnosis had been a mistake. Then he noticed the serious expression on his face and worried that the doctor was once again about to be the bearer of bad news. He turned to Janessa and said, "Would you excuse us for a few minutes?"

"Of course." She nodded. "In case I don't see you before you leave, have a safe trip."

"Thank you." As soon as Janessa left, he closed the door and turned his attention to the doctor. "Please sit down, Doctor."

"Thank you." He took a seat and then looked around the room, apparently making sure they were really alone.

"Is something wrong?" Stefano prompted.

"Belinda Parnelli, the nurse who ran the blood work on you at the hospital, is missing."

"What do you mean *missing*?"

"No one has seen her since she finished her shift at the hospital almost three weeks ago."

"She's been missing for almost a month? Why am I only hearing about this now?"

"I received a call from her brother a few weeks ago to let me know they had a death in the family and that she would be gone for a couple weeks. I was worried when she didn't show up this week, so I stopped by her house this morning to see if everything was okay." He took a steadying breath. "Her family said that they had received a phone call too, but the man who called them said he was from my office and that she was coming with me for a few weeks to take care of you here in Bellamo."

A vague image of the young woman with the quiet bedside manner formed in Stefano's mind. Confusion and concern mingled together. "Do you think she was kidnapped?"

"I'm afraid so."

"I don't understand. Who would possibly go to such trouble to kidnap a nurse? And why?"

"The police have been talking to everyone she knows. They have all confirmed what I already know. She has always been incredibly responsible and honest. She goes to chapel every Sunday." He hesitated a moment as though trying to control his emotions. His voice wasn't quite steady when he added, "If she had wanted to go away somewhere, she would have informed her family and me before she left."

"Do you have any idea what anyone would want with her? An old boyfriend maybe?"

Dr. Casale shook his head. "I'm sorry, Your Highness, but the only thing that makes her any different from the other nurses at the hospital is that she knows the results of your medical tests."

"I see." Stefano let the reality of the situation sink in. A young woman's safety could be in jeopardy because she knew he had Merid's syndrome. His concern for her welfare overshadowed the dread seeping through him. "Did you explain to the police why you think she was kidnapped?"

"Not in detail, but they are aware that she has access to private medical files on many of the prominent families in Meridia."

"Have the police found anything else to indicate what happened to her?"

"They believe she was abducted from the hospital, but they don't have any leads yet on where she might be now. Apparently her car was still parked at the hospital parking lot, and the call her parents received came shortly after she left work. Since no one has heard anything in the past three weeks, the police don't expect any kind of ransom demand, not that her family would be in a position to pay much anyway."

"This isn't a coincidence, is it?" Stefano's voice was tight, and he fought against the trepidation that the public was about to share his private turmoil.

"I'm sorry, sir, but I don't think so." Dr. Casale clenched his hands together, his voice compassionate. "I really am sorry."

"So am I."

Chapter 30

STEFANO STARED OUT THE PALACE window at the castle ruins to the west. More than four hundred years had passed since the civil war in France spilled into his country and ultimately destroyed the Fortier's first ancestral home. A fight over religion had been at the root of the conflict, a conflict he had never truly understood. His family had nearly been forced from power, his country nearly swallowed up by its neighbors, but the first King Stefano had refused to concede. He had used cunning and strength, loyalty and perseverance to defend Meridia's borders as well as its way of life.

Now Stefano found himself wondering how the citizens of Meridia would feel when they realized that someday their king would not share their religious beliefs. Would religion once again threaten to tear his country apart? Would the monarchy be endangered or even destroyed when Meridia's citizens discovered that one day they would be ruled by someone who was not of their faith?

He had thought he alone understood the inevitability of this, but now he wasn't so sure. The details behind Belinda Parnelli's disappearance had rolled over and over in his mind since last night when the doctor had given him the news. If she really had been the only other person who knew he had tested positive for Merid's syndrome, no one would have known she possessed sensitive information about him.

The certainty of this fact left Stefano with two theories, neither of them good. First was the possibility that she had shared the information with someone and that act had put her in danger. The second thought was that someone else already knew he had Merid's. The doctor had told him the test had been run once before. What if someone had intercepted the first results and for whatever reason was holding on to that information?

Even more disconcerting was the possibility that someone was actively collecting potentially damaging intelligence on him and his family. Even though the listening devices discovered in the chateau were only discovered in some of the common areas, no one could be certain that Garrett's religious beliefs were not transmitted to some unknown intelligence agency.

His family understood that Garrett's baptism would eventually leak. They all hoped to be able to control the information until they were best prepared to deal with any media fallout, but no one else in the family knew that Stefano too had a secret. The burden of that secret weighed heavily upon him, and he knew he could no longer carry it alone.

Turning from the window, he drew a deep breath and hoped he was doing the right thing.

His father was seated behind his desk when Stefano entered, and his mother was sitting in one of the chairs across from him. King Eduard looked up and offered a smile as Queen Marta stood to envelop Stefano in a hug. "Welcome home," she said.

"Thank you." Stefano held on to her a moment longer than expected, always appreciating her quiet strength and unwavering support. He smiled down at her as he drew away. "I've missed you the last few weeks."

"We have missed you too." Marta sat back down and motioned for Stefano to sit in the chair beside her.

King Eduard settled back into his seat. "Have you managed to make any headway on those financial matters?"

"Not yet." Stefano shook his head, and his stomach tightened as he added, "Alora is still filtering through the bank accounts."

Eduard's eyebrows drew together. "Is everything okay?"

Stefano took a deep breath and pushed the image of Alora to the back of his mind. "I have something we need to discuss."

The king straightened a bit, but his expression didn't change. "What is it?"

"After my accident, the doctor ordered some blood tests on me."

A flash of concern illuminated the king's face before he controlled it. "Yes, Dr. Casale mentioned that."

Stefano tried to keep his voice matter-of-fact, even though his stomach was twisted in knots. He glanced at his mother briefly before addressing his father once more. "Did he mention that one of the tests was for Merid's syndrome?"

Slowly, Eduard shook his head. "You were tested for Merid's years ago, before you entered the navy."

"The first test results are missing. The second test results were destroyed."

"Why . . ." Eduard's voice trailed off as awareness and denial lit his eyes.

Stefano drew a breath and forced himself to say the words, though he saw the knowledge on his father's face. "I have Merid's syndrome. I can't produce an heir."

Silence encompassed the room. Eduard swallowed hard, finally managing to ask, "You're sure?"

Stefano nodded. "Dr. Casale said they ran the test several times. He repeated it himself when he came to give me the news. All the results were the same."

Marta reached out and put her hand on his arm in an effort to comfort. "Stefano, I can't tell you how sorry I am. I thought that since we haven't had a case of Merid's for the past few generations our family was finally free of the disease."

"I thought the same thing, but obviously it's still very much a part of our family." Stefano drew a breath before continuing. "There is more you need to be aware of."

Eduard's expression was deceptively calm as Stefano explained the disappearance of Dr. Casale's nurse, his concerns about the missing test results, and the possibility that the news of Garrett's baptism could have been compromised.

"Father, I keep going over all the details in my head, trying to make sense of it all, but I keep coming back to the possibility that someone is sitting on this information so they can use it to serve some purpose in the future," Stefano said. "What I don't understand is who would gain from exposing our family secrets."

"You mean, who would benefit from creating chaos here in Meridia," Eduard corrected.

"You don't think Uncle Elam could be behind all of this, do you?"

"I don't know what to think." Eduard shook his head. "We are already concerned that Elam might have known about the listening devices, and I suppose it's possible he could have used his position as a family member to access your medical file."

"But why hold on to it for all of this time?" Stefano asked. "The initial tests for Merid's were taken more than ten years ago."

"Yes, but exposing the diagnosis back then wouldn't have gained him or anyone else anything except perhaps some money from the media.

Now that your brother is potentially vulnerable, it's possible someone plans to do more than cause our family a bit of embarrassment."

"Does Elam know Garrett is Mormon?"

"Not that I'm aware, but those listening devices were active until a few weeks ago. If he had any involvement with that, it's possible he or someone else picked up on that information," Eduard said. "And as much as I like Janessa, she is American. Even if no one knows about your brother, Liberté certainly can't be pleased about who he has chosen to marry."

Marta interrupted. "Eduard, I think it's time you have a talk with your brother."

"If he is involved, we need more than speculation to get information out of him. I need proof."

Stefano nodded in agreement. "Alora should be done with her analysis today or tomorrow. I'll call her this evening and see if she has found anything that might point a finger at Elam."

"And I'll speak with Janessa about enlisting her help to see if the CIA can do some more quiet digging for us," Eduard said.

"I also think we need to consider publicizing Garrett's conversion to the Mormon Church sooner rather than later," Stefano suggested.

"What good would that do?" Marta asked. "Garrett wants to keep his religion private as long as he can, and I don't know what good can come from turning his decision into a media circus."

Stefano's shoulders lifted slightly. "If we release the information, we can control how it is handled. If someone really is trying to use our private affairs against us, the best thing we can do is bring some of this out in the open."

"Stefano's right." Eduard nodded thoughtfully. "Especially now that we know the monarchy will someday pass to the son Garrett will hopefully give us, it would be best if the country start acclimating to the situation while the information can still be controlled."

"I thought perhaps Garrett and Janessa could come to the palace for the council dinner this weekend. It would give us some time together to decide how best to handle the announcement."

"We can make that happen." Eduard nodded. "Now tell me about Alora. I know Janessa is very fond of her, but are you sure she can be trusted?"

Stefano's stomach muscles clenched again. The look on his father's face told him he was fishing for information, but Stefano wasn't ready to confide in him about his feelings yet, not while Alora was still erecting barriers between them. Instead he simply nodded and said, "She can be trusted."

Chapter 31

ALORA STARED AT THE INFORMATION in front of her. Even after two days of research, she still wasn't able to put her finger on what was wrong with the financial picture as a whole. Her progress had slowed since Stefano had left the day before. Janessa had given her his cell number, but she was determined not to use it until she could find some clarity in her feelings for him.

When he first left, she had felt a mixture of relief and regret. Now she was riddled with doubts even though one thing was certain: she missed him.

Maybe she was overthinking their relationship. Obviously Stefano was doing fine without her since he hadn't felt the need to say good-bye before he left. At least he hadn't said good-bye to her. The boys apparently had ranked higher than her on Stefano's list of priorities since they mentioned he had said his good-byes after he finished his ride with Dante. She couldn't say why that irked her so much. She had told Stefano she needed space, but she hadn't meant *this* much space.

She opened a new spreadsheet and decided to deal with the data the old-fashioned way. She would organize it.

For several hours, she typed in data, listing bank transactions, expense reports, and contractors. Her progress was slow, but once she began manipulating the data, the patterns finally appeared.

"Signora?" Martino broke into her thoughts.

Alora looked up to see him standing in the doorway next to a man who appeared to be about her age. "Yes?"

"Jacques Neuville asked to see you."

Alora glanced down at the papers strewn across Stefano's desk. Instinctively she hit the power button on the monitor and flipped over the top page of the financial records she had been reviewing. Then she looked at the man beside Martino. "I'm sorry, but have we met?"

"No, signora, but I was hoping you might be able to help me," Jacques said.

"Help you with what?"

He glanced at Martino, who was still standing in the doorway like a silent sentry. "May we speak privately?"

She nearly granted his request automatically. Then a sense of uneasiness combined with logic. She didn't know this man, and from what she had observed after a month of living at the chateau, Martino was trusted implicitly by the royal family. She couldn't think of any subject that couldn't be discussed in front of him.

Alora stood but remained behind Stefano's desk. "I'm sure Martino can be trusted with anything you want to discuss with me."

"It is a private matter."

"Sir, since we have never met, we can hardly have any private matters to discuss."

His face flushed slightly, but he maintained his professional demeanor. He glanced at Martino and then bowed slightly to Alora. "In that case, I'm sorry I took up any of your time. Enjoy the rest of your afternoon."

Alora kept her voice neutral to mask her confusion. "Thank you. You too."

Jacques turned to leave, and Alora caught the odd expression on Martino's face. She went with her instincts and added, "Martino, after you show Signore Neuville out, may I speak with you, please?"

"Of course, signora."

A few minutes later, Martino reappeared in the doorway holding a small box wrapped in silver paper. "Was there something you needed?"

"Martino, who was that man?"

"He attended college with Prince Stefano. He now works in the oil industry."

"Do you have any idea what he wants to talk to me about privately?"

"I can't be certain, but there have been instances in the past when the media has printed private information shortly after one of his visits."

"You think he was looking for a story?"

Martino granted her a small smile. "I think you handled the situation perfectly. Prince Stefano would have been proud."

Pleasure, warm and sweet, filled her, and Alora returned his smile. "Thank you."

"Oh, I almost forgot. This came for you earlier." He crossed to the desk and handed the box to her.

Alora set it on the desk and ran a finger over the smooth paper. "Who is this from?"

"Prince Stefano."

She snatched her hand back and looked up at Martino. "Is he back from Calene?"

"No. He is still at the palace, but he asked that this be delivered to you." Martino motioned to the paperwork spread out on the desk and changed the subject. "Would you like for me to have some lunch brought up? I believe Paolo and your boys were going to ride down to the beach and have a picnic."

The ghost of a smile lingered on her lips as she remembered the boys' excitement that morning about their impending adventure with Paolo. "I forgot about that."

"I'll have Patrice send you something up from the kitchen."

Alora started to object, but then she considered how close she was to figuring everything out. "That would be wonderful. Thank you."

Martino nodded and then turned and left her alone.

Alora stared down at the package on her desk for a moment, curiosity eating at her as she wondered what was inside. With a shake of her head, she set it aside and turned the monitor back on. She had work to do, and she didn't have time to let her mind dwell on the man who was currently making her crazy.

She had prayed about him constantly for the past two days, but her answers were more confusing than her questions. Images of Stefano with her children, of them eating together like a family, continued to pop into her head with annoying frequency and only served to remind her how much she missed him. Too often she remembered the kisses they had shared and the sense of belonging she had found in his arms.

The muffled sound of a phone ringing broke into her thoughts. She looked over at the one on the corner of Stefano's desk wondering why it sounded so weird. Then she realized the sound was coming from the other side of the desk. Her eyes narrowed as she realized it was originating from the package Martino had delivered.

She picked it up just as the ringing stopped. A few seconds later, the ringing started again. "Oh, for heaven's sake," she muttered and ripped the wrapping paper away from the box and lifted the lid. Nestled inside was a cell phone.

Alora grabbed it and took a second to figure out which button to press to answer the phone. Then she lifted it up to her ear. "Hello?"

"Oh good. You got the phone." Stefano's voice came over the line.

Alora held the phone away from her ear long enough to look at it and take in the absurdity of the situation. "Why did you send me a cell phone?"

"Because you didn't have one."

"I don't have a villa in the south of France either, but that certainly doesn't mean you'd need to buy me one."

"You needed a phone. Now you have a phone." Before she could object, he changed the subject. "I was wondering if you finished your analysis of those financial reports."

"Actually, I'm almost finished," Alora said, trying not to be disappointed that he had only called her because of business.

"Did you find anything?"

She considered her earlier discovery and forced herself to give him the news. "I'm afraid so. Someone has hacked into your financial system." She paused before adding, "Stefano, these charges were very deliberate, made in a way that it would be easy to overlook."

"You're saying someone was embezzling from our accounts?"

"That's exactly what I'm saying. I found several abnormalities, all with proper documentation if you don't dig too deep below the surface. I still have a little work to do to trace who owns the accounts where the money finally landed."

"How long will that take?"

"Not long. I should be done in another fifteen or twenty minutes." She glanced at her watch to see that it was almost one thirty. "Do you want me to call you when I finish?"

"Actually, I'm going to be in meetings for the next couple hours." Stefano hesitated and then asked, "Would it be possible for you to bring the results here to the palace? I think my father is going to want you to explain this to him personally, especially if our suspicions are correct in who is behind this."

She wasn't sure what to think about an invitation to meet the king, so she keyed in on the latter part of his comment. "You think you already know who is stealing from you?"

"We think so, but we're not certain," Stefano said without elaborating.

"I suppose I can drive over there tomorrow after breakfast, but I'd need to be back around dinnertime to spend time with the boys."

"I'd prefer that you come tonight." Before she could object, he added, "If I have Brenna help get the boys packed, you could be here in time for dinner."

She blinked twice before she managed to decipher his words. "You want me to bring my children to the palace?"

"I don't expect you to come without them," Stefano said edgily. "Look, I know it's a bit of an imposition, but this is more important than you realize. Besides, I can have Brenna come with you to help with the boys while you're here. They wouldn't have access to the beach, but we do have horses and a swimming pool."

"I need to head over to the security office on base as soon as I finish this analysis."

"You can swing by there on your way."

"But I'll have the boys with me."

"Martino can make the arrangements so they can go on base with you."

"I guess that would work if you really think it's necessary—"

"I do," Stefano interrupted before she could make any more excuses. "I'll have Brenna get the boys ready for you so you can finish your analysis."

Before she could accept or refuse his offer, the dial tone sounded in her ear. Her breath hissed out as she hit the end button on the phone and eyed the garbage can beside the desk. Sorely tempted to dispose of the *gift* Stefano had sent her, Alora held it out for a moment. Then with a shake of her head, she slipped it into her pocket and tried to push Stefano out of her mind.

Chapter 32

STEFANO WALKED INTO HIS SITTING room in the palace and dropped his briefcase on an end table. He could admit to himself that he had found a certain grim satisfaction that he had managed to keep things professional when he spoke to Alora on the phone.

He knew he could have had her simply courier the report to him and then talk him through the specifics on the phone before he briefed his father, but the simple fact was that he needed her here. He missed her more than he wanted to admit, and he still couldn't quite put his finger on when everything had changed for him. Alora and her children had become important to him over the past month. Now he had to convince her that their relationship was one worth building upon.

He wondered for a moment what his parents would think of her, what they would think of Giancarlo and Dante. Alora's previous social outings with him made him think she could fit easily enough into palace life, both the stiffly formal state affairs and the warm family gatherings. He could easily imagine riding with the boys down to the ruins to let them climb and explore or dining with them and Alora at the table on his private balcony.

Determined to get through some of the work he had brought with him from his office, Stefano dropped into a chair and pulled out a file. His eye caught a glimpse of blue, and he stared down for a moment before pulling the book Janessa gave him out of his briefcase. He knew Janessa meant well, but he didn't know how a book that was written several hundred years ago could possibly help him understand Alora any better.

He flipped the book open and skimmed through the introduction. As he reached the bottom of the page, a passage caught his eye. In it was an invitation to read and ponder the book followed by the invitation to pray to God to see if it was true. He reread the paragraph a second time and considered.

Apparently Mormons really did believe that individuals could get answers to their prayers. Remembering Janessa's suggestion that this book might help him understand Alora better, he settled back in his seat. Maybe he could spare a few minutes to read. After all, understanding her beliefs might give him the insight he needed to help her get past this hang-up she had about him having a different religion.

Flipping the page, Stefano began to read.

* * *

She was living in a dream. There was no other explanation for what was happening to her. Alora admired the passing scenery through the limousine window while her children debated which animated movie they wanted to watch on the portable DVD player across from them.

Never in her life had she imagined riding in a limousine or having a driver. Even when she had worked for the CIA, she had never worked the kind of assignments that warranted such extravagancies. Now she was watching the quaint houses in Bellamo come into view while Patrice's husband, Enrico, drove the limousine toward the naval base. As soon as she dropped off the paperwork Janessa needed, they would continue on to Calene.

Her plans to drive herself had been shot down by Patrice and Enrico as well as Martino. As Martino pointed out, she was transporting classified documents, information that needed to be protected. Enrico had then gently reminded her that children travel best while entertained, something he was certain he could accommodate if they were in the right vehicle.

Feeling outnumbered and too tired to argue, Alora had let Enrico and Martino load her luggage into the car, watched Brenna climb into the front seat beside Enrico, and then settled back for the ride.

As Alora looked out at the Bellamo coastline, she considered what it must have been like for Stefano as a child, growing up with nearly unlimited wealth, having a summer home that was so large it needed a You Are Here map to keep its occupants from getting lost. Did he appreciate the stunning beauty of this tiny country his family ruled, or was he so used to the incredible views that he didn't notice anymore?

After spending so much time with him, she already knew that despite growing up with an army of people who tended to his needs, Stefano knew his servants by name and habitually thanked them when they completed their duties. Looking back to her first day at the chateau, she marveled that she was now on a first name basis with Stefano. It was odd to think that when she moved to Meridia she hadn't even expected to meet him. Now she was struggling to balance their friendship with budding romantic undertones.

Stefano was right when he said she was scared of what she was feeling for him. She kept expecting that her prayers would help her get past the feelings he stirred in her, but over and over, her thoughts kept turning to the many days they'd spent together before he ever kissed her, before she had been forced to admit that whatever attraction she had felt for him at first had deepened into something else, something almost tangible.

The car pulled to a stop, and the boys shifted to look out the window. "Can we come in with you, Mama?"

Alora considered for a minute. "I suppose so. You just have to promise to be quiet. People are trying to work inside."

"We promise," Giancarlo answered for both of them.

"Okay, then. Come on."

Enrico pulled the car door open for them. Alora climbed out of the limousine and turned to him. "We shouldn't be too long."

Enrico nodded. "I'll wait right here."

"Okay." Alora moved toward the security office as a slender, dark-haired man walked outside. He held the door for them, his eyes narrowing as Alora and her sons moved closer. Alora thought she saw a spark of recognition in his eyes, but as she studied the long, thin face, she couldn't recall ever seeing the man before. She muttered her thanks as she passed through the door.

When she glanced over her shoulder to find him still staring at her through the glass door, her stomach twisted uncomfortably. Grateful that her children were safely beside her, she walked deeper into the building, eager to dispense her business at hand.

* * *

"Are you sure these are the right coordinates?" Janessa asked Levi skeptically. He had succeeded in using the transmitter data to extrapolate where the signal had been broadcasting to. She wasn't sure what she had expected to find, but this little wooden shack overlooking the naval base definitely hadn't been it.

Levi nodded. "Langley verified the information."

"This doesn't feel right." Janessa looked over at the local policemen taking their positions near the front of the structure. She then turned to study the landscape below. From this vantage point, she could see the Meridian side of the naval base and the beach that stretched along the front of the chateau as well as the gardens and part of the chateau itself.

"This cabin does have the perfect view for someone trying to keep tabs on the day-to-day operations at the base and the chateau," Levi offered.

"Yes, but why?"

"It could have been someone with the paparazzi."

"Maybe, but this technology isn't exactly common for photographers." Janessa shook her head.

"Well, there's only one way to find out." Levi motioned to the police officer nearest him.

Methodically the half dozen men worked their way forward with their weapons drawn. Then the man in charge yelled out in Italian, "You're surrounded. Come out with your hands up."

Silence followed.

A signal from the lead detective put the man nearest the door into motion once more. He took a step onto the front porch, and a click sounded beneath him as though he had stepped on a brittle twig. Then the ground shook, and the policeman blasted through the air away from the cabin as it burst into flames and debris filled the air.

Her heart racing, Janessa ducked instinctively as three police officers were knocked to the ground and two others struggled to keep their footing. Just as one of the officers rushed to the side of their fallen comrade, another blast echoed. Janessa turned to see flames spear up from the security building on the naval base below, the same building where her base office was housed.

* * *

Stefano sat across the table from his father as they studied the reports the CIA had provided on Elam and his family. He tapped a finger on the list of Elam's income. "Did you know he was receiving an income from the church?"

"I knew he was getting some sort of a stipend because of his position there, but I didn't think it was this large." Eduard shook his head. "If he's really getting a hundred thousand euros a year, I don't understand why he needed help with Philippe's wedding. With his trust fund, he should have had more than enough."

"His income seems like it should support him well enough, but look at his bank accounts. They're practically dry."

"Where's the money going?"

"I have no idea." Stefano shook his head. "Would you be willing to let Alora take a look? She's got quite a knack at tracing money."

Before Eduard could respond, his office phone rang. As Eduard reached for the phone, Stefano's cell phone also began to ring. Stefano glanced at the caller ID to see that it was Garrett calling. With a nod to his father, he stepped out into the hall to take the call. "Hello?"

"Janessa just called. There's been a bombing at the naval base." Tension vibrated through the phone. "The security building was leveled."

His breath came out in a *whoosh*, and his chest tightened as he forced himself to ask, "Alora and the children. Were they still there?"

Garrett's voice was suddenly unsteady. "I thought they were at the chateau."

"I'll call you back." Stefano hung up abruptly and immediately dialed Alora's number. The phone rang a half dozen times before going to the generic voicemail account. He hung up and hit the redial button. Seconds stretched out, and Stefano found himself praying to whatever god would listen that Alora and her children were unharmed.

Again, no one answered the phone. His hand trembled as he ended the call, and he had to force himself to draw a breath. He started down the hallway toward the closest stairwell. His idea to drive to Bellamo was quickly pushed aside. Instead, he fumbled with his phone and headed for the helicopter pad.

He was halfway down the stairs when his phone rang again. He looked at the caller ID, hoping to see Alora's number. It was Garrett's. "Any news?"

"They're okay."

Stefano's grip tightened on the banister. "You're sure?"

"Yes. I just talked to Enrico. They left for Calene before the bombs went off. They'll be at the palace within the hour."

"Thank God."

"I already have."

Chapter 33

HER BREATH CAUGHT WHEN THE palace came into view. The structure dominated the high cliffs that overlooked the village, the Mediterranean glistening below. White stone gleamed beneath the evening sun, turrets, towers and battlements spearing into the sky. Alora pointed out the window. "Boys, look."

Giancarlo leaned toward the window, and his eyes widened. "Wow!"

"It's a real castle." Dante shifted closer. "Can we go there?"

Alora smiled. "That's where we're staying tonight. The palace is where Prince Stefano lives."

"I thought he lived with us," Dante said.

Alora felt his confusion and disappointment. "I think he lives here at the palace most of the time. He was only at the chateau so his arm could get better."

Dante's lower lip poked out. "But I want him to stay with us."

"I know, sweetheart." Alora ran a hand over his dark hair. "Don't be sad. Hopefully you'll see him in a few minutes."

Instantly his mood brightened. "Really?"

"He might be in meetings," she warned him and hesitated a minute before offering a promise she knew wasn't hers to make. "But I'm sure Prince Stefano will visit with you for a few minutes."

"I hope he's not in meetings," Giancarlo offered. "Meetings are boring."

"They certainly can be," Alora agreed. "Now, do you both remember how to act when you meet new people?"

"Yes, Mama," both boys answered.

"Good." She looked back out the window as they began their winding climb through thick trees and then emerged a few hundred yards from the castle gate.

Armed guards stood at attention. One moved into a guard booth when they approached, and another stepped toward them as the car came to a stop. Alora reached for her purse, fully expecting to need her identification. To her surprise, he only glanced in the backseat before saying something to Enrico. Then, apparently satisfied, he stepped back and motioned for another guard to open the gate.

She didn't have time to wonder at the lack of a security check. She was too enchanted by the vision in front of her. Three uniformed servants stood at the bottom of the wide marble steps that ascended to massive wooden doors. Towers speared to various heights, giving the palace a mystical look. Two guards held position on either side of the entrance, and more guards were visible at the far corners of the building, as though poised for an attack.

The moment the car pulled to a stop, a servant opened the car door for them. Taking a deep breath, Alora stepped out and motioned for her children to follow. She slipped the strap of her briefcase over her shoulder and grabbed her sons by the hand to prevent them from running off the way they had when they'd first arrived at the chateau.

Two of the servants moved to the back of the car to collect luggage, and the one who had opened the car door for her motioned to the front door. "This way, signora."

Her heartbeat pounded in anticipation. She tried to convince herself that it was because she was nervous about meeting the king and queen, but in the back of her mind, the thought took seed that she was more excited about seeing Stefano.

She felt the history exuding from the walls the moment she stepped inside the massive front hall. An impressive chandelier hung above them, but her eyes were drawn to a marble statue of two doves perched atop a birdcage situated to her left. A suit of armor was displayed at the hallway opening. A wide archway to her right revealed an enormous room, a second archway running through the center. The subtle scent of lemon and fresh flowers hung in the air.

"You must be Alora," a woman's voice called out.

Alora turned to see an elegant, dark-haired woman approach through the doorway to her left. She was dressed in trim beige slacks and a cream-colored blouse, and Alora caught the subtle appraisal as she approached. It wasn't until the woman smiled and her eyes warmed that Alora saw the resemblance to Stefano and realized she was the queen.

"Yes, Your Majesty." Alora curtsied, shifting her attention briefly to make sure her sons bowed as they had been instructed.

"And who might these two young men be?"

"These are my sons, Giancarlo and Dante."

"I am delighted to meet you," Queen Marta said kindly. "I imagine you are both hungry after such a long trip."

Both boys nodded but didn't speak.

"Eduard and Stefano have a dinner appointment, but I thought perhaps you would like to join me for dinner on the terrace."

Alora recognized the queen's tone, the same tone she had heard often when Stefano asked a question disguised as a command.

"It would be our honor to dine with you."

"Excellent." The queen turned her attention to the servant who had shown them inside. "Miguel, please let the kitchen know our guests have arrived and we are ready to eat."

"Yes, Your Majesty."

Marta motioned for them to follow her into the enormous room to their left. "This is our main salon, where we do most of our entertaining."

Alora's eyes were drawn to the ornate ceiling twenty feet above her head. A look of amazement lit her face when she looked back at the queen. "It's incredible."

"I've always loved this room. It gives me a feeling of permanence, maybe because it has changed so little over the centuries." She motioned to the wall of windows interspersed with three sets of French doors that lined the far wall. "The terrace is right over here."

Alora released Giancarlo's hand when they reached the door, and he moved to open one of the doors for them.

The queen's face lit up with a smile. "Why, thank you."

"You're welcome," Giancarlo said, turning to give his mother a satisfied smile as the queen continued forward.

Alora and the boys followed the queen outside onto the stone terrace. The view captured her attention immediately. From high on the cliffs, she could see the rambling village on the hillside below, red-tiled roofs contrasting against the greenery of the native foliage. The evening sun shimmered off the Mediterranean, catching on the waves and the cliffs below.

"What a perfect view." Alora stared for a moment until Dante started tugging her toward the table set up a few yards away. She glanced at the queen to see her smiling at her.

"I've always thought so myself." She settled onto a cushioned seat and motioned for Alora and the boys to join her. "Now tell me, boys, how do you like living at the chateau?"

The simple question was all it took. Dante immediately launched into stories of his favorite horse to ride, and Giancarlo proudly informed the queen that he could now swim all the way across the pool by himself. As Alora watched Marta interact with her sons as if they were members of her own family, once again the reality crashed over her that her children would never know what it was like to have grandparents of their own.

* * *

Marta walked toward her husband's office, considering what she had discovered over the course of the evening. Her curiosity had been piqued after learning that Stefano had escorted Alora to several events over the past few weeks. The photographs that had appeared after their visit to the museum exhibit together had provided little information other than the fact that she was attractive and poised even though she didn't appear terribly comfortable in front of the camera.

At dinner, Marta had discovered Alora to be polite and engaging. She also noted how skilled she was in sidestepping topics she didn't want to address. Her children were surprisingly well mannered for their ages, although Marta hadn't missed the gleam in their eyes when they had walked by the pool. Undoubtedly, they could be a handful if they wanted to be, especially the younger one.

Stefano's decision to have Alora hand-deliver the financial reports made her wonder if perhaps her son had developed more than a working relationship with the young widow. She knocked twice on her husband's office door and then pushed it open without waiting for a response. As expected, her husband and their older son were deep in discussion.

"Are you two about done with this for the night?" Marta asked as both men stood when she entered. "I thought now might be a good time to meet with Alora about her financial analysis."

"They're here?" Stefano asked, relief tinting his voice.

Marta nodded, her suspicions heightened. "If you can find a stopping place, I can have Miguel send for Alora."

Stefano shook his head and spoke hastily. "I can go get her." He looked over at his father. "That is, if you don't mind taking a short break. I'd like to say good night to the boys before they go to bed."

"Go ahead." Eduard nodded. "We can finish this in the morning, and I'm anxious to hear what this Alora has found that everyone else seems to have missed."

The moment Stefano left them alone, Eduard looked at Marta, his eyebrows furrowed. "What was that all about?"

"I think our son is smitten with Janessa's new assistant."

Eduard shook his head. "He probably just wants to see for himself that she's okay."

"Why wouldn't she be?"

"Two bombs went off today in Bellamo, one of them at the naval base and another at a remote cabin. Nine people were killed and thirty-four more were hospitalized."

"That's awful." She moved closer to lay a hand on his arm. "Do you know who did it?"

"Not yet." Eduard shook his head. "I hope I didn't make a mistake by allowing the United States access to our waters."

"You can't let an isolated incident undermine your decisions."

"I hope it was an isolated incident." Eduard shook his head. "I feel like every time we turn around, everything is falling apart."

"Hold on a little longer. We'll make it through this just like everything else we've faced."

He reached out and pulled her close. Marta linked her arms around his neck and prayed that their country would be able to weather this latest storm.

Chapter 34

STEFANO KNOCKED ON THE DOOR to Alora's guest quarters. He could hear muffled voices followed by rapid footsteps. Then the door flew open, and Dante launched himself into Stefano's arms.

"You're here!"

Relief shot through Stefano. He drew Dante close and breathed in the lingering scent of chlorine and kid shampoo. "I am here." He caught a glimpse of Alora out of the corner of his eye, and his heartbeat quickened, but he kept his focus on Dante. "Are you being good for your mama?"

"Uh huh." Dante nodded rapidly. "We got to ride in a mimosine."

"A limousine," Stefano corrected him gently as Giancarlo reached for his free arm and pulled him into the room.

"Mama let me bring my Legos with me. Do you want to come play?"

Stefano lowered Dante back down to the floor before speaking to Giancarlo. "I would love to play, but I'm afraid your mama and I have some work to do."

"Oh, okay. Maybe you can play tomorrow."

"We'll see," Stefano agreed, wishing his life could be so simple again. He looked up to see Alora staring at him with a carefully guarded expression. He fought the urge to cross to her and gather her close. "Are you ready to meet with us?"

"Yes." Alora picked her briefcase up off a chair and turned to Brenna, who was sitting on the couch. "Brenna, I'm not sure how long this will take. Could you please make sure the kids are in bed by eight if I'm not back by then?"

"Yes, signora."

"Thank you." Alora reached out and gave Dante a hug and then kissed Giancarlo's forehead. "You boys be good for Brenna."

After exchanging good-byes with the boys, Stefano escorted Alora into the hall. He reached for her arm and felt her stiffen. Though he ached to draw her close, he forced himself to remain as he was. Her expression wasn't readable, and he couldn't tell if she had stiffened because she didn't want to be near him or because she did. The silence between them grew heavier as he guided her down the hall. Stefano stopped a few yards from his father's office and turned to face her. "Is something wrong?"

She shook her head, but her eyes didn't meet his. "No, nothing."

"Alora . . ." Stefano stared at her until reluctantly she looked up at him. "What's wrong?"

"Why should anything be wrong?" Alora asked. She waved a hand to encompass the palace, and her shoulders lifted. "I'm staying in a beautiful palace. My children got to ride in a limousine today and then have dinner with the queen of Meridia. Everything is great."

"And?"

"You didn't say good-bye." She blurted out the words and then paled as though she didn't mean to say them. She drew a breath, and when she spoke again her voice was calm, edging toward professional. "I thought we were . . . friends. I didn't appreciate finding out secondhand that you had decided to leave the chateau."

"I see." A glimmer of hope stirred inside him. "Then I should apologize."

"Yes, you should," Alora agreed, a hint of anger still vibrating through her voice.

"I am sorry I didn't say good-bye. I didn't know if you would want to see me before I left."

Alora's cheeks flushed, and her eyes lowered for a moment.

Stefano reached for her then, pulling her close to satisfy his need to hold her, to prove to himself that she was whole and alive. That she was his.

He felt her arms come around his waist and cling for a moment before she shook her head. "Stefano, don't." She pulled free and motioned down the hall. "I thought your parents were waiting for us."

"They are." His eyes were dark as he stared down at her. "Perhaps we can talk later."

Alora gave a slight nod and then followed him into his father's office. Even though her posture didn't change, he sensed her nerves when his father stood to greet them. She dipped into a curtsy. Gently, Stefano placed a hand on her back as he offered an introduction. "Father, this is Alora DeSanto."

Eduard extended his hand. "My son tells me you have some information to share with us."

"Yes, Your Majesty," Alora said as she shook his hand. She shifted her briefcase from her shoulder and then gave the king a wary look. "I'm afraid I do."

"Please sit down, and you can walk us through your findings."

Stefano pulled a chair out for her, and they all sat down at his father's worktable. Alora slipped several sheets of paper from her briefcase. She looked apologetically at the queen as she slid a copy to Stefano and another to the king. "I'm sorry. I only brought two copies."

"What are we looking at here?" Eduard asked as Marta shifted closer so she could read the paper with him.

"Stefano asked me to conduct an in-depth audit of your household accounts, specifically for the expenses of the gala event held at the chateau." Alora tapped a finger on her own sheet. "The initial findings were that everything was in order, but when I began tracing the funds used to pay the expenses, I found several irregularities."

"Like?" Stefano prompted.

"Your main expenses for the gala that were drawn out of your household accounts were security, catering, flowers, and music." Alora pointed to the top sheet of her report. "A physical check was cut to the caterers for the exact amount of their contract, but for the other three categories, the payments were made via electronic fund transfers."

Alora's eyes lifted to meet Stefano's, and then she looked at the king. "All three of the accounts that received the payments were dummy accounts."

"What do you mean *dummy accounts*?"

"The accounts were set up in the names of the various contractors you hired, but the authorized users on the accounts didn't belong to anyone within those companies," Alora told them. "The money was transferred into these dummy accounts, and then the amount that was actually billed by the various companies was paid to them. The difference remained in the dummy accounts, and a few weeks later, the money was siphoned off and transferred again, only this time the funds went to a numbered account in the Caymans."

"Why didn't the other auditors catch this?"

"There wasn't any reason they would. The invoices on file all matched the amounts that were paid," Alora said. "My guess is that the amounts on the original invoices were replaced before the payments were ever made.

The auditors would have verified those invoices to the payment amounts and seen that the money went to bank accounts that they believed belonged to the contractors. They wouldn't have had access to dig any deeper, nor would they have had any reason to believe they needed to."

"How much money are we talking about?"

"At this one event, it was just over two hundred and forty-seven thousand euros." Alora glanced at Stefano. "The bank only allowed me access to the past eighteen months of records, but I did find similar anomalies last year as well. It's possible this has been going on for some time."

Stefano's jaw clenched. "Do you have any idea who's behind this?"

Alora nodded. "I'm afraid I know exactly who's behind this. I also have an idea of how we can prove it."

* * *

Alora walked out of King Eduard's office nearly an hour after she had presented her initial analysis. The royal family clearly had a lot to consider, and she didn't envy them their task of deciding how to handle the fact that someone so close to their family had been stealing from them, most likely for years.

The office door snapped closed, and she looked up to see Stefano standing next to her. "We need to talk. Privately."

Even though the commanding tone put her on edge, Alora didn't argue. As much as she didn't want to admit it, she had been looking forward to this opportunity to be alone with Stefano, to somehow define what their relationship had become since she had seen him last.

He took her arm and guided her toward a narrow staircase, the scent of potpourri mixing with traces of Stefano's cologne. When they reached the single door at the end of the hall, Stefano pushed it open and led her outside onto a lit pathway that cut through the wide patch of grass. He nodded to the guard who stood just outside the door and continued toward the gazebo located in the center of the yard.

The moonlight reflected on the structure that had been built of the same white stone as the palace. Thick columns supported the cupola top, and several stone benches were positioned inside. Stefano led her through the wide, arched entrance and then released her arm when he turned to face her.

Shadows played over his face, and she couldn't read his expression. Could it be that he had decided she was right when she told him they didn't have a future together? Was that why he hadn't said good-bye when he left? Questions burned on her tongue, but she couldn't force herself to ask them. Instead, she looked up at him, braced for what was to come.

He stared at her as though he too was searching for the right words. Several long seconds ticked by before he finally asked, "Why did it bother you that I didn't say good-bye before I left?"

Alora had pondered that same question herself the past few days, but she offered him the simplest truth she could put into words. "I thought we were friends."

"We are friends." He stepped toward her, his hand linking with hers. "But I want more."

Alora looked down at their hands, hers narrow, the tan line from her wedding band no longer visible. A large sapphire ring adorned his right hand, identifying who and what he was. Impossibly, their lives had merged, and the thought of moving forward without him in her future sent a sense of panic skittering through her. Not prepared to analyze her own feelings, she turned the conversation back to him. "Why didn't you say good-bye before you left?"

"I hoped that if I gave you some time alone you might miss me."

"Oh." His admission should have irritated her on principle, but she could only wonder how he had come to know her so well.

He ran his thumb over the back of her hand, his eyes locked on hers. "Did it work?"

Her shoulders lifted. "Maybe."

His lips twitched, and he edged closer. "Good."

She lifted a hand to his chest, surprised to feel his heart beating as rapidly as hers when he appeared so composed. "I still don't think there can be a future between us."

"Then we'll have to live in the moment." His lips brushed hers, once then twice.

When he released her hand so he could pull her closer, she leaned into the kiss. She was past pretending that she didn't want this, that she didn't feel for him what she hadn't dare let herself feel in a very long time. His hand trailed up her back to tangle in her hair. Chills ran through her, and she pulled back to look up at him.

Decisions would have to be made, issues about their differences would have to be faced, but for tonight she wouldn't think of the obstacles between them. Surely it wouldn't hurt to live in the moment just this once.

"This scares me, what I feel for you," she said.

"You don't have to be scared. I'm not going anywhere."

"No, but I am. I will be leaving for the chateau in the morning." Alora looked past him to the palace standing so solidly on the cliffs. Then she shifted, and her eyes met his once more. "I know your home is here, but will you be coming to visit us anytime soon?"

"My father wants me to stay until after parliament's first legislative session. It is the only time our entire government body is gathered in one place. As heir to the throne, I shouldn't be there with him because of potential security concerns, but I will need to remain here in Calene."

"When will that happen?"

"Next week."

"We'll miss you."

"Stay." Stefano said the word as though he was surprised it escaped his mouth. Then he kissed her gently once more. "Stay here at the palace for a few more days."

"Janessa needs me at the chateau."

"My father has asked Garrett and Janessa to come to the palace. They will be here at least through the weekend. Besides, I would feel better if you aren't at the chateau until the financial issues are resolved."

The thought of staying longer, of spending more time with him, was appealing, but she also had to consider the practicality of the situation. "I only packed for one night."

"Call Patrice tomorrow and ask her to send some more of your things. Or if you would prefer, Janessa can take care of it for you. She can bring whatever you need when she comes tomorrow."

"I guess that would work . . ."

"Good." Stefano smiled. "Does that mean I can talk you and the boys into eating breakfast with me tomorrow?"

Her smile was instant. "We would all love that."

Chapter 35

"WHAT IS THE MEANING OF this?" Martino looked at Garrett, disbelief and indignation on his face. "I have been loyal to this family for more than thirty years. You can't possibly believe I would steal from you."

"Martino, I'm sorry, but the evidence is compelling. I'm afraid you'll need to come with us." Garrett placed his hand on Martino's arm. He could feel the fury vibrating from him, but Martino nodded stiffly and moved forward without another word.

Garrett escorted Martino out of his office to where Levi was waiting with two uniformed police officers. As Garrett released Martino's arm to turn him over to the police, he leaned closer to the older man and spoke quietly. "Martino, I promise you, the truth will come out."

Martino didn't look at him, but he gave a curt nod before falling into step with the men who had come to take him away.

Garrett let out a shaky breath. He still couldn't believe the holding accounts Alora had discovered had all been in Martino's name. He watched Martino disappear down the hall and then pulled his phone free to call his brother. "It's done. Now it's in your hands."

Stefano's voice was sympathetic. "How did Martino take it?"

"About as well as can be expected," Garrett told him. "I sure hope you know what you're doing."

"So do I."

* * *

Stefano hung up with his brother and immediately dialed Luigi Ovalle's phone number. The man answered on the second ring.

"Your Highness, what can I do for you?"

"Luigi, I need your assistance with a rather delicate matter."

"Of course. What do you need?"

"As you may already know, Martino was just taken into custody. It appears he may have been involved in some questionable financial transactions in relation to the gala this summer."

"Martino? I find that difficult to believe."

"So do I," Stefano agreed. "From what I understand, inflated bills were submitted to replace the originals, which were lower amounts. The only way to prove conclusively who was behind this fraud is to find the original invoices or the blank invoices used to create the new bills."

"You want me to look for them?"

"Yes. If Martino really is guilty, they should be hidden somewhere in his room or his office."

"I'll see what I can find."

"Let me know if you uncover anything."

"Of course, Your Highness."

* * *

Alora stared out the window at the drizzling rain, memories of last night still occupying her thoughts. Her concern that she was falling for a man who wasn't LDS was forefront in her mind, but she couldn't deny that her prayers seemed to have led her to this point. Every time she thought of life without Stefano in it, she felt hollow inside. She knew there were plenty of women out there who had managed to stay active in the Church after marrying someone who wasn't a member, but she also knew they faced challenges she never hoped to understand.

She shook her head to clear her thoughts. She knew she was worrying about a future that was unlikely in the best of circumstances. Despite the attraction she felt for Stefano, the circumstances that had brought them together were coming to an end. In a matter of weeks, he would relocate permanently to the palace, and she and the boys would have to adjust to life without him at the chateau. She dreaded the time when that would happen, as much for her sons as for herself. They had so enjoyed having breakfast with Stefano this morning, even though an important phone call had forced him to leave them earlier than he had planned.

Already Alora could see the change in him since their time at the chateau. His duties weighed more heavily on him here at the palace, and she imagined his free time would be even more limited than before. The demands on his schedule would surely affect their relationship sooner than later. Undoubtedly time and distance would erase whatever closeness they now shared, but even with that knowledge, she found herself looking forward to enjoying this time together.

He had called shortly before noon to let her know he wouldn't be able to meet her for lunch because of meetings. Feeling awkward about wandering around the palace, she had let Brenna bring lunch up to their rooms instead of venturing out to the kitchen. Now that their dishes were cleared, Alora found herself restless.

Giancarlo climbed onto the window seat beside her and cuddled onto her lap. "Mama, I'm bored."

"Why don't you go watch a movie?"

"We already watched a movie."

"Do you want me to read you a book?"

He shook his head. "I want to play outside."

"I know, honey, but it's too wet to play outside. I don't want you to get sick."

"Can we go see the horses?" Dante asked, climbing up to sit on the other side of her.

"Maybe tomorrow, if it's sunny out."

"What can we do today?" Giancarlo asked impatiently.

"Maybe we can play a game," Alora suggested as someone knocked at the door.

Dante jumped up to answer it.

"Hello there," Stefano greeted him before his eyes swept over the room and landed on Alora. "I thought maybe you would all like to walk around the palace for a bit before I have to get back for my next meeting."

Giancarlo jumped out of Alora's lap as she nodded. "That would be great. I'm afraid we've been spoiled by the nice weather over the past few weeks. The boys definitely aren't used to staying inside."

"Boys, why don't you go get your shoes on, and we'll find something for you to do."

"Okay!" Giancarlo raced into the bedroom, followed by Dante.

"Have I ever told you that you have excellent timing?" Alora asked with a smile.

"I gather they were getting a little antsy?"

She nodded. "Oh yeah."

Stefano moved closer and lowered his voice. "Do you have any religious objection to your children learning how to shoot? We have a firing range in the east wing."

"I don't have a *religious* objection to it, but I think they may still be a bit young to be handling weapons."

"It's laser, not live fire," Stefano told her. "I promise, it's perfectly safe."

"I suppose that would be okay," Alora agreed.

When the boys returned, Stefano led them through a maze of hallways until they reached a glass-encased room with targets on the far end. A stocky man stood in what appeared to be a control booth. When he saw them coming, he stepped into the hall to greet them.

"Are these the young men who want to learn to shoot?"

"That's right." Stefano nodded. "Giancarlo and Dante, this is Pedro. He is the shooting instructor here at the palace. He trains all our guards."

"Come this way, and we'll set you up." Pedro put a hand on each of the boys and nudged them into the shooting area.

Alora watched as Pedro instructed the boys on gun safety before he helped each choose a weapon. He then taught them how to hold the modified rifles and how to stand. Alora couldn't help but grin as she watched Dante fire all of his pretend ammunition in a quick burst, while Giancarlo carefully squeezed off one shot at a time.

Pedro set them up for a couple more rounds, correcting them as they progressed.

Alora glanced over at Stefano, who was watching through the glass beside her. "He's very good with them."

He nodded. "I thought this would help break up the boredom for them. It's never easy being cooped up inside when it rains."

"Especially for those two," Alora agreed. "I wasn't sure if we were going to see you today, especially after what happened yesterday."

Stefano looked at her inquisitively. "How did you . . . ?"

"Enrico got a call from your brother when we were on our way here."

Stefano let out a sigh. "We lost nine people yesterday, and dozens were injured."

Alora's voice lowered. "Tragedies like this are always hard to come to terms with."

"But you did." Stefano looked at her intensely. "How is it that you've been able to move past everything you've been through?"

Something in his stare told her he knew more than what she had told him, that perhaps he knew much more about her than she had realized. Her voice lowered to a whisper. "How did you know?"

"The background check from when you first started working for Janessa." Stefano reached for her hand. "I look at you, and I'm amazed at how you are with your children, how you are so cheerful around them even though you're the only family they have left."

"You're seeing me as I am now. It's taken me a long time to get here," Alora admitted. "Losing my family tore me apart, but I finally had to accept that I'll be able to see them again someday and that they wouldn't want me to spend my life pining for them. I do the best I can to live the life they would want me to live." She nodded at her sons. "That includes helping them learn to enjoy life."

Giancarlo held a hand up victoriously when he made his first bull's-eye.

"It looks like they've got that down." Stefano gave her hand a squeeze and nodded at the shooting range. "You know, you can try too if you like."

"That's okay."

"You aren't afraid, are you?"

She heard the challenge in his tone and recognized the gauntlet he had thrown. Unable to resist, she nodded. "Maybe I'll give it a try."

Pedro printed out copies of their results, and the boys came out waving them like they had just gotten straight As on their report cards.

"Signora DeSanto would like to try as well," Stefano said.

"Do you already know how to shoot?"

Alora shot a smug look at Stefano before nodding. "I know the basics."

"This way, then." Pedro helped her select a weapon and then stepped aside.

She lifted the rifle, adjusting her stance for the weight difference between a fully loaded weapon and one equipped with laser. Then she set her sights, took aim and fired methodically until her laser ammunition was expended. Once the round was finished, she set the rifle back in the rack and walked back into the hall, where Stefano was waiting with Dante and Giancarlo.

"Didn't you want to try another round?" Stefano asked.

"No thanks. I think that should do it." Alora shook her head as Pedro came out of the control booth with a printout. He looked at her skeptically, and then he handed her the report. She didn't have a chance to look at it before Stefano took it out of her hand. His eyes widened, and Alora fought back a grin when she saw what he was staring at. A black target was dotted with white spots where her shots had landed, a single shot at the bull's-eye surrounded by seven other shots so the target resembled a daisy.

"Did you do that on purpose?" Stefano asked. Even though he was quite certain she had worked for the CIA, he suspected she had worked in an administrative capacity. He hadn't considered that marksmanship would be one of her skills.

Alora shook her head and gave him a blank look. "I'm sure it was just beginner's luck." Then she turned to Pedro. "Thank you for teaching the kids. They really enjoyed it."

"If the sun doesn't come out tomorrow, bring them back, and we'll go a few more rounds."

"I doubt I'll be able to keep them away."

Chapter 36

STEFANO WALKED INTO HIS FATHER'S office and saw Martino sitting stiffly on the couch beside Garrett. Janessa and his father were seated in the chairs across from them. "Have we had any success?"

"We have." Garrett nodded. "Luigi took the bait. The hidden cameras caught him planting the evidence in Martino's private quarters not ten minutes after I told him what we were looking for."

"The police are bringing him in now," Martino added. "He thinks they are escorting him to the palace to deliver the evidence to Prince Stefano. I guess he'll find out soon enough that he's really being taken to the police station here in Calene."

"I'm sorry we had to put you through this, Martino," Stefano said apologetically.

Martino gripped his hands together. "I appreciate that your family went to such lengths to clear my name."

"We never believed you were guilty," Stefano assured him before turning his attention to his father. "Now that we've proven that Luigi was behind the fraud at the chateau, perhaps it would be wise to allow Alora access to the other bank accounts we were concerned about this morning. It would be nice to know if the two situations are related, and we can't be sure that Luigi will be forthcoming with information."

King Eduard glanced over at Martino briefly and then nodded. "Go ahead and send for her. Make sure she has everything she needs."

"I'll have her work out of my office." Stefano looked over at Garrett. "Let me know if you find anything else out."

"We will."

* * *

"What exactly am I looking for?" Alora asked as she took the seat in front of Stefano's computer.

"Any correlations between the information you found earlier and these accounts." Stefano handed her a list of a half dozen bank accounts.

She read the owner information and then looked up at Stefano. "You think your uncle is behind the missing funds?"

"That's what we need to find out," Stefano said stiffly. "We certainly don't want to accuse him of any wrongdoing without proof."

"Okay." Gone was the man who had kissed her in the moonlight. This man was all business, coated with a layer of impatience. Swallowing a sigh, Alora keyed in the code to allow her access to the accounts. She focused on the information in front of her and jotted down a few notes on the pad of paper Stefano had given her.

Stefano's phone rang, and he settled down in the chair across from her and started talking about some details for the upcoming legislative session. She tuned him out as she focused on the information in front of her. She noted the source of the various incoming funds and then started on the expenditures. Only twenty minutes later, she circled an account number and looked up at Stefano, who was currently reading through a thick report.

"I think I found what you're looking for."

"Already?"

She nodded. "At least one of these accounts is transferring money to a numbered account in the Cayman Islands. It's the same account as the one the embezzled funds were transferred to."

"Is there any way to identify who owns the account?"

"I seriously doubt it's your uncle. He wouldn't have a reason to siphon money out of his own accounts, especially since he's the sole owner of this one. That means you've got two logical scenarios."

"Which are?" Stefano prompted.

"Either Prince Elam has been paying Luigi for some reason, or they're both sending money to the same person."

"Do you think this has anything to do with the bombing yesterday?"

"I don't know. It depends on what your uncle has been paying for." Alora shook her head. "I'm afraid all I can tell you is where the money came from and where it went."

"That's a lot more than what we started with," he told her. "I'm going to give my father this latest information. Hopefully he'll be willing to bring Elam in now for a little heart-to-heart."

"Do you want me to keep digging and see what else I can find?"

Stefano nodded. "I'm sure we're all especially interested in that numbered account in the Caymans."

"I'm not promising anything, but I'll do what I can."

* * *

When Stefano entered his father's office once more, Martino was no longer present, and his mother now sat on the couch beside Garrett.

"Did you find Alora?" Janessa asked.

Stefano nodded. "She's still looking through Uncle Elam's bank accounts, but she's already linked money transfers from one of his personal accounts to the same account the embezzled funds were sent to."

"Are you sure?"

Stefano nodded.

Eduard reached for his phone and immediately called his brother. Stefano expected his father to demand that Elam come to the palace immediately, but to his surprise, he issued an invitation for him to join them the following evening for the council dinner, along with a request to meet with him following the event. He hung up and looked at Stefano. "Have Alora gather as much information as she can. I would like her to join us at the meeting with Elam."

"I'll extend your request." Stefano thought of the last time he had made arrangements for Alora to join him for a social event and glanced over at Janessa. "Any chance Alora had you pack something suitable for her to wear to the council dinner?"

Janessa shook her head. "I'm sure I can find something for her to borrow."

"Nonsense," Marta interrupted. "We can't have her settle for a borrowed gown. My designer is scheduled to arrive tomorrow morning to meet with Janessa and me about her wedding dress. I can have her bring something from her shop for Alora."

"We'll need to let Signora Vorneaux know that Alora is LDS too. She won't wear anything sleeveless either," Janessa told her.

"I'll call her and make the necessary arrangements," Marta promised.

"There is one more thing we need to discuss." Eduard focused on Garrett. "We are concerned that someone is gathering information on our family, potentially damaging information." He hesitated a moment as though searching for the right words. His voice was tight when he continued. "Your brother and I feel that it would be best if you announce you have converted to the Mormon Church."

"What?" Garrett's eyes widened. "I thought you wanted me to keep that private as long as possible."

"I did, but there is evidence that someone may be trying to undermine the very fabric of this monarchy. Coupled with the terrorist attack yesterday and the possible vulnerability of my brother, if all our secrets came to light at the same time, the media could be used to turn our citizens against us or at least cause enough confusion that we would be vulnerable."

"I don't understand." Garrett shifted forward in his seat. "My baptism doesn't matter in the overall scheme of things. I'm second in line to the throne. Stefano's future family will be the concern of the kingdom."

Stefano looked from his brother to his father, the unspoken question visible in his father's eyes. He looked around the room at the people who were most important to him. They were all here except for Alora and her children. He drew a steadying breath, and then he spoke to Garrett. "My sons will never rule." Regret filled Stefano's voice. "Yours will."

"What?"

"I have Merid's syndrome." He started to say he would never have children, but the image of Giancarlo and Dante flashed into his mind. The clarity that he could be a father even if he couldn't have children in a traditional sense gave him a feeling of comfort. "I can't ever have a child who will be of royal blood."

Silence hung in the air as Garrett absorbed the news, confusion shifting to awareness and compassion. "You're sure?" When Stefano nodded, Garrett shook his head. "How long have you known? You never said anything."

"Only a few weeks. My original test results are missing. The results in my medical file belonged to someone else."

Before Garrett could offer his sympathies, Eduard spoke once more to Garrett. "Obviously your brother's news is very private, but we believe his medical records may have been compromised. Your religion will become public knowledge eventually. I think it best if we leak it in a way that is within our control."

Still stunned by the news, Garrett rubbed a hand over his face. "What do you suggest?"

"I feel it would be appropriate for all of us to attend the Meridian cathedral on Sunday to pray for the victims of the bombings. Afterward,

I think you and Janessa should go to your church," Eduard suggested. "If you let the press follow you, they will undoubtedly be waiting for you when you come out, and you can give a statement about your new religion."

Garrett seemed to struggle with his father's suggestion, but after a moment he nodded. "If that's what you want, that's what we'll do, but what happens if the news about Stefano is released at the same time? It could still have the same result."

"We are changing the impact of your story by releasing it ourselves. As for your brother, his news was only recently acquired. Hopefully it won't come out, but if it does, I think we can turn the person holding it into the villain for selling private medical information. Besides, by attending services before going to your church on Sunday, you will be showing respect for the religion of your land as well as the religion of your heart."

"I hope you're right."

A rapid knock sounded at the door. Stefano moved to open it, concern shooting through him when he found Alora on the other side, her face pale. He reached for her hand and drew her inside. As soon as he closed the door once more, he asked, "What's wrong?"

"I finished following the money trails out of Prince Elam's personal accounts, and I managed to hack into the bank account in the Caymans."

"And?"

"I still don't know who owns the Cayman account, but I can tell you that Hector Ambrose was paid from it." Her words came out in a rush, and her eyes were wide. "The timing indicates that the payments would have been for the bombing in Bellamo."

King Eduard shifted uncomfortably. "You think my brother could be involved with the bombing?"

"I can't be certain," Alora said, clearly distressed by her findings. "Besides the money transferred from your household accounts and Prince Elam's personal accounts, I traced several more deposits from a bank in Libya. It's possible that Prince Elam was using that account to launder funds so they couldn't be traced back to him, but it's also possible that he was being blackmailed by whoever is behind it."

"Do you know where the other money came from?"

"It was routed through several different accounts, from all over the globe. I don't know who owned the account the money originated from in Libya, but I did uncover a name on a bank the money was routed through in Singapore." Her eyebrows drew together as she looked down at the pad of paper she held. "Caspar Gazsi."

Stefano's eyes widened. "The president of Caspian Oil?"

Alora looked at him, confused. "Caspian Oil?"

Stefano nodded. "The Libyan company that wants to drill for oil off our shores."

Janessa shifted in her seat uncomfortably. "Director Palmer also mentioned that Gazsi is associated with Liberté, the dissident group here in Meridia."

"You think he might be working with my brother?" Eduard asked.

"There's no way to tell for sure." Alora shrugged. "Either way, your brother probably knows more about who hired Ambrose than we do."

"We will be meeting with Elam tomorrow after the council dinner. I want you to be there."

"If you wish," Alora said hesitantly.

Eduard nodded. "Stefano, please make sure Alora makes it back to her room, and then I have some things I still need to discuss with you before dinner."

"Yes, Father."

Chapter 37

"YOU DON'T NEED TO WALK me back," Alora said as soon as they left the king's office. "I'm sure I can find my way to my room."

Stefano took her by the arm and started down the hall. "The palace can be a very confusing place."

Her mind was still so consumed with the information she had uncovered that she didn't hear the underlying challenge in his voice. "I'm sure you have a lot to discuss with your father. Besides, I have a really good sense of direction."

"Have you always been that way, or did you pick up that skill while working for the CIA?"

"Excuse me?" She stopped walking and turned to face him. "What are you talking about?"

He nudged her forward again. "I was just wondering how extensive your training was while you worked for the U.S. government."

Her heartbeat quickened, but she fought to keep her posture relaxed. "I worked in their embassy as a finance clerk. That's all."

"Alora, there's no need to stick to a cover story with me," Stefano returned mildly. "You didn't learn how to track down fund transfers like that by working as a finance clerk, and I've seen you shoot. Besides, I'm well aware of Janessa's background and training with the CIA."

Alora kept her expression carefully blank. "I don't know what you're talking about."

"Of course you don't." Stefano nodded knowingly. He steered her toward an intersecting hallway, but she stopped and looked over her shoulder. "Where are you taking me? My room is that way."

"We need to talk."

She stepped away from him. "Stefano, I need to go get the kids ready for dinner, and your father is waiting for you."

"Just give me a few minutes." Stefano reached for her hand and gave it a gentle squeeze.

Alora debated for a moment, weighing the ramifications of confiding in Stefano about her previous job. If he knew about Janessa, he clearly had earned the trust of someone high up in the CIA. Realizing that the conversation was inevitable, she nodded and let him lead her by the hand down the hallway. After making several more turns, he pushed open a French door that led directly onto a covered balcony.

Drawn to the view, Alora crossed to the railing and stared out at the gardens and the cliffs that lay beyond. The clouds hung low in the sky, and a light rain still fell steadily.

"I understand you have been trained not to divulge who you worked for," Stefano began calmly. "But knowing Janessa's background, I already know that the employer you listed in Paris is a front for CIA operations. Janessa's résumé reads the same as yours."

Alora remained silent, her eyes still fixed on the gardens.

"I can ask Director Palmer to send your complete file, but I would much rather hear about your background from you."

Alora let out a sigh. "If you talk about this in front of anyone else, I'll deny it."

"Fair enough." Stefano nodded. "But you did work for the CIA in Paris and so did your husband, right?"

"Yes, we both worked for the Agency." Alora shifted so she was facing him. "Carlo was second generation CIA. Both of his parents worked there, and I met him when I was on my mission in France. He started writing me, and we were married shortly after I returned home. We lived in the United States for about a year. Then right after Giancarlo was born, my father-in-law arranged for Carlo to be transferred to Paris.

"My husband was working with the locals there, tracking a terrorist cell, and my father-in-law was convinced Carlo could help stop whatever the group planning. We bought a house on the outskirts of Paris, and money was tight, so I started working part time as a bookkeeper at the embassy. My mother-in-law had retired from active service, and she volunteered to babysit for me. It seemed like the perfect situation."

"But somewhere along the line, the CIA recruited you."

"Yes." She nodded. "Before my mission, I worked in a bank in Zena, so I knew my way around banking software, and I had a knack for tracking fund transfers. Carlo and his father helped push through my security clearances and made the arrangements for me to have the proper training. I was never an agent, so most of my skills were acquired on the job."

"I've seen you shoot. You didn't learn that on the job."

She granted him a small smile and shook her head. "My father taught me when I was young. Then shortly after Dante was born, Carlo insisted that I needed to know how to defend myself. He took me to the shooting range with him several days a week, and I took a series of self-defense classes." Alora hesitated as the memories took over. "At the time, I thought he was just being paranoid, but I realize now that he was afraid the terrorist cell had discovered who he really was."

"Is that who set the bomb that killed him?"

"We think so." Alora shrugged. "I spent months trying to make sense of it all, trying to figure out if Carlo was the target or if maybe it was my father-in-law. In the end, the truth was that it didn't matter. They were both gone, and so was the rest of my family."

"Why was everyone together at your house?"

"My family came to Paris to spend the holidays with me, and my in-laws had decided to spend the day with us." Alora's eyes glistened with tears. "It was Christmas Eve."

"Alora, I'm so sorry." He drew her into his arms, holding her close as he felt her tremble. After a moment, he shifted so he could see her face. "How did you and the boys survive?"

"Dante had strep throat." She shook her head and let out a short, humorless laugh. "At the time, I was so frustrated that he was sick for his first Christmas. It turned out that the trip to the doctor saved our lives."

"I'm so sorry about your family."

Alora leaned into him, drawing comfort. She thought of the information she had uncovered earlier and shifted so she could look up at Stefano. "You don't think your uncle could really be behind the bombing in Bellamo, do you?"

"I don't know what to think anymore," Stefano admitted. "But I do imagine it will be difficult for all of us to deal with him at the council dinner tomorrow night since we're all anxious to find out the truth."

"Does your father expect me to attend dinner with you too?"

Stefano nodded. "I hope you don't mind."

"This seems to be a recurring theme, but I don't have anything to wear. I didn't think to have Janessa pack my formal dress."

"My mother is taking care of that." Stefano explained the plans for his mother's favorite designer to provide her with a gown.

"Stefano, that's too generous."

"Consider it a small token of our appreciation for all your help," Stefano told her. "After all, you're the one who finally proved that my father's suspicions held merit."

"I hope all of this comes to an end soon," she said softly. "I hate seeing everyone so tense."

"I have a feeling it's going to get worse before it gets better, especially when the media finds out that my brother is Mormon."

Her jaw dropped. "What?"

"He was baptized a couple months ago." His shoulders lifted. "The plan is that he'll make an announcement on Sunday. Hopefully the situation with my uncle won't complicate matters."

Alora shook her head as she absorbed this latest information. "I know a lot of families have their share of secrets, but yours definitely has more than I expected."

"I just hope we can survive them."

* * *

Stefano stood between Garrett and Martino in the observation booth at the police station. Luigi was already seated in one of the two chairs, his hands clasped tightly in his lap.

"It's still hard to believe he worked for us for almost thirty years without raising any suspicions," Martino said as a police officer entered the interrogation room.

"I wonder how long he's been skimming money out of our accounts," Stefano commented. "Alora has only gone back two years so far."

"It looks like we're about to find out."

The interrogator took his seat across the table from Luigi. "Mr. Ovalle, I understand you've been working for the royal family for some time now."

"That's right. Nearly thirty years." Luigi looked at him with confusion on his face. "Why was I brought here? I was supposed to deliver some very important documents to Prince Stefano at the palace."

"We just have a few questions for you in relation to the chateau manager's arrest earlier today," he assured him. "Now, I understand you've worked closely with Martino in your event planning duties. How long have you been in this position?"

"Two years."

"And before that?"

"I was Prince Elam's personal assistant."

"Why did you change jobs?"

"When Prince Elam relocated his offices a few years ago, my current position became available. It seemed like a good time for a change."

"What do you know about the bombing at the naval base in Bellamo?"

Surprise illuminated Luigi's face before he managed to control it. "I don't know anything about that."

"The funds embezzled from the royal household accounts ultimately ended up in the hands of the man who planted the bomb," the inspector informed him. "The documents in your possession indicate you may have had some involvement."

"I found these invoices in Martino's private quarters."

"Documents you planted."

Luigi paled. "I don't know what you're talking about."

"There's no use denying it. We have your actions well documented on video," the inspector said smugly. "What we want to know is who else was involved with the bombing."

"This is absurd. I demand to talk to my lawyer."

"Things will go easier for you if you cooperate."

Luigi shook his head, his expression belligerent. "I have nothing to say to you."

Chapter 38

KING EDUARD SAT AT THE head of the oval table in the library, his wife already seated by his side. Marta reached out and squeezed his hand in a gesture of comfort, but tonight nothing was going to settle this rage inside him until he uncovered the truth. The idea that his brother could be involved in an attack against his own country was absurd, but the facts Alora had laid out for them raised too many questions, questions that could no longer be ignored.

He had hoped that Janessa's friend had been wrong, that perhaps Alora had not been as skilled as Janessa had believed her to be. Unfortunately, the in-depth background he had received on Alora just that morning revealed that Janessa's faith in her friend was well founded.

He hadn't been aware of her previous employment with the Central Intelligence Agency, but oddly enough, that knowledge gave him a sense of comfort. Clearly, she had been trained to keep confidences. A personal call to Director Palmer had revealed that Alora had not only been one of theirs, but she had also specialized in tracking laundered money.

When Stefano led Alora into the room, Eduard didn't miss the way Stefano's hand lingered on her waist as he showed her to her seat or the look in her eyes when she settled beside him. He wondered now if his wife was right, that Stefano had developed feelings for Janessa's new assistant. When Elam entered the room, Eduard immediately dismissed that thought and focused on the more pressing issue.

Janessa and Garrett followed him into the room and closed the door behind them. As soon as everyone was seated, Eduard slid Alora's report to his brother.

"Can you explain this?"

Elam's eyebrows lifted arrogantly, and he took his time in sliding the paper closer so he could read it. When he looked down and saw the summary of his bank transfers, outrage lighted his face. "What is the meaning of this? Being king does not give you the right to poke into my personal affairs."

"It does when it involves acts of terrorism."

"What are you talking about?"

Eduard forced the words out. "The money you have been transferring to the Cayman Islands was used to fund the bombing in Bellamo."

Elam's face paled, and he looked at his brother now with wide eyes. "I . . . I didn't know that's what he was using the money for."

"What have you done?" Eduard asked with anguish in his voice. "What have you done to our country? To our family?"

"It was our family I was trying to preserve." Elam's jaw tightened. He pushed out of his seat and strode to the window. Then he glanced back at the door as if suddenly realizing his freedom was no longer entirely his own. He drew a deep breath and turned to face Eduard. "I have Merid's syndrome."

Surprise rippled through the room, and Eduard shook his head. "That isn't possible. You have a child. And how does that have anything to do with these acts of treason?"

"I have a child who is not my own. Philippe was conceived through in vitro fertilization. He doesn't carry Fortier blood."

Silence lingered for a long moment before Eduard spoke once more. "But why hide this, especially from me?"

"Do you have any idea how hard it is to find out you can't father a child? That your humiliation will be displayed in front of the public for their amusement?" Elam shook his head. "I couldn't do it, and Victoria wasn't willing to spend her life living with the speculation of why we couldn't have children."

"I can understand your desire to keep the information private, but there is no shame in facing something you cannot control."

Elam looked back at his brother and then seemed to realize he had spoken his secret aloud in front of a crowded room. "You couldn't possibly understand."

"Then explain it to me," Eduard insisted. "Why were you transferring money to the Caymans? Who were you paying?"

"My old assistant helped me make the arrangements for the fertility treatments years ago. He overheard the doctor give me the news and offered to help. Then shortly after Philippe was born, he ran into some financial trouble. He suggested that I help him out. After all, I wouldn't want anyone to find out that Philippe wasn't really my son."

"Luigi Ovalle was blackmailing you?" Stefano asked with a shake of his head.

Elam nodded.

"Did you know he was also embezzling funds from our household accounts?"

Again, he nodded. "His demands for money were getting beyond what I could afford. That's when he started asking for other favors."

"Like helping hide the listening devices in the chateau?" Janessa asked now.

"I didn't know that's what he was doing. He just wanted me to make sure a certain contractor got the remodeling job." Anguish showed on his face when he looked at Eduard. "I swear I didn't know what he had done until after the equipment was found."

Stefano leaned forward. "But it was you who knocked the hole in the wall in your old office."

Elam's voice was low. "Yes."

"Were the household accounts the only ones you were skimming from?"

He lowered his head and shook it slightly. "I had a good deal of latitude with my expenses with the church."

King Eduard's jaw clenched. He shifted his attention to Stefano and Alora. "I believe another audit is in order."

Alora's eyes met his, and she nodded but remained silent.

Janessa shifted forward in her seat. "What do you know about Ambrose?"

"I don't know who that is."

"What about other people Luigi associated with?" Janessa pressed.

"I don't know. All I cared about was keeping him happy so I could live my life in peace."

"I don't think peace is what Luigi Ovalle had in mind for any of us."

* * *

"What happens now?" Alora asked after Elam had been escorted out of the room.

"We'll have Elam join us tomorrow at church services," King Eduard told her. "Then he will be invited to remain at the palace until we can be certain Luigi acted alone."

Since two guards had been called to accompany Elam to his quarters, Alora guessed he would be closely supervised. She also realized for the first time that she was being included in this very private family matter as though she belonged.

"Do you think he was acting alone?" Janessa asked. "Director Palmer raised some concerns about Liberté trying to undermine the monarchy here in Meridia. One of the names that came up was Caspar Gazsi."

"He certainly has a lot to gain if we were forced from power," King Eduard admitted. He stroked a finger along his chin and then spoke to Janessa. "Could you make a call to your director and see if he has any new information? Perhaps with the full resources of the CIA, we can also find out who owns that account in the Caymans."

"I will get a message to him right now. Since it's the weekend, we probably won't get any information until late Monday or early Tuesday though."

"I understand, but the sooner the better." King Eduard stood, and everyone else followed his lead. "I think it's time we all retire for the night. I will see you all at church tomorrow morning."

Chapter 39

ALORA SAW STEFANO APPROACH AS she emerged from her room with Dante and Giancarlo. "I didn't think I would see you until after we got back from church."

"I thought I would come with you today."

Alora looked at him quizzically. "We would love that, but I thought you already went to church today."

"Yes, but Janessa and Garrett are going to attend the Mormon Church this afternoon, and I thought I would join them."

Remembering that Garrett was planning to announce his membership today after their services, Alora realized Stefano's decision to attend was likely a gesture of support for his brother. Still, she found herself looking forward to having someone to sit with who was over the age of six.

Stefano led the way outside and then ushered them into the backseat of a waiting limousine.

"Where are Janessa and Garrett?" Alora asked when the car started pulling forward.

"They're going to meet us there."

She thought of the events that had unfolded last night and his family's plans to attend church together this morning. "Do you mind if I ask how things went with your uncle this morning?"

"He played his part adequately," Stefano said before turning his attention to Giancarlo and Dante. "Did you boys have fun with Brenna last night?"

Dante made a sour face. "She made us eat all our vegetables, even the broccoli."

"The trials of childhood," Alora said dryly. "Last week he liked broccoli but he didn't like carrots."

"Maybe tonight we can just have pizza," Stefano suggested.

"I love pizza!" Dante's eyes lit up.

"Do you realize you just offered him his favorite food?"

"That works in my favor." Stefano winked at Dante. "It's one of my favorites too."

* * *

King Eduard leaned back on the long sofa in his sitting room and rubbed both hands over his face. His world was hanging by a thread, and his stomach was eating itself up as he waited to see who was going to grab a pair of scissors first.

"Everything is going to be okay," Marta insisted, lowering onto the couch beside him.

Eduard shook his head. "Our country has withstood wars and invasions. We've survived famines and droughts. Now public perception could be the one thing that destroys us."

"It's not going to happen." Marta took his hand and squeezed. "You are an incredible leader, and our people love you. We're going to make it through this."

Eduard thought of his sons who were both currently headed to the Mormon Church. He shifted and looked over at his wife. "And what is it with our sons and Mormon girls?"

"You know very well you can't choose who you fall in love with." She shifted beside him and gave him a knowing look. "If you could, you would have married that snobby little duchess from England instead of me."

"Yes, but at least you're from Meridia. Janessa isn't royalty or Meridian. I didn't think that would matter much since we expected that the monarchy would continue through Stefano's children. Now . . ."

"Now things have changed," Marta finished for him.

"You don't think Stefano is really serious about Alora do you?" Eduard asked now, his eyes troubled. "I never dreamed that both our sons might choose foreigners."

"Foreigners who speak our language and have embraced our culture," she reminded him. "And yes, I think Stefano is very serious about Alora."

"This is a nightmare. Everywhere I turn I learn of something else the press can use against us."

"Let the public relations people figure out how to spin the story. Be happy that both our sons have found somebody to love."

* * *

Stefano took his seat in the pew beside Garrett. Only once before had he stepped foot in a Mormon church, and that had been the day of his brother's baptism. He thought now, as he had then, how simple everything seemed. The pews were padded, the floor carpeted, but the walls were bare. Nowhere did he see any ornate statues or crucifixes. The windows were simple glass rather than the stained glass works of art that adorned the cathedral he had attended just that morning.

The bishop who stood up to conduct the meeting wasn't wearing fancy robes as he'd expected but was dressed like everyone else. He referred to some ward business, and Stefano watched as hands were raised to approve the two new Sunday School teachers whose names had been read. Then he presented Garrett's name for a confirming vote to receive the office of elder. Surprise rippled through the congregation, but everyone's hand went up to approve the action, and their surprise quickly melted into acceptance.

When the sacrament was blessed, two teenagers performed the ordinance, and then several boys who appeared to be about thirteen passed the bread to the congregation on trays. Dante and Giancarlo were clearly well versed in these unique customs since they took their bite-sized piece of bread and passed the tray with ease. The process was repeated with the water, and Stefano didn't miss that Alora put a steadying hand on the water tray when Dante took it from his brother.

The oddities continued when the bishop stood up again, but instead of delivering a sermon, he announced the members of the congregation who would be giving talks that day. The first speaker, a teenage girl, spoke about prayer. Her voice was sure and steady, her message similar to the words Stefano had read in the introduction to the Book of Mormon. The theme continued through the meeting as a young couple delivered their talks.

As the congregation sang the closing hymn, Stefano looked around the chapel, struck by the fact that all these people truly believed God not only listened to their prayers but that He also answered them.

* * *

Garrett stepped out of the meetinghouse, saw the reporters hovering outside, and instantly prayed that he would find the right words. He thought of the blessing he had received less than an hour before when he had been ordained an elder in the Melchizedek priesthood. He couldn't remember the words exactly, but he remembered the feeling of comfort, the surety that everything would be all right.

Aware of the members of the congregation who were still exiting the building, Garrett moved away from the doors and toward the waiting paparazzi. The minute they realized Garrett was willing to speak to them, they started firing questions at him. Rather than respond, Garrett simply held up a hand and waited for the voices to quiet.

He felt Janessa's hand on his arm, and he sensed his brother's presence behind him. Out of the corner of his eye, he could also see Alora and her children standing nearby.

"I have some news I would like to share," Garrett began. "Several weeks ago, I was baptized into The Church of Jesus Christ of Latter-day Saints."

The flurry of questions immediately intensified.

"Did you convert for Janessa?"

"How can you fulfill your royal duties if you no longer belong to the Meridian Church?"

"What does your family think about your decision?"

Again Garrett held up a hand to silence the crowd. "As all of you should already be aware, the royal family does not have any administrative power over the Meridian Church. Regardless, my choice to become a Latter-day Saint in no way diminishes my respect for the Meridian Church and the dedicated people who belong to it. As far as why I chose to be baptized, the decision was mine alone. It was the culmination of years of study and prayer that began before I met Janessa."

Stefano stepped forward until he was standing beside Garrett. "The citizens of Meridia have embraced the religious freedom we all enjoy. Everyone in my family hopes all of you will support Prince Garrett in his decision to honor both the religion of our land as well as the religion of his heart."

After waiting a brief moment to allow the photographers the opportunity to take pictures, both princes, Janessa, Alora, and the boys moved away from the press and headed for their cars.

"What do you think?" Garrett whispered to Stefano.

"I think we handled it as well as possible. Now all we can do is wait and see how the press spins the story." Stefano put a hand on his brother's shoulder. "Some prayer might help too."

* * *

"Who are all those people?" Giancarlo shifted in his seat and pressed his nose to the limousine window.

Alora's eyes widened when she saw the crowd that had gathered outside the palace gates. She guessed there were more than two hundred people, some with cameras and others simply looking on. "Are they all out there because of Prince Garrett's announcement?"

"I'm afraid so." Stefano nodded. "We hope this will all die down within a few days. Otherwise, the opening council session is going to be rather difficult for the family."

Several guards had already positioned themselves along the drive leading to the palace to keep the crowds back as the limousine slowed and the gates opened. Their car entered, followed by Garrett and Janessa's limousine and several cars carrying security personnel. When the limousine door opened, Stefano exited first and then reached a hand down to help Alora from the car. The boys scrambled out behind her as photographers pressed their camera lenses through the front gate.

Her hand still caught in Stefano's, Alora reached out instinctively for Dante's hand. Stefano reached for Giancarlo, and together they started up the stairs to the palace entrance.

Alora spoke quietly when she asked, "Did you expect the press to show up so quickly?"

Stefano nodded. "I was afraid they would. Let's get the kids inside, and then we'll go see what the initial reaction is to the news."

A guard opened the door for them, and Alora was surprised to see King Eduard descending the stairs as they entered. "Stories are already popping up all over the Internet."

Stefano sighed. "We expected that."

"Our press secretary released our official statement a few minutes ago. Your mother has requested that we all dine together in the family dining room this evening. Until then, I suggest we start analyzing this media storm before it gets out of hand."

Alora noticed the disappointed looks on her children's faces as they realized Stefano wasn't going to be able to join them for pizza after all. To her surprise, Stefano nodded down at Giancarlo. "Father, I'm sorry, but I already promised the boys that we would have pizza together tonight."

Something flashed in King Eduard's eyes but was quickly gone. He took a step closer and looked down at Giancarlo and Dante. "Stefano, I don't believe I've been introduced to your young friends."

"Father, this is Giancarlo and Dante DeSanto. Giancarlo and Dante, this is my father, King Eduard."

Alora swallowed a sigh of relief when both boys bowed to the king.

"So it's pizza you want for dinner tonight?"

Both boys looked up with wide eyes and nodded.

King Eduard turned to a servant standing nearby. "Anna, please inform the kitchen that we would like pizza on the menu for this evening."

"Yes, Your Majesty."

"Oh, we wouldn't want to intrude on your family dinner," Alora said quickly as Anna curtsied and started down the hall.

"Nonsense." King Eduard waved away her concerns as Garrett and Janessa walked inside.

"We're drawing quite a crowd," Garrett said, a hint of nerves humming through his voice.

"Well, if we have people who wish to see the royal family today, perhaps we should take our afternoon tea out on the front balcony. It will do our citizens good to see that we expect life to continue normally."

Giancarlo tugged on Alora's hand and lowered his voice. "Mama, I thought we weren't supposed to drink tea."

Before Alora could answer, Janessa leaned down and said, "Don't worry. I'm sure there will be some lemonade you can drink instead."

"Oh, okay." Giancarlo seemed to accept her answer.

Then Alora watched with amazement as her children were ushered up the stairs with the rest of the royal family. Within five minutes, Queen Marta joined them on the wide balcony and a servant wheeled a serving cart out with an assortment of finger sandwiches, scones, and cookies, in addition to tea and lemonade.

As everyone settled around a large wrought-iron table, Alora glanced out at the stunning view of the village below and was struck again with a sudden appreciation of her situation. Here she was in the company of royalty as they looked out over their storybook kingdom. She saw Giancarlo say something to the queen, and then Stefano laid his hand lightly on her shoulder before sitting beside her.

An unexpected sense of belonging rushed through her, along with a sense of anticipation. As she glanced down at the reporters gathered at the palace gates, she prayed that the people of Meridia would accept Garrett's choice.

Chapter 40

"Have you seen the news?" Caspar demanded.

"Yes," he said, his voice surprisingly calm. "It appears the royal family has jumped the gun, so to speak."

"I'm not talking about that. Luigi was arrested."

A small sigh escaped him. "They must have found something."

"What are we going to do if he talks?" Caspar asked edgily.

"He's not going to talk. He wouldn't dare."

"Even if he doesn't expose us, Prince Garrett's announcement throws everything off." Caspar paced across the room and shook his head in frustration. "You said yourself that the timing needs to be perfect."

"His secret was going to come out in a couple days anyway," he said dismissively. He knew his destiny, and he had no doubt that everything would fall into place in the end.

"How can you be so calm? I have a great deal of money tied up in this venture," Caspar reminded him. "If I can't start drilling by year's end, I will be ruined."

"Don't worry, my friend. You help get me into power, and you'll be richer than you ever dared imagine." His mind calculated quickly, and he smiled. "In fact, we may be able to use today's events to our advantage."

"How?"

"You leave the media problem to me. A few well-placed phone calls will turn it in our favor. For now, I have another job for you before you leave town."

* * *

Stefano searched through Internet articles on his laptop while Garrett and Janessa did the same on the other side of his father's worktable. His mother had insisted on going for a walk with Alora and the boys after dinner while the rest of them dealt with the business at hand. From behind his desk, Eduard shook his head. "Well, the news has definitely gone global."

"I know. There are already thousands of results on the Internet search engines." Garrett looked up at him. "A lot of them are pretty neutral though."

"That's a good thing," Janessa offered.

"You need to look at this one." Stefano shifted his laptop so everyone could see it before pressing the button to view a news video clip. In it, Archbishop Leone reacted to the news.

"I understand Prince Garrett has the freedom to change religions, but I am relieved that he will never take the throne. I feel it would be inappropriate for him to rule this country when he doesn't belong to the church this kingdom was founded on. I would hope that if the day ever did come when he would ascend the throne that he would step aside and let someone else rule who is more connected to our citizens."

"I suppose it could have been worse," Janessa sighed.

"Yeah," Stefano muttered. "He could already know that a Mormon will rule someday."

His cell phone rang, and he pulled it out of his pocket and answered it. His jaw tensed as he listened to the police chief's latest report. He was only on the call for a couple minutes before he said good-bye and looked up at his father.

"That was the police. They received an anonymous tip about an hour ago."

Garrett's eyebrows drew together. "About what?"

"Apparently someone noticed something odd at the home of my old classmate Jacques Neuville." Stefano drew a deep breath. "They just finished searching his house, and they found Belinda Parnelli's body hidden in a freezer."

Janessa looked up at him, horrified. "Who's Belinda Parnelli?"

Stefano's stomach clutched at the thought that this young woman was dead because of her involvement with his medical treatment. He took a moment to make sure his voice was steady. "She's a nurse who was kidnapped several weeks ago."

"Do you have any idea why?"

"She's the one who ran the tests on me for Merid's syndrome."

Silence hung in the room for several long seconds.

Janessa was the first to speak. "You think someone is going to publicize your medical problems?"

Stefano nodded. "Mine and Uncle Elam's. With everyone buzzing about Garrett being Mormon, the announcement that Uncle Elam and I cannot have children could destroy the monarchy."

"We're not going to let that happen," Eduard insisted. "We already have Luigi in custody. Now it looks like we've found his accomplice. We may have silenced everything before they could use the information as they wanted."

"I still don't understand what their motivations were and why they didn't publicize the news as soon as they received it," Janessa said skeptically.

"I have to think their motivation was profit, but I don't know why they were sitting on the information," Stefano said. "Jacques could have stood to gain a lot if we had approved that offshore oil well. If our family was forced from power, it's possible the ruling council might have overturned that decision."

"And we already know Luigi was keeping Elam's secret so he would keep getting paid," King Eduard added. "My guess is that Luigi found out about Garrett's baptism somehow, probably through one of those listening devices. Somehow he decided to team up with Jacques, and together they planned to exploit our family and get rich at the same time. Hiring Ambrose in a way that the payments could be traced back to Elam was just one more way to undermine our family's integrity."

Garrett shook his head. "It's hard to believe that people would try to unravel centuries of tradition for money."

"Hopefully everything is contained now," Eduard said. "If all goes well, the media frenzy about Garrett's new religion will die down within a few days, and when we walk into the council chambers on Thursday, we will be able to get back to business as usual."

"Father, there is one thing I think we may need to change for the upcoming council session," Stefano said.

"What's that?"

"In the past, you've always had me remain behind at the palace in the event of any kind of tragedy."

"Yes." Eduard nodded. "Many countries follow similar protocols to make sure that in the event of a natural disaster or a terrorist attack someone will survive to rule."

"And it is a good policy," Stefano agreed. "But in light of my medical situation, I feel Garrett should be the one to remain behind."

Eduard opened his mouth as if to object and quickly closed it again.

Stefano continued. "Most of our citizens are not aware of these security procedures, and keeping Garrett out of the spotlight this week might help us stay focused on the needs of our country instead of what the newspapers are printing."

Slowly Eduard nodded. "Garrett, your brother's right. Stefano will someday rule, but you are the future of the monarchy."

* * *

Alora knew she was taking advantage of having an in-house babysitter, but tonight she needed to have a little time to herself outside of the confines of her room. Besides, she couldn't deny that she had been disappointed when she had opened her door tonight to find Brenna standing on the other side instead of Stefano. Since Giancarlo and Dante had already fallen asleep, Alora had decided to take Brenna up on her offer to sit with the boys for a few hours.

Alora started down the hall, not sure if she should explore the palace a bit more or if she should try to find Stefano. She had been a bit disappointed that he had been unable to join her and the boys on their walk after dinner. Alora was astute enough to appreciate that the royal family had deliberately avoided speaking about the possible political ramifications of Garrett's baptism while her children were present. She also could admit that she had been surprised when the queen had chosen to join them for their Sunday evening walk.

Stefano had remained with the rest of the family to help deal with their current political affairs while Queen Marta had been the perfect hostess, showing them around the grounds and giving the boys the chance to get some fresh air. They had kept to the far side of the palace, away from the palace gates and the prying eyes of the press and public.

When they had reached the yard near the gazebo, Alora's thoughts had instantly turned to Stefano. So much had happened over the past few days. She had so enjoyed having him sit beside her in church today, but she knew it was an isolated event. Even if this blossoming romance did continue, he wasn't likely to attend church with her again.

Alora thought of the paparazzi still camped outside the palace gates, and she realized that even if Stefano was willing to go to church with her, such an event would likely feed this current media frenzy.

Tension hung thick within the walls of the palace, but she was touched to see the royal family's constant dedication to their country and their love of their citizens. Those same qualities were among those she had admired about her husband.

Even though Carlo had spent most of his career undercover, his love for freedom and his overwhelming desire to protect Americans from any perceivable threat had dominated his actions throughout their marriage. Ultimately his choice to dedicate himself to his country had taken him from her. Stefano would never work undercover, nor would he ever try to infiltrate a terrorist group, but Alora recognized that a certain amount of danger accompanied his public role in Meridia. Otherwise he wouldn't have so many guards assigned to him.

She looked down at the cell phone in her hand and considered. She knew she could call Stefano to find out where he was, but the prospect of interrupting him while he was meeting with his father made her uneasy. She reached the hallway leading to the royal offices and hesitated. Just as she convinced herself that she would be intruding if she went looking for Stefano, she saw him in the hall.

Her heartbeat quickened, and she moved toward him. "Are you all done for the night?"

He nodded, and Alora noticed the line of tension on his brow. "There's nothing more we can do for now."

"I gather the initial reaction isn't good," she said cautiously.

"We're seeing mixed reviews. It actually isn't as bad as we expected."

"Then what's wrong?" Alora asked. "You look upset."

He let out a sigh. "I just found out that one of my old classmates may have been involved with the bombing. And it appears that he was responsible for the death of a young woman."

"I'm so sorry. Were you close to either of them?"

Stefano shook his head. "I'd only met the woman a few times, and Jacques was always more of a rival than a friend. Still, I never thought him capable of something like this."

"Jacques?" Alora repeated, an uneasiness coming over her.

"Jacques Neuville," Stefano elaborated.

Her eyebrows drew together. "I met him a few days ago."

He took a step back. "Where?"

"In your office at the chateau. I was working there after you came to the palace. Martino brought him in and said Jacques had asked to see me."

"What did he want?"

"I don't know." Alora shrugged. "He asked to see me privately. When I refused to send Martino away, he decided to leave."

"That's odd."

"I thought so. I don't even know how he knew who I was."

"He could have seen some newspaper articles from when we attended the exhibit together, but I don't know why he would have asked to speak with you."

"I know it's been a long day for you, but do you think you might want to go for a walk? Brenna is watching the children for a little while."

Stefano slipped his hand into hers. "I can't think of a more perfect way to end the day."

A slow smile crossed her face. "I'm glad you think so."

Chapter 41

"LOOKS LIKE YOU'RE IN THE SPOTLIGHT again." Marta dropped the newspaper on Stefano's desk.

"Me?" Stefano looked down at the image in the center of the page. A photographer had snapped a picture of him returning from church the day before. In it, he and Alora were linked with the boys, all four of them holding hands and looking very much like a unit. The caption asked the question, *Has Prince Stefano found an instant family?* A small smile lighted his face as he looked up at his mother. "Well, this is definitely not what I expected on today's front page."

"Your father was quite pleased about it." She took a seat across from her son. "Alora and her children seem to have caught the interest of the media and, in so doing, have succeeded in taking some of the attention away from your brother."

Stefano considered the implications of this, both the fact that his relationship with Alora was giving the press something to balance the stories on Garrett and his concern that she would now be dogged by the paparazzi. "I think it would be wise to assign guards to Alora for the foreseeable future. She's not accustomed to dealing with the press."

"That would be a good idea."

"I'm surprised the press didn't key in on her religion."

"There were a couple comments in various articles about how she had attended church with you and your brother, but it appears that no one has managed to confirm that she is the same religion as Garrett and Janessa."

"That's probably a good thing right now."

Marta shifted closer so she too could see the newspaper now spread out on Stefano's desk. "You know, this really is a nice picture."

"Mmm hmm," Stefano murmured in agreement, his attention still on the article.

"Alora's children seem to be very fond of you."

Stefano looked up at his mother now. He recognized the look on her face, the same one she always had when she was digging for information. "Mother, are you prying?"

"Absolutely," Marta said with humor in her voice. "Tell me everything."

Stefano shook his head. "I don't know that there's much to tell."

"You can do better than that," Marta insisted with a delighted laugh. "It's obvious that you're taken with this girl, and I'd have to be blind not to see the way she looks at you."

A ripple of excitement pulsed through him. "How does she look at me?"

She gave him a knowing smile. "Like a woman in love."

His eyebrows lifted. "I think you're getting ahead of yourself, Mother."

"I'm not so sure," she said and then moved to stand. "I will tell you that I like her. I think she is a very bright young woman, a wonderful mother, and she carries herself with a great deal of class."

Stefano smiled fully. "I'm glad you approve."

"And when the day comes that you decide she is the one you want, I would be honored if you gave her the engagement ring your father gave to me."

Stefano's jaw dropped at her assumption. Then he managed to grasp at the one fact he wanted most to forget. "Mother, even if I do someday marry, your ring should pass down through Garrett and Janessa's children since I can never have any of my own."

"Nonsense. Alora's boys will be as much your children as you are mine. Take your mother's word on that." Then with a definitive nod, she turned and sailed out of the room.

*　*　*

King Eduard took his seat at the head of the conference table in the library. He watched his two sons pull out chairs for Janessa and Alora and considered for the first time that his family might finally be complete. If his wife was right, Stefano had found his bride-to-be even if he didn't recognize the fact yet.

He had thought that Stefano's obvious fascination with Alora was a passing fancy, one that had been born from his weeks in close proximity to her at the chateau. After seeing them together several times the past few days, and especially after seeing Stefano with Alora's children, he was starting to trust Marta's instincts.

When Stefano had asked for this family meeting to start at nine so he and Alora could put her children to bed first, any lingering doubts had vanished. Whether Stefano realized it or not, he was already thinking of Alora as part of the family and, in his subtle way, expected the rest of them to include her as well.

As soon as everyone had taken their seats, he asked, "Where do we stand?"

"We have confirmed that Caspar Gazsi has left the country," Janessa began. "Apparently he drove to Monaco last night. From there, he's believed to have flown to Libya."

"His sudden departure would make it seem that he was involved and realized that we might be on to him," Garrett offered.

Eduard nodded, considering. "Has the CIA come up with any information on that bank account in the Caymans?"

"Not yet. They did an initial report, but it didn't reveal anything that Alora hadn't already told us about," Janessa said. "There is one thing that concerns me though."

"What's that?"

"No one seems to be able to find any links between Jacques Neuville and Luigi Ovalle. They didn't have any common acquaintances that we can find, and there aren't any financial links between them."

"Jacques definitely knew Caspar Gazsi though," Stefano reminded her. "Maybe Gazsi is the link. Or perhaps they were all members of Liberté."

"Maybe," Janessa conceded. "Jacques Neuville wasn't identified as being part of the dissident group, but I suppose it's possible he was able to hide his association with them."

"Were the police able to get anything out of Jacques or Luigi?" King Eduard asked.

"Luigi still isn't talking," Garrett offered. "As for Jacques, he adamantly denies any involvement. He insists he's being framed."

"Is it possible that he's telling the truth?" Stefano asked.

"It's doubtful." Garrett offered his brother a sympathetic look. "Assuming the oil rights are the motivation behind everything that's going on, Jacques would have just as much to gain as Caspar Gazsi if the restrictions on offshore drilling were lifted."

"When the police questioned him about why he came to see Alora, he admitted that he was looking for a story to sell to the tabloids." Stefano shook his head. "I don't know why he would admit to that and deny everything else. Seems like he would deny everything if he were guilty. Also, the police said Belinda Parnelli's body had been moved."

"We already suspected that," Garrett said. "With where her body was hidden, she definitely would have been killed somewhere else first."

King Eduard interrupted the speculation and addressed Janessa. "Is it possible that we have identified everyone involved, or does the CIA believe a threat still exists?"

"The Agency is skeptically optimistic," Janessa told him. "Since the bombing already occurred, and we've been able to find the financial backers, it's possible the threat is over. Of course, that is assuming their plan was to blame Prince Elam for the bombing and then release potentially damaging information on both Garrett and Stefano to try to topple the monarchy."

Eduard noticed her hesitation. "But?"

"I don't know. I just think the naval base was an odd choice for a target." Janessa shifted forward in her chair, and her eyes met his. "Logically, they would have tried to come after you so there would be no one left to rule."

"Maybe they did," Stefano suggested. "If my car accident was caused by someone running me off the road, maybe I wasn't the one they were after. With the tinted windows, it could have been any of us inside."

"Yes, but the bombing occurred after that." Janessa shook her head. "Maybe I'm being paranoid, but I'd feel a lot safer if we keep the extra security details for everyone until we're sure this is all behind us."

Eduard nodded. "I'll make sure of it."

Chapter 42

ALORA SETTLED A FOOT ON the bottom plank of the split-rail fence surrounding the riding ring. Unlike the stables at the chateau that Paolo ran practically by himself, the palace stables had an abundance of stable hands. Currently, two of them were in the ring, one instructing Giancarlo and the other working with Dante. Another was in a larger ring working one of the horses through a series of jumps.

She glanced at the palace in front of her and could almost feel the whirl of activity and tension emanating from within. Today was the day. The legislative council session would begin within a matter of hours. Security guards buzzed everywhere as cars were prepared to transport King Eduard and Stefano to the council chambers, while the paparazzi, with their zoom lenses, crowded the front gate.

The past several mornings, she had been surprised to find as many stories about her and Stefano in the papers as there were about Garrett's baptism. Yesterday's highlight had been a photograph of Stefano taking her hand when he'd walked with her out to the gardens the day before. Today a photograph of her sitting by the pool watching her children play took center stage, the caption reading simply, *A new royal family in the making?*

She wished she could say she was unaffected by the headlines, but since seeing the photo of her family walking into the palace with Stefano, her confusion about her future with Stefano continued to mount. At times she found herself dreaming of a future together, of having a man in her life who was kind and caring, a man who already treated her children as though he loved them as his own. Then her doubts would creep in, always circling back to the fact that they didn't share the same religion.

Her prayers continued to confuse her, especially late at night when she found herself trying to figure out what she really wanted as well as what Heavenly Father wanted for her. She was already afraid that they wouldn't be the same thing. Deep down, she already knew where her dreams were taking her, and all of them included Stefano.

What would it be like, she wondered, if a future developed between them? How would it affect her children to have a father who was royal but not Mormon? What about any future children they might have together?

She thought of the headlines about Garrett; after three days, the speculation about the impact of his baptism was not more political than religious. Would Stefano allow her to raise their children as Latter-day Saints, or would the politics of Meridia make those decisions for them?

Her heart ached at the knowledge that Stefano's first responsibility would always be to his country, that his position could very well prevent them from moving forward as a couple. When she saw him crossing the wide lawn toward the stables, she tried to push aside her doubts. For now, she needed to be a friend to him, to give him support at this stressful time. Next week she could take the time to consider what would come next.

"Are you leaving already?"

"In a few minutes." Stefano lifted a hand to wave at the boys as they circled the ring. "I was hoping you might come with me."

"Come with you?" Alora repeated.

He nodded. "I just thought that if you're going to make Meridia your home, you might want to see how our government operates."

"I would like that." She glanced down at the jeans and button-up shirt she was wearing. "How soon are you leaving? I need to change."

"You have about a half hour." Stefano motioned to the palace. "Go ahead. Brenna will be out here in a few minutes. I'll keep an eye on the boys until she gets here."

"Thanks." Alora reached up to give him a kiss and then stopped suddenly. They were standing here in broad daylight with her children and several stable hands nearby as well as the paparazzi lingering around the corner. She dropped back on her heels, suddenly self-conscious. The casual kiss she had intended would have been too familiar, too much like the way she would have acted with Carlo.

Before she could take a step back, Stefano put his hand on her arm and held her in place. Awareness lit his eyes, and he hesitated for only a split second before he leaned down and kissed her cheek. "I'll meet you in the front hall in a few minutes."

Alora nodded, her eyes darting to where her boys were still riding. They didn't seem to notice that Stefano had kissed her, or if they did, they didn't seem to care. A bit flustered, Alora started across the lawn. She had taken several steps before she realized she needed to tell the boys where she was going. As though reading her mind, Stefano nodded toward the boys as she turned around. "Don't worry. I'll let them know what's going on."

"Thanks." Alora turned toward the palace once more, her stomach fluttering with an odd sensation that she recognized as hope. For the moment and for as long as it lasted, her family felt complete again. Before her doubts could wash away that feeling, she focused on preparing for her next outing with the prince, a prince she now thought of as her own.

* * *

Stefano watched Alora approach, her simple blue dress falling nearly to her ankles. Her dark hair was tied back at the base of her neck and ran down her back in a sleek ponytail. Silver earrings carved in the shape of seashells were clipped onto her ears, but her wrists and neck were bare. "Are you ready to go?"

She nodded and motioned down to her dress. "Am I dressed okay?"

"You look perfect." He took her hand and leaned down for a kiss. "Our car is waiting outside. My father left a few minutes ago. He said he had a few fires to put out before the session begins."

Alora nodded, waiting until they were settled in the backseat of a limousine before she asked, "Is everything okay?"

He started to brush his concerns aside, but instead he pushed the button to raise the privacy window between them and their driver. "There's talk that Bernardo Campesi, the president of the council, is going to try to enact a law today. The new law would prohibit anyone from ruling Meridia unless they are a member of the Meridian Church."

"That doesn't seem right." Alora shifted so she was facing him more fully. "If your citizens can choose their religion, surely the monarchy should have the same privilege."

"I don't disagree, but there are those who are trying to strengthen the ties between the Meridian Church and the government. We believe the archbishop himself is behind this legislation."

"What does he hope to gain by this?" Alora asked. A touch of regret reflected in her eyes. "You still belong to the Meridian Church. It's your son who will rule someday."

Stefano saw the opening she had given him to confide in her, but he wasn't ready for the changes the truth would surely bring. "The future is never certain. Some believe my car accident was really an attempt on my life. It's possible that somebody was trying to get rid of me and then use our secrets to oust my family from power. If the press got wind of my uncle's activities and the fact that my cousin isn't of royal blood, our country could find itself in turmoil."

"I still don't understand how a bunch of bad press could possibly topple a monarchy that has been in power for centuries. Even if someone had managed to get to you and all of these skeletons got out at the same time, your father and his council would still be able to rule."

Stefano recognized the truth of her statement, considering for a moment what would happen if his family was forced from power. Laws were in place to allow the ruling council to take control of the government so the country and their military would remain intact.

The limo pulled to a stop, and a moment later their driver opened the door for them. Guards shifted into place as they exited the vehicle and moved into the council building. Even as they headed for the conference room where he expected to find his father, Alora's words continued to play over in Stefano's mind.

She was right. If something happened to his family, the ruling council would be able to step in and take over the government. A large majority of the council members had supported both his father's decision to allow the United States to build their naval base as well as his resolution to deny offshore drilling.

Alora tugged on his arm and nodded in the direction of a dark-haired man who was walking toward the stairwell. "Do you know that man?"

Stefano shook his head as the man looked over at Alora. "I've never seen him before. Why?"

"This is the second time I've seen him recently. He looks at me like he knows me, but I don't know him."

Stefano started to brush it off, certain that he had probably seen her in the newspaper. Then the man glanced their way again, and something in his eyes sent a ripple of uneasiness through him. "Where else have you seen him?"

"At the naval base." Awareness flashed in her eyes. "Stefano, I saw him right before I came here. Right before the bombing." The concern visible on her face heightened. "You don't think he could . . ."

"The council chambers." It all became clear in that instant. "If a bomb went off during today's legislative session, it could take out the entire government."

"You don't really think someone would be able to plant a bomb here, do you?" Alora asked, her eyes wide.

"I know someone has been sitting on damaging information about my family, and it's never made sense why they haven't already used it against us." Stefano's words came out in a rush. "The only explanation is that they were waiting for something."

"And you think they were waiting for today."

Stefano nodded. "I want you to wait here. I'm going to go see who that guy is." He motioned to one of his guards. "Stay here with her."

Then Stefano headed for the stairwell with his other guard following closely behind him. Together the two men disappeared through the stairwell door.

Chapter 43

A KNOT OF TENSION FORMED at the base of her neck as Alora watched Stefano leave the reception area of the council building. A familiar helplessness flooded through her as she considered what could happen if Stefano was right. This building and everyone in it could be reduced to a pile of rubble in an instant. She wasn't prepared to let that happen.

If the man Stefano was following really was the bomber, then they were safe as long as he was still in the building. She didn't know if they were both being paranoid or if their instincts were right. Either way, she wasn't going to stand by and watch from the sidelines. She took two steps toward the stairwell before the guard reached for her arm.

"Signora, the prince asked you to wait here," he reminded her.

"I just want to make sure everything is okay." Alora pulled free of his grasp and continued forward. "You're welcome to come with me."

"I think it would be best if you stay here in the lobby."

Alora shook her head, the tension in her neck spreading. Her pace quickened as she crossed the marble floor, the guard following her. She pulled open the stairwell door to reveal two sets of stairs, a narrow set of stairs leading to the basement level and another wide staircase leading upstairs. The air was warm and stale on the landing, the faint scent of cigarette smoke and disinfectant hanging in the air.

She took a step toward the wide staircase and hesitated. If someone really was planting a bomb, they would likely go for the basement, not the upstairs.

She stood silently for a moment, listening for footsteps, and was surprised she didn't hear any—nor did she hear any voices. Uneasy, she started down the stairs. She sensed movement beneath her, followed by an odd muffled popping sound.

"Signora," the guard began, but Alora held up a hand to silence him.

They reached the lower landing, Alora squinting as her eyes adjusted to the dimly lit room. Then she saw a body sprawled near a doorway on the far side of the room. She rushed forward and crouched down beside the guard who had accompanied Stefano into the stairwell. Blood seeped through his shirt, and Alora quickly checked for a pulse.

"He's still alive. Give me your jacket."

Her guard stripped off his jacket and handed it to her. Alora pressed it to the wound. "Now go get some help," Alora ordered him. She went with instinct and added, "And evacuate the building."

"Evacuate?"

"Do it." Alora's tone was quiet but held authority.

"Yes, signora." He turned and rushed back up the stairs.

The wounded man stirred. "The prince," he said weakly. "He has the prince."

Alora's breath caught, and she fought for calm. "Stay still. Help is coming."

As she started to stand, she glimpsed the weapon holstered at his waistband. She pulled the weapon free as the guard nodded weakly in approval. She didn't have time to decide whether to move forward or wait for help before she heard movement in the next room.

* * *

King Eduard sat at the head of the conference room table and stared down the senior members of the ruling council. Two of the seven men sitting at the table were behind the new legislation regarding a religious requirement for any future king, and at least one more appeared to be wavering.

"This is completely unacceptable," Eduard said, determined to win this fight. "You are saying that our citizens can have religious freedom but the king cannot. Surely you see how inequitable this is."

"Your Majesty, I understand how conflicted you must feel regarding Prince Garrett's decision," Bernardo Campesi began.

Eduard interrupted before he could continue. "Both of my sons are perfectly capable of ruling this country—and ruling well. Your job is to make sure *no one* is allowed to undermine the monarchy."

Shouts sounded in the hallway, followed by pounding footsteps. Before Eduard could respond, the fire alarm sounded.

"A fire?" Eduard considered the recent security concerns, immediately wondering if this was a trap, some kind of scheme to get him and Stefano out into the open.

The door burst open, and a guard rushed in. "We must evacuate immediately."

"Are you sure the fire is real?"

"It isn't a fire, Your Majesty. We believe there is a bomb." The guard motioned to the door and looked at the other men in the room. "This way. The side entrance has been secured for your safety."

Eduard let the guard lead him out of the conference room and into the hall. He glanced toward the lobby, where another guard was directing people out the front doors while keeping the hallway clear for him to make his escape safely. Guards' barked orders echoed toward him, and he could feel the panicked energy vibrating through the air.

Voices melded together in a dull roar, the volume increasing as he made his way to the side door.

"Where are Stefano and Alora?" Eduard asked the guard who was currently gripping his arm. "Have they already made it out?"

"I'm not sure, sir. It was one of Prince Stefano's guards who alerted us to the problem."

"Find out where he is," Eduard demanded, his stomach clutching with worry. "Find my son."

* * *

Alora turned slowly. Her heart froze in her chest when she saw the glint of metal pressed to Stefano's head. Fear filled his eyes—fear for her, fear for himself. Yet she could also see Stefano's steely determination.

"Stay where you are, madame." The familiar man spoke in French, but Alora barely registered that detail. Her entire focus was on Stefano and on the gun pressed to his right temple. The man standing behind him was an inch or two shorter than Stefano, his left arm gripping Stefano around the throat.

"Let her leave," Stefano managed to say, his eyes dark and focused on Alora. "You don't need her."

"Who are you?" Alora asked before he could respond. She said the words first in Italian, and then repeated them again in French. "*Qui êtes-vous?*"

He laughed now, his laughter hard and brittle and proud. "You don't know?"

"Why should I?" Alora studied the face, a dozen thoughts whirling through her mind, including the fact that she couldn't recall seeing him before that day in Bellamo. "And how do you know me?"

"I am Ambrose," he said haughtily. His eyebrows lifted arrogantly as he added, "I saved your life one Christmas Eve."

Her world froze. "What?"

He cocked his head slightly to one side and looked almost apologetic when he said, "I have a soft spot for children."

Her right hand lifted, the weapon cold in her hand as she trained it on the man holding Stefano.

"Now, you don't want to do anything foolish."

"You killed my family?"

"I saved your life." He spoke brashly. "Someone else might have waited for you and your sons to get home before detonating the bombs."

She straightened her arms and took aim. Only Ambrose's head was visible behind Stefano. Even with all her CIA training and the hours of shooting practice, she couldn't be sure she could take the shot. She knew how to kill in theory, but she had never done so in reality. "Let Stefano go, and I'll return the favor."

Ambrose laughed again. "You'll return the favor? I don't think so."

Her voice was like steel. "Last chance."

"No, madame. This is your last chance." The first hint of doubt crept into his eyes when Alora released the safety, her eyes remaining steadily on his. Then Stefano's arm shifted ever so slightly, and Alora felt an uncomfortable sense of anticipation. "Put down the—"

Stefano's elbow plowed into Ambrose's stomach, and Stefano leaned to the left. A split second later, Alora squeezed the trigger. Ambrose's head jerked back before he dropped to the floor, a spray of blood misting Stefano's face and clothes.

Alora lowered the gun, and immediately, her body began to shake.

Stefano didn't look at the dead man behind him. He reached for Alora and pulled her close. "It's okay." Her arms came up to encircle his waist. "You did it. Everything is okay now."

She drew a jagged breath, fighting back the tears that threatened. Her body still trembled, and she could feel that Stefano wasn't much steadier than she was. She heard movement in the other room, and a moment later a guard stepped through the doorway.

"Your Highness, are you okay?"

Stefano nodded and then spoke to Alora. "Let's get you out of here."

"What about the bomb?" Alora motioned in Ambrose's direction.

"He was planting it on the underside of the gas line when we walked in on him." Stefano motioned across the room. "That's how my guard was shot. When he heard you coming down the stairs, he grabbed me."

Alora looked up at the guard. "Call in the bomb squad anyway, just to be safe."

He looked at Stefano. When Stefano gave a subtle nod, he pulled out a phone and made the call.

"Come on." Stefano shifted, keeping an arm firmly around her waist. "I want to get you back to the palace."

Chapter 44

STEFANO STRIPPED OFF THE BLOODY clothes the moment he stepped into his private quarters. He balled them up and dropped them into the trash can. Then he stepped into the shower to erase the evidence that he had nearly died less than an hour before. If only he could erase the memory of Alora standing in front of him holding that gun, if he could forget the look on her face when she learned that the man threatening him had been responsible for destroying most of her family.

He hadn't been sure that she would be able to pull the trigger when the opportunity arose, and he hated that she had been the one put in that position. Never before had he been forced to literally put his life in someone else's hands, and he could say with surety that he hoped to never repeat the experience.

No sooner had he finished dressing than a knock came at his door. Before he could respond, his brother walked in.

"Have you heard anything yet?" Stefano asked.

"The bomb squad found three bombs in the building." Garrett leaned against the back of the couch in the sitting room. "Unfortunately, they missed one in the parking garage."

"Was anyone hurt?"

Garrett shook his head. "Everyone had already been evacuated. The parking garage is a mess, but the structure itself only sustained minor damage."

"Sounds like we got lucky."

"Janessa doesn't think it's over."

Stefano's eyebrows drew together. "What do you mean? Ambrose is dead, and we've arrested the two men who hired him."

"Maybe." He folded his arms across his chest. "The link between Jacques and Luigi is still pretty thin. Janessa and the CIA have tried to find something more to tie them together besides knowing Caspar Gazsi, but the more they dig, the more convinced Janessa becomes that Jacques is being set up."

"It's possible that Gazsi was the only one working with Luigi. Together they could have decided to hire Ambrose," Stefano suggested. "Any of the three of them could have killed Belinda Parnelli."

"That's the CIA's take on the situation." Garrett nodded. "They're still trying to identify who that Cayman account belongs to, but other than that, there isn't a whole lot more to go on."

"I hate waiting."

"Me too." Garrett pushed away from the couch. "You gave us quite a scare today. Maybe you should take a day or two off and let the rest of us deal with today's situation."

"I need to work."

"Are you okay? Really?"

His instinct was to hide his weaknesses, to gloss over his fears, but he and Garrett were more than brothers. They were friends. Slowly Stefano shook his head, and he could feel his throat closing up as he thought of Alora. "I keep seeing Alora standing in front of me, imagining what would have happened had she not recognized Ambrose in the lobby. Her children would have been orphaned. Hundreds of people would have died."

"I know you aren't much into religion, but just this once, maybe you need to recognize that the Lord had a hand in how things played out today," Garrett said softly.

"I'm sending Alora and the kids back to the chateau."

"Why?"

"I think it's safer for them there. If this isn't really over, I want to make sure she isn't anywhere near me."

"Stefano, are you sure that's what you want?"

"Of course it's not what I want, but this is what's best for her." Stefano took a step toward the door. "I don't have time to deal with this now. We have work to do."

* * *

"You want me to leave?" Alora looked at Stefano, stunned, hurt, and confused. When he had walked into her room, all she had wanted was to be held, to be told that everything would be okay. Instead, Stefano stood rigidly in front of her demanding that she leave the palace.

"I want you to be safe."

"There are guards everywhere. I am safe."

"Alora, please." Stefano's shoulders drooped slightly. "I'll feel better when you are back at the chateau, away from everything that is going on here."

"Did I do something wrong?"

"Of course not." Stefano shook his head, impatience and a barely leashed fury evident on his face. "You just saved my life."

"And as a thank you, you're sending me away." Her voice shook as she found herself caught in a tangle of emotions. She held her hands out in front of her and looked down at them. "I killed a man today, a man who not so long ago destroyed my life. I have to live with that, both with what I've done and the fact that I have yet to feel any regret."

Sympathy flashed in his eyes. "Do you think Ambrose felt regret about killing your husband? Your family?"

She shook her head, her eyes filling with tears. "That doesn't change the reality though. There is a person who is no longer living because of me."

"And there are hundreds of people who are *still* living because of you, including both of us." He ran a finger gently down her cheek. "My brother seems to think the Lord had something to do with how things played out today. Maybe you were supposed to recognize Ambrose so he wouldn't succeed."

"It's hard to imagine that the Lord would put me in the position to kill someone, even for His purposes."

"Why not? It happened in your Book of Mormon," Stefano pointed out. "What was his name? The man who killed to get those plates? Nephi?"

"That was an exception. The Lord doesn't normally work that way." His words caught up with her, and confusion lit her eyes. "You've been reading the Book of Mormon?"

"A few chapters." His shoulders lifted. "I figured it couldn't hurt for me to understand a bit more about your religion."

Momentarily distracted, Alora asked, "What do you think so far?"

"It's interesting reading." Again he shrugged. "I can understand why Garrett would think the Lord might have interfered against someone as evil as Ambrose."

"I guess." She let out a sigh. "I keep thinking I should be feeling something more than I do. Remorse, regret, justice. Something. Right now, I just have this hollow feeling inside of me like I've woken up from a dream that isn't completely my own."

"Give yourself some time. Go back to the chateau and spend a few days with the boys. That will help put things back into perspective."

"You're probably right."

Stefano nodded and then hesitated as though he was suddenly at a loss for words.

"Is something wrong?"

"There's just something I need to know." Stefano's eyes darkened and stayed fixed on hers. "When you pulled the trigger, did you do it for revenge or did you do it to save me?"

She looked up at him through damp eyes. Hadn't she been asking herself that same question since the moment she had ended Ambrose's life? The first tears spilled over, and she found the answer for both of them. "I couldn't go through it again."

"What?"

"Losing someone." Her voice lowered to a whisper. "I couldn't lose someone else I loved."

Surprise, wonder, joy. She could see them on his face as he reached for her hand to pull her closer. He lowered his lips to hers, unspoken promises pouring into the kiss. She braced for the briefest moment, afraid to hope, afraid to dream for what they could have together. Then she felt her heart open to him.

She was lost and wasn't sure any longer if she wanted to be found. Against all logic, she felt a sense of rightness as his lips trailed up to brush against her cheek then her temple. Then his arms tightened around her, and he just held on.

Though doubts lingered, Alora refused to let them fully form. For now, she needed Stefano too much. For now, she needed to live in the moment.

Chapter 45

"WE CAN HIRE SOMEONE ELSE," he said, desperation and frustration humming through his voice. He still couldn't believe Ambrose had failed, that the impending audit might very well expose his involvement. How had they come to this point? "Surely the potential payoff is worth investing a little more money."

"It's too late," Caspar insisted. "Interpol already knows I was involved. Most of my funds have been frozen, and the moment I leave Libya, I'll be arrested."

"We can't stop now." His voice was stern now, controlling. "The council session has already been rescheduled. If we wait much longer, we'll lose the support of the citizens of Meridia."

"We've already lost their support," Caspar countered. "You said your countrymen would be up in arms when they found out about Prince Garrett. That didn't happen."

"They can be made to understand how serious Prince Garrett's decision is. We just have to take care of the council, and then we'll expose the princes."

"I'm through with your elaborate plans," Caspar told him. "I can't function in Meridia now that I'm on Interpol's watch list."

"I never thought you a coward."

"I never thought you a zealot."

His jaw clenched, and he felt a consuming need to have control. King Alejandro had chosen him more than two decades before to lead this country in what mattered most, and then he had yanked that power away. When King Eduard had ascended the throne, he had abided by his father's wishes, effectively limiting his reach in all things.

The royals were naïve, too far removed from the citizens to know what was really important. But he knew. He understood that they needed one of their own to rule. They needed him. "Someone has to save this country from the monarchy. If you won't help me, I'll take care of things myself."

* * *

Alora walked barefoot along the water, the surf splashing over her toes, causing them to sink deeper into the sand. Giancarlo and Dante sat on the beach a short distance away building a sand castle under Brenna's watchful eye. The chateau stretched out behind them, looking as perfect as it had the day they'd arrived, late summer roses scenting the warm, humid air.

Except for the servants going about their duties, the chateau remained oddly quiet. Janessa and Garrett had stayed at the palace with Stefano, all of them working diligently to prepare for the rescheduled council meeting that would take place in just a few days. Alora, on the other hand, found herself with nothing but time.

Janessa had insisted that she take a few days off, and the household staff seemed determined to make sure she followed that counsel. Levi and Martino had practically banned her from her office, despite the arrival of the church's financial records, and Patrice was hovering over her like a mother hen.

Stefano called her each night in time to say good night to the children, and every night she could hear the strain in his voice. She hated knowing he was shouldering so much responsibility, that there was nothing she could do to ease his burdens.

The water surged up and over her ankles, dampening the hem of her cotton dress. A dog barked in the distance, but Alora didn't recognize that the sound was out of place until Giancarlo and Dante rushed toward her.

Dante pulled on her hand and pointed. "Mama! Mama! Look!"

Alora turned to see Stefano walking down the steps to the beach, a golden-haired puppy squirming in his arms. For a moment, she simply stared, afraid that if she blinked he would disappear. Stefano hadn't said anything about coming to the chateau when she had spoken to him the night before, but there he was moving toward them.

Even from across the sand, she could see the tension in his shoulders, but as the boys raced toward him, he smiled and winked at her. He set the puppy on the sand and handed the leash to Giancarlo.

"Don't let him get away from you."

"Whose puppy is he?"

"He's yours," Stefano told him with a grin. "Yours and Dante's."

"Really?"

Stefano chuckled. "Yes, really."

Delighted squeals pierced the air, accented with thank yous and excited barks and yips from the newest addition to the family.

"Make sure you keep him on the leash," Stefano warned as he crossed the few feet to where Alora now stood. He motioned to Brenna to supervise the children and then lowered his voice. "I hope this is okay."

"This is a wonderful surprise. Thank you." She reached out and squeezed his hand. Then her eyes narrowed fractionally. "But what are you doing here? I thought you had to stay in Calene until after the council session next week."

"My father decided it was time to send us away in case there's another incident."

She lowered her voice as Stefano led her farther down the beach away from the children. "Are you expecting more trouble?"

"I hope not, but Janessa doesn't think this is over yet," Stefano told her. "Jacques Neuville was released last night. His alibis weren't as tight as they would have liked, but he consented to a lie detector test, and he passed it with flying colors."

"Why did he come to see me that day?"

"He was looking for a story, something to sell the tabloids to give him some extra cash." Stefano shrugged. "He won't be welcome at any royal events again, but he isn't a killer."

"You think someone else is still out there."

"I don't know what to think. I'd feel better if we knew for sure who that account in the Cayman Islands belongs to. Your friends at the Agency believe it could belong to Luigi, but if they're wrong . . ."

"Then there's still someone out there who is trying to hurt your family."

"It's possible." He motioned to the chateau. "For now, Janessa and Garrett will return to their work at the naval base and start the process of rebuilding the security offices. I will work with the public affairs office to monitor the political climate regarding my brother's announcement. As for you, my father is anxious for you to start on the church audit."

"You realize this audit is a huge job, especially with only one person."

"Martino has volunteered to help you," he offered and gave her an apologetic look. "My father doesn't want any outsiders involved in this audit, considering the sensitivity of the information we expect to find."

"I understand completely."

"For now, what do you say we go get the boys ready for dinner?"

"You realize that we're not going to be able to pull them away from that puppy, don't you?"

Stefano chuckled, and some of his tension seemed to ease. "I'm thinking pizza out on the front lawn. We can have a picnic."

"Sounds perfect."

* * *

Incompetents. Imbeciles. He gripped the steering wheel and wondered how everything could go so wrong. For years he had been plotting and planning, always waiting patiently for the time to be right.

Years of preparation, and now he had nothing. He drew in a breath and let it out slowly.

His instructions had been specific, outlining each step down to the letter. Now, instead of the chaos that was supposed to be taking place in Meridia, both the royal family and the ruling council were safe, and life continued exactly as it had for centuries. Or so everyone thought.

Gone was the time when the royal family was only a figurehead, when the real power had been held by him and his predecessors. King Alejandro had been too power hungry to let him keep what was rightfully his, and Eduard had shared in that hunger.

A change in dominance had been within his grasp. Only last week he had held all the weapons in his hand that he could possibly need to overthrow the monarchy, but now the citizens of Meridia were proving to be much more fickle than he had ever thought possible. They actually believed the story that the explosion at the council building was the result of a gas leak. Could they really be so gullible?

And how could Meridians be so blind as to think Prince Garrett's religion was of no consequence? That his marriage to an American wouldn't affect them all? How could they be so enamored with the idea of Prince Stefano's new girlfriend and the idea of him walking into an instant family?

His jaw clenched as he thought of Prince Stefano, the man who had ruined everything. He had stood by so smugly when his brother announced his betrayal to the Meridian Church, supporting a decision that would alter everything for generations to come. His sources also revealed that Stefano had been the one responsible for stopping Ambrose.

His knuckles turned white as his grip tightened on the steering wheel. He had no choice now. It was up to him to make sure the country saw the royals for who they really were. It was up to him to make them pay.

Chapter 46

"THE BOYS ARE GOING TO sleep well tonight." Stefano leaned back on his elbow and watched the boys tumbling around on the grass with their new puppy they had named Roscoe.

Alora shifted beside him on the picnic blanket. "They're definitely going to need baths."

"Oh yeah." Stefano chuckled as the puppy climbed up and licked Dante's cheek. He turned his attention back to Alora, and he looked uncharacteristically nervous. "After we get the kids in bed, I was hoping we could spend some time together."

"I'd like that," she said, smiling at his assumption that he would once again share the boys' bedtime ritual with her.

He nodded and seemed to relax a little. "I'll make the arrangements with Brenna."

An engine sounded, and Alora shifted her attention to the car that pulled up to the front gate. "I wonder who that is. No one has any appointments scheduled for today."

Stefano straightened, his eyes narrowing when he saw the older man with his round glasses and owlish face. "That's odd. It looks like Archbishop Leone."

Alora's tone cooled. "Isn't he the one pushing to make sure royalty stays within the Meridian Church?"

"He is." Stefano stood up. "Maybe he's here looking for some reassurances that he will still be able to perform the marriage ceremony for Garrett and Janessa. By law, they'll have to marry in the Meridian Church to make their marriage official."

An uncomfortable feeling quivered in her stomach. "I would have thought he would have come to see them while you were all still in Calene."

"You would think." Stefano offered her a hand up.

The guard at the gate waved the archbishop through, and a moment later he came to a stop in the circular driveway beside them. He climbed out of the car, his customary robes flowing nearly to the ground, beads of sweat visible on his forehead. He bowed to Stefano, and an odd smile lit his face.

"Your Highness, isn't this convenient. I had hoped to speak to you today."

"Archbishop Leone, it's good to see you." Stefano reached out and shook the older man's hand. "What brings you to Bellamo?"

"I have an appointment with Janessa about her wedding plans." The archbishop waved vaguely toward the chateau.

Stefano's eyes narrowed. "That's odd. She didn't mention it."

"Really?" He tucked a hand into the folds of the traditional religious robe. A thick crucifix hung from his neck on a heavy gold chain. He glanced over Stefano's shoulder and said, "I arranged it with her assistant."

Alora's discomfort grew. This religious leader was standing in front of the heir to the throne and lying. For what reason?

A gentle breeze stirred the scent of the sea and roses. Giancarlo giggled. The puppy barked. Alora's heart thudded uncomfortably in her chest as she considered why the man in front of her was really here.

"Alora, why don't you take the boys inside?" Stefano suggested mildly. Something in his tone told her he was just as suspicious of the archbishop as she. "You can let Janessa know the archbishop is here to see her."

Alora was torn between distancing her children from this man and not wanting to leave Stefano alone. With some reservation, she nodded and called out to the boys. "Giancarlo, Dante, it's time to go inside."

"Do we have to?" Dante asked, rolling over on the grass to look at her.

"Yes, you do." She fought to keep her voice calm, already thinking ahead to when they walked to the entrance. She would speak to the guards, have them make sure Stefano stayed safe.

Archbishop Leone's eyes lingered on Alora, but he addressed Stefano. "I don't believe I've been introduced to your friends."

"I'm sorry," Stefano said, clearly trapped by protocol. "Archbishop Leone, this is Alora DeSanto and her sons, Giancarlo and Dante."

"Good to meet you." Alora gave him a polite nod. She waved at her children. "Come on, boys."

Giancarlo struggled to pick up the puppy, and both boys crossed the lawn to stand beside their mother.

The archbishop shifted slightly so he was between them and the door. "You don't have to rush off on my account."

"Oh, we're not," Alora said, her eyes lifting to where two guards stood at the front entrance. "The boys need to go inside and get their baths."

She started to guide the boys around the archbishop to the entrance, but he shifted once more to block their path. Then he looked at Stefano and said blandly, "Perhaps we can all go for a walk together." He shifted the folds of his robe, the evening sunlight gleaming off the pistol in his hand.

Alora gasped. A bubble of panic threatened as she noticed the slim silencer attached to the end of the gun. She grabbed both boys by the arm and pulled them behind her. The puppy slipped out of Giancarlo's arms and dropped to the ground with a whimper.

"Mama," Giancarlo said in protest, clearly unaware of the danger facing them.

Stefano gaped at the archbishop, incredulity in his voice when he asked, "You?"

"Now, we don't want to cause any alarm for the guards." He shifted closer to Alora, smiling as though they were having a friendly chat. He gave a meaningful glance at the children. "And you don't want anyone to get hurt."

"What do you want?" Stefano moved to Alora's side so that together they were shielding the children.

"I want you to pay for ruining my plans." His voice was evil, contrasting with the cheerful smile on his face. "Whether your friends pay with you is up to you."

"Let them go, and I'll come with you," Stefano said, his voice surprisingly steady. "You don't need them."

"Oh, but I do," he countered. "Do you think I'm a fool? If I let them go, they'll alert the guards. And they look like an excellent insurance policy against you trying anything stupid."

"Stefano." Alora breathed his name in a whisper. Helplessness flooded through her and warred with her protective instincts.

"Everything will be okay." Stefano squeezed Alora's arm. Then he leaned down and picked up Giancarlo.

"You keep right on thinking that."

"What's going on?" Giancarlo looked up at Stefano with innocence and curiosity.

"We're just going for a little walk. Remember, just like when I took you for a walk when you got into trouble with your mama."

Dante squirmed when Alora lifted him into her arms. He pointed at the grass. "Mama, the puppy."

"The puppy is fine. He wants to stay outside a little while longer." Alora fought for calm, confused when Stefano started toward the wooded side of the chateau. She thought for sure he would head toward the gardens, where they were more likely to be seen.

"Why are you doing this?" Stefano asked, his voice low and tense. "What can you possibly gain?"

"Power. Revenge." His eyes gleamed with it, with greed and madness. "Once, your family was loyal to the church. Decisions about Meridia were shared between the king and the archbishop. This country has suffered since your family changed that."

"Those changes were made decades ago," Stefano said, confused.

"Yes. Your grandfather approved my appointment as the reigning archbishop, and within months, he took away my power." Hatred seethed through his voice. "I would have been content to share the illusion that he ran the country, but he was too greedy. Little by little he made changes, always taking away from the church's influence and adding to his own. Within a year, I was powerless."

"Surely you can't blame us for something we didn't have any control over," Stefano insisted.

"Your father had his chance to change things, but he refused." Leone shook his head and spoke derisively. "And then your brother abandoned our faith. I can't let this country blindly accept his decision, knowing that someday we will have a Mormon king. I won't let that happen." He motioned toward the trees. "Once you're gone, our citizens will see the truth. They'll see that it's the church that should lead them. Not your family."

Stefano glanced over his shoulder as he led the way down an overgrown path, and the archbishop took up position behind them. "Surely you understand the guards will know it was you if anything happens to any of us."

"Oh no." He shook his head. "I will be the one who runs for help, alerting the guards to that nasty man who jumped out of the bushes when we were all enjoying our walk." He let out a hard, brittle laugh. "And to think I came here expecting only revenge. It seems the Lord wants me to prevail after all. I will have the power that is supposed to be mine."

Alora stopped midstride. "The Lord would never want this."

Beside her, Stefano lowered Giancarlo to the ground and turned to face the archbishop once more. "I won't let you hurt these children. I won't let you hurt Alora."

"You have no choice." He glanced back at the guards, who were still barely visible at the front gate. A few more yards and they would be out of sight. A few more yards and the archbishop could carry out his plans.

Dante whimpered and clung tighter to Alora. Giancarlo gripped the back of Stefano's leg. Alora buried her face in the soft folds of Dante's neck, breathing in the scents of little boy and grass. She would not let anything happen to him or Giancarlo. Even if she had to sacrifice herself, she was not going to let this man hurt her children.

As though sharing a similar resolve, Stefano turned to face Giancarlo and then squatted down in front of him. He pulled him close for a hug. "It's going to be okay." Then he lowered his voice, and Alora thought she heard him whisper something in his ear.

Standing back up, Stefano reached over and put a hand on Dante's back. His eyes dark, he said simply, "Don't be afraid."

Dante whimpered again, and Stefano motioned to Alora. "Let Dante walk. He's too heavy for you to carry."

"It's okay . . ." Alora started.

Stefano's voice became brisk and commanding. "Let him walk."

Shocked by his tone, Alora obeyed. Then Stefano spoke to Giancarlo. "Take your brother's hand."

Giancarlo swallowed hard, his eyes wide with fear. They started walking once more, the boys leading the way around a sharp bend in the path, the bend that would hide them from everyone on the chateau grounds. Stefano nudged Alora forward so he was effectively shielding her from the archbishop.

Her heart racing, Alora stopped on the edge of the guard's view. "Stefano, we can't let him do this. We can't . . ."

She felt a hand on her back. Before she could finish her sentence, Stefano pushed her toward the trees and shouted, "Run!"

Chapter 47

ADRENALINE SURGED THROUGH STEFANO WHEN the archbishop's hand lifted and tried to take aim. Stefano was too fast for him.

Stefano grabbed for the gun, pushing the barrel downward just as a shot fired into the ground. The sound was little more than a puff in the wind, not loud enough to be heard from any distance. Dust stirred into the air from where the bullet struck the ground.

Alora screamed, guards shouted, and Stefano tightened his hand around Leone's wrist to keep the gun pointed toward the ground. His heart raced as he listened to Giancarlo and Dante running away from them, quickly realizing that Alora was still a few feet away. "Alora, run!"

Leone turned and twisted, struggling to loosen Stefano's grip. The older man was stronger than he looked, grappling with Stefano to maintain possession of his weapon.

"You're going to pay," he muttered and swung out with his left hand.

The blow connected with Stefano's right temple, hard. Pain exploded behind his eyes, but his hold on the archbishop's arm didn't loosen. He fought to keep Leone's hand pinned to his side, praying that Alora would get to safety before Leone got off another stray shot.

In the distance, he could hear the guards' rapid footsteps coming toward them, melding with the fading footsteps he knew belonged to Dante and Giancarlo. Help was coming, but Stefano knew the guards were still more than a hundred yards away.

He heard Alora rustling in the bushes behind him, and he caught a glimpse of the weapon she now held. A branch the size of a baseball bat was cocked behind her shoulder, her hands gripping it tightly.

The guards' shouts grew louder, but Stefano knew they wouldn't be able to get a clear shot without the risk of hitting him. The archbishop's struggles became more fervent, Stefano countering each move. Leone twisted, attempting to elbow Stefano as Stefano tried to maneuver for control of the weapon.

A thud sounded when Alora swung her makeshift weapon, connecting with Leone's back. He yelped in pain, and the force of the impact sent both men stumbling forward. The gun dropped to the ground, and both men scrambled for it.

Then the guards were at the edge of the path, shouting orders.

"Hold it right there!"

"Don't move!"

The archbishop ignored the guards, fighting with a single-mindedness that defied logic. He managed to grasp his weapon once more, swinging it toward the guards in a bold move. He squeezed the trigger, his shot forcing the guards to take cover at the entrance to the path. Then in an equally audacious gesture, he whirled back toward Stefano.

Stefano saw his intent and dove to the left. A single gunshot followed, the bullet tearing through the fleshy part of Stefano's upper arm. He cried out in pain, the burning sensation overwhelming all of his senses.

At first he didn't notice Alora move forward or that she was still wielding the tree branch. Then he looked up at the older man, expecting him to shoot again, but he saw that the archbishop's attention and his weapon had shifted toward Alora. A split second before the archbishop managed to take aim, Alora swung the tree branch at him again, only this time, she let go and sent the length of wood flying through the air.

The archbishop ducked, narrowly avoiding being struck in the head. Ignoring the throbbing in his arm, Stefano took advantage of the distraction, tackling him around the waist and knocking him to the ground. Again, they grappled for control of the weapon, rolling around on the dirt as Stefano held Leone's right arm to keep him from grabbing the gun.

Footsteps sounded again, and he heard a guard shout at Alora to stand clear.

"You'll never beat me," the archbishop panted. "I have nothing to lose."

They were both up now, the gun still out of reach. Stefano elbowed Leone in the gut. He kept his gaze on the weapon, all the while praying that Alora was fleeing toward safety. He stepped backward, his heel catching on a protruding tree root. His loss of balance was enough for the archbishop to once again gain an advantage.

The archbishop pushed off of Stefano and managed to keep his footing as the prince tripped and fell to the ground. His eyes were dark with pure evil when he lifted the gun, his finger on the trigger.

Stefano scrambled backward, Alora screamed, and the guards opened fire. A heartbeat later, the archbishop dropped to the ground.

* * *

Stefano stood in the doorway of Giancarlo and Dante's room, staring at the two boys now tucked safely into their beds. Giancarlo had been beyond brave when he had followed Stefano's instructions. He had led his brother to safety, both of them taking refuge in the old tree house in the woods.

When he and Alora had found them, they were shaken and scared, but they were safe.

Stefano and Alora had carried them down the path to the stables before circling back to the chateau. The boys had been traumatized enough without having to see the archbishop's body lying on the edge of the woods.

The paramedics had tried to convince Stefano to go to the hospital to get his wound treated, but he had refused to leave Alora's side. Martino had indulged him by requesting that the local physician make a house call and treat him at the chateau. Four stitches and some bandages later, Stefano was able to turn his focus back to trying to help Giancarlo and Dante reclaim their sense of security.

Bedtime had been a long and drawn-out process tonight as one prayer had led to another, the boys struggling to understand the danger they had faced. Then Garrett had arrived and given the boys some kind of blessing. Alora explained that it was a way to help the boys find peace and comfort, that the ritual could only be performed by certain priesthood holders within her church.

Though he couldn't claim to understand the ritual, the boys seemed to have found some solace and were now finally asleep.

Alora tucked the covers more tightly around Dante and then repeated the process with Giancarlo. With an audible sigh, she walked toward the door, where Stefano stood. Without a word, she slipped her hands around his waist and leaned into him.

"It's okay now," Stefano murmured, drawing her close. "It's all over."

"I've never been so scared in my life."

"I find that hard to believe."

She shifted, pulling back enough that she could see his face. "You saved my children today. You saved me."

"I love your children," Stefano said quietly. He drew a breath and added, "And I love you. The three of you are everything to me."

Alora's hands tightened on his back, and she looked up at him.

Stefano's fingers trailed down through her hair, tangling in it as he searched for the right words. "I know you worry about our religious differences, but I love you, and I want you in my life. Please tell me we can build a future together. " Before she could answer, he leaned down and brushed his lips across hers. "You have my heart, Alora. If you walk away from me, away from us, you'll do more than break my heart. You'll shatter it."

Her breath caught, and the truth of his words reflected in her eyes. Her hand lifted to rest on his chest as though to steady herself. "I keep praying about what I should do about my feelings for you, but I don't seem to be getting any answers."

"Maybe you aren't asking the right questions."

"Maybe you're right." She let out a nervous laugh. "I keep asking if I should walk away from you, but every time I do, you're right there in front of me, and I know I want to be with you."

"Surely God didn't put us together only to ask us to stay apart," Stefano said almost desperately.

She hesitated, her expression becoming more serious. "I keep wondering if you might ever open yourself up to the gospel the way your brother did. Then I have to remind myself that for you to ever truly discover the joy of the gospel, you'd have to do it for yourself, not for me."

His eyes narrowed at that. "I want to learn more about your religion, to understand how God can answer personal prayers, but I don't think my country is ready to have two princes walk away from the Meridian Church."

"I know." Sadness and regret hummed through her voice.

Impatience flowed through him. "Are you really going to let this stand between us? We can make a life together, Alora." He waved impatiently around the room. "We already have."

"All my life, the main thing my parents wanted for me was to grow up and be happy. Part of that happiness was to get married in the temple, to raise my children in the gospel."

"You already did get married in the temple, and I would never get in the way of what you want for your children. If raising them Mormon is important to you, then it's important to me."

"What about any children we might have together?"

Stefano pulled out of her arms and crossed to the balcony. He looked out at the sea for a moment, staring into the darkness. Life seemed so simple here, but for him, there would always be complications. His voice was low when he turned back to face her and forced the words out. "There won't be any."

She followed him onto the balcony, her hair catching in the breeze. "What do you mean?"

"I can't have children." Stefano kept his eyes on hers. "The royal line will continue through Garrett's children. Someday this country will have a Mormon prince. One day, his son will rule."

"I don't understand."

"I have Merid's syndrome," Stefano said, almost choking on the words. "It's a rare disease that has affected my family for generations."

Concern flashed in her eyes. "Are there other problems? Does it cause you any pain?"

"No, nothing like that." He shook his head, unexpectedly relieved by her selfless reaction. "Most of the symptoms are minor, some odd allergies and an occasional problem with balance. They're so minor that until recently, I didn't even realize they were connected. Unfortunately, the one symptom that is irreversible is infertility."

"Stefano, I'm so sorry."

He took her hands in his. "I know you will have to make a lot of sacrifices if you are to marry me. We wouldn't be able to give Giancarlo and Dante brothers and sisters, at least not in the traditional sense. Your privacy will cease to exist in many areas of your life. And I know how concerned you've been about the idea of marrying outside of your religion."

Tears welled up in her eyes. "Are you asking me to marry you?"

Nerves battled in his stomach. "I'm asking if the question would be a welcome one."

Something changed in her countenance, as though she had suddenly found the peace she had been searching for, as though the answers to her prayers had finally been revealed. She offered him a tearful smile, her posture relaxing ever so slightly. "I think it would."

He reached into his pocket, his fingers curling around the ring box nestled within the folds of fabric. He drew it out, his lips curving when he saw her eyes widen. "This is the ring my father gave my mother." He flipped open the box to reveal the square cut emerald surrounded by diamonds. He pulled the ring free and took her hand. "I hope you'll accept it. And me."

She swallowed hard, her eyes lowering to her finger as Stefano slid the ring into place. Then she looked up at him and nodded. "Yes." She reached up and pressed her lips to his. "Yes, I'll have you."

The weight of the last few days vanished, and he lifted her in his arms, despite the twinge of pain caused by his injury. He whirled her around as his lips covered hers. Then with a grin on his face, he set her down and said, "Let's go tell the children."

Humor shone from Alora's eyes, but she shook her head. "If you wake them up, they'll never get back to sleep tonight."

Stefano glanced toward their room, remembering how long the boys had struggled to fall asleep. He pushed aside the little seed of disappointment and nodded. "You're right." He turned his gaze back to her. "Tonight we're a couple." He pressed his lips gently against hers. "But tomorrow, we're a family."

About the Author

ORIGINALLY FROM ARIZONA, TRACI HUNTER Abramson has spent most of her adult life living in Virginia. She is a graduate of Brigham Young University and a former employee of the Central Intelligence Agency. Since leaving the CIA, Traci has written several novels, including the Undercurrents trilogy, *Royal Target*, *Obsession*, and the Saint Squad series.

When she's not writing, Traci enjoys spending time with her husband and four children. She also enjoys coaching the local high school swim team.